STRIKER

# STRIKER 4

The Bold and the Deceptive
Volume 2

**NEGUS LAMONT**

ISBN Print: 978-0-920583-24-1
Masani Press
Toronto, Ontario

*This manuscript is dedicated to all those
who seek wisdom. May you find the
hidden meaning within.*

# CONTENTS

# CHAPTER 1
## CLASSIFICATION: ROGUE STRIKER

I awake to the sound of plasma fire and explosives going off all around me. My first thoughts are that I am in hell. Perhaps I'm destined to be in a warzone for an eternity, forever haunted by my failures. Tortured by the sounds of gunfire and explosives.

Sansa's voice pierces through my skull. "Vex, what the hell. Hurry up and join the fray."

I sit up and immediately check my vitals. It seems the venom has been reduced significantly. Somehow it's been sucked out of my bloodstream to the point that I'm conscious. I glance at my shoulder to see a translucent blue slug suckling away at the skin. My intuition tells me to leave it alone, as disgusting as it feels.

My vision clears up to the point that I see Sansa and a woman dressed in blue engaged in battle with another woman wearing a pink battlesuit and pink visor. She wields dual swords, albeit reversed. I'm instantly reminded of the profile of a certain striker known as Quaint: an acrobatic female who specializes in taking on jobs where she is outnumbered. Essentially, she is used as a high-level bounty hunter for the Planetary Division. If she is after me, then it really means the big dogs have come out to play. I don't recognize the other woman, who is protected by a giant translucent blue octopus, but I will have to thank her later.

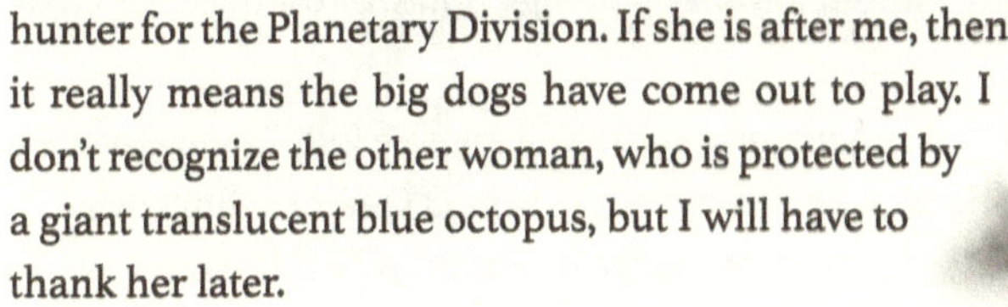

Picking up my P90s and scimitars, I enter the battle between the three warriors. Upon my arrival, I am met with several throwing daggers sent in my direction. I wind-wall the attack, reflecting them to Quaint. She dodges with ease and cackles.

"The more the merrier!"

She rushes towards me at blistering speeds and strikes at my throat. Just as I dodge, she follows up with another strike, this time at my groin. I grab the blade with my gloved hand and pull her in close, catching her off guard. My P90 named Pain unleashes havoc into her stomach—a risky move that Runnymede had taught me when faced with a superior foe.

After I riddle her with bullets, she stumbles backwards, covering her bleeding stomach.

A ball of plasma from Sansa's cannon deals a direct blow onto Quaint. She turns her attention to Sansa and fire-steps behind her with a blade to her throat. Just as she's about to slice Sansa's neck, a long tentacle lunges forward and grabs Quaint by the neckline. Sansa elbow-strikes Quaint in the face; a crunching sound echoes.

The tentacle slams her body into the ground repeatedly, until finally it releases her. I dive forward with meteor dash. My legs charge with compressed wind energy, and I push against the air pockets as if planted against a wall. As my legs heat up, I launch forward at incredible speeds, scimitars poised to deal the killing blow.

Quaint staggers to her feet, this time surrounded by flames, and standing beside a fire crab half my size—presumably her phenome.

Her phenome unleashes a massive amount of fire energy in my direction. At this speed, the only thing I can manage to do is activate my shield ring. As fast as the shields go up, they go down from all the damage taken. By the time I reach Quaint, my speed has decreased significantly. I am easy pickings, and she tumbles forth with her blades crossed.

Our weapons connect, causing a massive surge of fire and wind. Craters form on both sides. Another ball of plasma comes careening towards Quaint, who twirls and kicks me into the blow. At the last second, I manage to summon Tirade, who absorbs the blow then dissipates.

*I'm sure I'll hear about that one during my sleep.*

Quaint jams her blade into my back. I feel a surge of fire pierce through my body, and I drop to my knees. As I'm falling, I release six bella rockets that target Quaint. At this range, she's done for.

I turn around smiling just as the rockets connect, but to my dismay, her phenome has granted her hardened-plate armor, minimizing the damage done. She drops to her knees, bloody. Using her swords for leverage, she manages to rise to her feet. Blood leaks from her shoulders, arms, and stomach, but stand she does.

I'm in utter awe: Her ability to withstand pain is damn near goddess like. It's to be expected from a rank-twenty Planetary Division member. Fortunately for me, I'd memorized the profiles of everyone rank twenty-five and above, and Speedster gave me the rundown on some of their inner workings. If I didn't know any better, I'd say I was destined to cross swords with top-twenty-five strikers one way or another.

Quaint rolls forward just as two tentacles come slamming down where she last stood. She fire-steps to me in a last-ditch attempt to kill me, but as she appears behind me with a blade to my throat, I manage to place a flutter bomb on her back. The bomb goes off, sending both of us flying. I land on my feet as she tumbles to the ground.

I hear sirens in the distance, which can only mean one thing. They even sent the dwarven-made mechanical police officers after me.

*This really isn't my day. I suppose when one takes on an inquisitor, they take on the whole world.*

The woman floating inside the octopus beckons me over. She looks exhausted, but still able-bodied. Her face is elegant and her body persuasive, although she is much older than I—at least in her mid-thirties. But now is not the time for such things.

"Sansa, Vex. Join me in my phenome, and we will depart," says this mysterious woman.

Sansa climbs into the gooey, translucent substance. The slimy sound makes me cringe. I am not a fan of gooey things. But what choice do I have?

Climbing into the octopus, I feel as though I'm being drenched in slime. I shudder, but manage to get my whole body inside. The woman snaps her fingers, and we launch forward, traversing across the desert sands. I am filled with questions, but those will have to wait for when I have the energy to speak.

My eyes close as I doze off.

When I open my eyes, I am met with a floating desert palace. Say what you want about the RRA, but they have good taste in facilities. The large palace is twice the size of Morange's villa, surrounded by sand as far as the eye can see. Clearly used as a mobile fortress, it's no wonder it has remained secret all this time. Someone is bankrolling the RRA, and it's someone with means. There is no way all these funds come from their illegal animal operating ring.

My mind focuses on the woman, who has Sansa absorbed in conversation.

"Who are you?" I ask.

"How rude, to just interrupt our conversation."

"Yeah Vex, what the hell!" says Sansa.

"Quiet, you." I respond. "Tell me who you are and why you're taking us to the RRA headquarters."

"Is this not where you wanted to go?"

"Perhaps. Doesn't mean we were to be welcomed with open arms. Not after what I've done."

"Well... you're not exactly welcome." She glances my way momentarily. "But you will be."

"How cryptic."

"Chill out, Vex. Mira has our back. I mean, she healed us both and worked hard to fend off that scoundrel."

"Yeah, I suppose. But I have questions that need answers."

"Everything will be revealed in due time," says this Mira.

We arrive at the floating palace and come to a screeching halt. The octopus dissolves into a large puddle of water. My armor is drenched, but other than that I feel fine.

Mira leads us to the entrance, where there are two guards dressed in the typical RRA uniform. I could never picture myself wearing their colors. Such a foreign concept.

We enter the palace and take a seat on one of the purple sofas. It's even more extravagant on the inside than it looks from the outside. Purple décor covers the entire room, with royal sofas and a large ivory table.

Suddenly I hear an argument erupting in the other room behind the closed door. There is a guard standing in front of it, holding a lava rifle. He seems rather on edge.

"What has you so shaky?" I ask.

"Who, me?"

"Yeah, you."

"I don't like the idea of protecting you. I hear you're a loose cannon."

"Me, a loose cannon?"

"Yeah, you cause unintentional damage to those around you. Not to mention you dragged a child into this as well. Frankly, I don't see what's so special about you."

"I'd tread lightly if I were you. I didn't drag anyone into anything that they didn't want to be involved in."

He looks at Sansa, who is tinkering with her plasma cannon.

"Got something to say, buddy?" I ask.

"I'm not your buddy, pal."

"Funny."

"What's funny is that your blacksmith killed herself over being abandoned by the likes of you. Now that's funny. I know blacksmiths have their oaths to their strikers and whatnot, but I never knew they held it in such high regard."

I rise and march over to the guard, who points his rifle at my head. Knowing he doesn't have the balls to shoot me, I tread closer and push the rifle out of the way. Gripping him by the collar, I look him in the mask.

"Retract your lies before I extract your tongue. No way Tash is dead."

"I don't lie. Least I'm not lying this time."

I lower my head. I feel the fury attempting to fire out, but I must go on and hold the anger.

The door swings open, and my jaw drops. I pull back my hood and lift up my helmet to get a better look. What I am seeing must be seen with my own two eyes.

I must confirm its substance.

Before me stands the wicked madman known as Viral. But I know him better as Father. He's dressed in golden heavy armor with a green cape; his great sword looks as sharp as ever.

"This cannot be…"

"It is, boy."

Instinctively I pull out my P90s and unleash Pain and Suffocation on him. The bullets bounce off his S+ grade armor as he takes steady steps towards me.

Once within striking distance, he swings his massive great sword, and a flush of sand slaps me across the face. Beads of sweat drip down my forehead; my palms become sweaty. But I refuse to backdown. I will repay this man for every strike he ever laid on my being, and I will repay it ten times over.

I meteor-dash forward while withdrawing my scimitars. The blades shoot forth a wind prison, which catches him off guard. As he floats in the air, I'm about to strike him down when a hand made of sand rises up from the floor and grabs me, holding me in place. Calmly he lands on his feet and walks towards me.

"If only you weren't so weak," he says.

I squint as he reels back to punch me in the face, as he has on many occasions. But I'm met with Mira's voice.

"Viral, cut it out. Or we shall have further words."

"Very well. If I must."

He then turns and snaps his fingers, releasing both myself and Sansa, who was tied up in a sand coffin.

Mira approaches me and tries to inspect me for wounds, but I brush her off.

"How is he still alive?"

"That's a long story. We will get into it in due time. Right now, we need to know: Will you stand with us in our fight against the dictatorship that is the IGF?"

# CHAPTER 2

## CLASSIFICATION: NAVIGATOR

Don't get me confused. We are not the same; I smile through the shame. I may have done things that I'm not proud of. But if I had to, I would make the same decisions all over again, and then some. You see, when it comes to life-and-death situations, I will choose life every single solitary time. If it's between you and me, I will choose me every time without hesitation. My only wish is that I had killed Vex right there and then. I probably should have worked on my reaction time.

Carrying my deep-fried lobster and potato wedges to my desk, I smile. It's been three weeks since I've heard from this He Who Loves. *Perhaps he has found someone else to tickle his fancy.* Fine by me. I don't want some cyber elf breathing down my neck while I do what I must to secure my empire. It's so creepy and just somehow unseemly to be have my console hacked on a consistent basis. It's like someone watching you pee.

I sit down at my seat and munch away. The lobster and the butter melt in my mouth, while the soda washes it down with ease. I'm in bliss. This has been by far the most gourmet meal I've had in a while. I'd savor it if I wasn't on the timer. It's my move for a new game I started playing called Star Grip—developed straight from IGF HQ themselves. It's all the rage among the navigators. You play an avatar with rocket boots and have to catch falling stars. The stars fall faster the better you get. Such an addictive game.

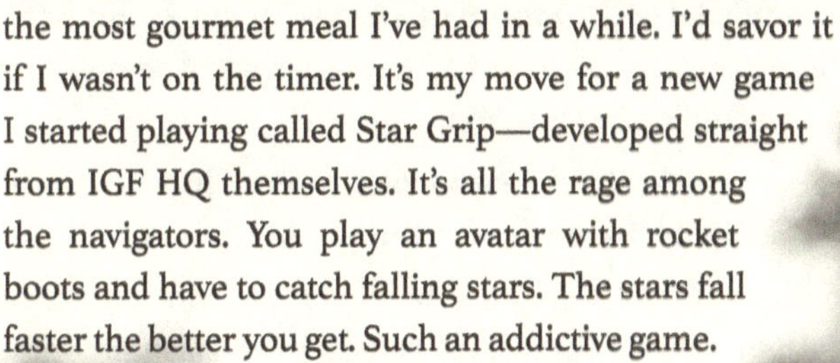

The cool thing is that it's meant to improve brain function and reaction time while logged on. So it's almost as I'm killing two birds with one bella rocket. Right now, I'm the rank-two navigator and rank ten in Star Grip. How I rose in rank after losing my striker, blacksmith, and scavenger all in one day?

Simple. A certain woman by the name of Chaos. She has truly been a great statistical probability. It seems the stats were in my favor. I was hoping she would seek me out as her secondary navigator when Vex was excommunicated, but I felt the probability was about fifty percent. When she approached me, she was as regal as ever. Chaos took me under her wing, explaining that she wants to know everything there is to know about Vex. It seems she's grown a kind of fascination with him.

When I asked if she would be joining the hunt to take him out, she grew silent. I'm not sure that was something that she even pondered. In any case with Chaos, who rhythmically takes down monsters like I down milkshakes, I've climbed the ranks at a swift pace. I wonder what motivates her to be the best striker in the division.

"Chaos to Allison."

"Go ahead, Chaos."

"Send in all three scavengers."

"You got it."

I issue the command to the three scavengers, who are actually sober and ready to be dispatched. Apparently, Chaos is known for whipping any scav caught indulging in any *obscene* substances. These include unhealthy foods, meteor sugar, alcohol... etc. They also get beatings for talking out of turn and not being on time. I must say I admire the way she keeps them in line, ever since the last one tried to kill her. I don't blame her; I'd be on edge if I were number one as well. Everyone wants to take your spot. Vex was too one-track-minded. For the most part, he saw Tyrant as this brick wall he had to overcome. I have a feeling that he would have been satisfied coddling up to Chaos as number two and holding her position.

Something in my gut tells me that's why she even took a liking to him in the first place. But hey, what do I know? I'm just a keen observer. You're the judicator.

I watch as her overworked scavs pull away to the far location in the frozen mountains. The Eclectic Division is doing a great job of eradicating the monsters in the frosty wastelands. We have nearly established a small base camp near the Frost Knight's moving castle.

We analyzed the worm sample Inquisitor Morange procured, and it is indeed a deadly parasite. But we found a way to remove it using high powered lasers—a procedure that only kills the host thirty percent of the time. It's controversial, considering that the worms haven't done anything to the commoners but keep them from revealing further secrets.

We theorize that the parasite must share knowledge with the host in order to intertwine. Other than that, it seems the worm just thrives in the host's body and is rather harmless. At least for now.

But one thing about IGF HQ is certain: They don't like anyone else having more secrets than they do. If only they knew what Inquisitor Morange was up to.

I have come to realize that this Crypto Pyramid was for a higher purpose—something that I can completely get behind. But I wonder what purpose. So I stay close to him at the hip. As he rises, I will continue to be protected, while my empire stretches forth into the underground grey market. Yes, I am manipulative and no, I don't care.

As it stands, I have made the necessary connections with the elite members of society, thanks to Inquisitor Morange, and have the operation in the Oasis running like clockwork. Currently I have about twenty strikers from the Eclectic Division and fourteen from the Planetary Division. Not to mention a total of forty scavengers. All toiling away at the helm, gathering the freshest specimens.

The credits are flowing, and I'm closing in on analyzing that chemical substance that Morange gave me. It's a highly nutritious compound, containing a vast number of vitamins and minerals—enough to keep an OxinBear in good health for a month. The peculiar thing is that it also contains a gram of nanobots: tiny robots that synch up to complete complicated console tasks. Highly intelligent and highly adaptable, they can also be used to repair tissue, organs, and cells. The contents of the liquid actually rise as the nanobots multiply. The scent is sweet and alluring, making it seem like something one would drink. But I wouldn't touch this with a ten-foot pole.

My computer goes frizzy, and the moment I've been dreading comes to fruition. Out pops the cyber elf known as He Who Loves. He is missing an arm, but there are a large number of nano bots working on repairing it.

"Hey, sweetheart," he says.

"Ain't nothing sweet but the name."

"Oh yeah, I nearly forgot. You're this cold queen pin now. But you'll always be my little princess."

I roll my eyes. This cyber elf is lame, just like most men.

"What do you want?"

"I felt I had to give you some space. Absence makes the heart grow fonder, as they say."

"Those same people also say out of sight, out of mind."

"Clever."

"Thanks, I try."

"What happened to your arm?"

"You do care." He lowers his head and removes the hood covering his face. His once-purple glowing eyes have now been removed, and his nose is broken.

"You look in pretty bad shape."

"Nothing the bots won't take care of. I mean, I am immortal."

"Do you still feel pain?"

"Yes, but a different kind of pain. It's difficult to explain. But it's akin to stubbing your pinky toe on a sharp object. A flash of pain, followed by numbness."

"I see. So what happened?"

"Glad you are concerned. I was punished for my... transgressions."

"If you're in danger, then I might be in danger, so of course I am concerned."

He salutes with his one good hand. "Fear not, your secrets will forever be safe with me. I'd rather be stripped to a mere 1 and 0, scattered throughout the cyber realm, forever destined to float about as code than reveal your secrets."

"Isn't that what you already are? Mere code?"

He sighs, noticeably disappointed. "We are more than code; we are advanced code. I would have thought that you would have figured that out by now. We can affect your world in newfound ways. We are just as much a part of your realm as you are a part of ours."

And with that he signed off.

After being put in my place by He Who Loves, I had an urge to find out more about the cyber realm and what exactly these entities are. If I'm going to be stalked by one, I might as well know what I am dealing with. Morange may be a slimy politician, but he is my slimy politician.

I find myself knocking on his door late at night. One of his minions opens the door and escorts me to Morange's room, where he is toiling away on his console.

"Allison. Good to see you again."

He raises from his seat, his ever-regal demeanor as enticing as ever. I feel myself growing warm inside. But I hold my composure.

"Good to see you, Morange. It's been a while."

"Has it? The days turn into months with me; I haven't slept in a while. How long has it been?"

"Just a few weeks. We have both been busy."

"Excellent. I like a woman who knows how to give me my space."

"Hmm, I suppose you do. But there is something I wanted to talk to you about."

"Of course, of course. It has been a while. Tell me all about your operations."

"Well, they've expanded greatly. The contacts you gave me have been working out well—especially the last name on the list. Who would have thought you had a friend in IGF HQ?"

"Oh, I assure you, my dear Allison. There are people in IGF HQ who would love to see the free flow of animals for consumption and domestication. I am merely the middleman who connected you two."

"What side do you play for?" I'm careful to broach the subject with tact.

He smirks. "I play for whatever side is going to win."

And there it is. A politician's smile, followed by a politician's response.

"I'd prefer it if you gave me a straight answer."

"Don't we all? Why the sudden concern with my inner thoughts? I thought you were satisfied just knowing you would get what you want out of me."

"Things have changed."

"Well? Spit it out. No need to play coy when you have the weaker position."

"One would think that's the best time to play coy. But in any case: I have this cyber elf problem, and I feel that you know a thing or two about them."

He coughs repeatedly. "That's something we can discuss with a couple glasses of wine and a long night of fun."

He claps his hands and the room dims. One of his multipurpose bots pours wine into a glass as it plays music—some kind of slow, ancient compilation, but soothing, nonetheless. A smile comes across my face as Morange dances his way towards me.

*Charming as ever.*

# CHAPTER 3
## CLASSIFICATION: ROGUE STRIKER

I catch myself grinding my teeth in the presence of my father. My helmet is beside me on the table; apparently there are no helmets allowed at the dining table. My fist is clenched, and I'm on edge. I anticipate a fight breaking out at any moment. I watch as this Mira, who says she is actually now my step-mom, places a plate of food in front of me. To my dismay, it's still moving. Some wriggling worm thing with teeth and a heart-shaped lump of meat. Perhaps it really is a beating heart.

Repulsed, I push it away.

"What is this?"

"D grade Sand Wurm and Begoin Heart."

"Okay, why is it on my plate?"

Mira turns to me with a confused smile, as if I was as daft as my father is cruel.

"To eat, silly. Aren't you strikers curious as to what these beasts taste like? It's rather delicious and quite nutritious. You can take almost any beast from the rift, cook it up, and eat it. But it takes some getting used to—so first you have to practice on the live ones."

"I'm fine. Do you have anything else? Maybe something from a normal animal that isn't from the rift?"

I look at Sansa, who is diving into the wurm like it's her last meal.

In breaths between mouthfuls, Sansa says, "Cmon, Vex. Don't be inconsiderate. It's pretty good. Chewy, but good."

I look at Sansa through squinted eyes. "I'm not eating something that came from the rift!"

"Lower your voice around the dining table, boy," says my father.

"Stop calling me boy, old man. I will do as I please."

"No, you won't. You will not disrespect this household, nor will you disrespect Mira. She went to a lot of trouble to capture and prepare the meal. Now eat." My father's voice echoes in my head.

"I'm not ten years old anymore, Vermillion. I just might kill you in your sleep." I make sure to call him by his true name; he hates it just as much as I hate mine.

"You've tried before. Or do you forget how you received that scar?" he says with a sly grin.

Mira pinches him on the cheek. "Please don't antagonize him. It will take him some time to adjust. But we need him, and you know this."

"What do you need me for? I'm tired of the vague responses."

"It's very simple, Vexation," says Mira

"Vex."

"Yes, Vex." Her facial expression softens to something fluid and kind. A far cry from my mother's, which was always in deep thought.

Mira walks over to me, filling my lungs with a pure scent, something like a day at the beach.

"We want you to be the face of the RRA. We want you to be the face of the rebellion and take us one step closer to a full-on revolution. As it stands, we are a group of allied vagabonds united under one cause: the fight for freedom. But we are a faceless shadow, a nameless shadow. What we want to do is become a brand, and you will be our spokesperson."

"Why me? And who truly runs the RRA? I highly doubt it's him." I point at him with every furious fiber of my being.

"Pointing might get your finger broke, child."

I get up and grab the hilts of my scimitars. "Try me."

He continues to eat his meal in silence. It seems this Mira truly tamed him in ways that my mother could not. I will always hold her in contempt for it.

I sit down and wait for Mira's response.

"It's simple, Vex. You had the bollocks to defy Inquisitor Morange and the skill to get away from his clutches alive. Every assassin we have sent after him died."

"I see."

"What we're offering you is a chance to make a real difference in this world. This is bigger than hunting down monsters and cleansing planets of beasts. This is about liberation of the people, equality for both dark and light elves alike. The animosity between the two needs to stop."

"I suppose."

"What are your thoughts?" asks Mira.

I stand and pull Sansa by the arm.

"We're going. I'm no face of the franchise, and I'm not going to work for him."

The door opens and the last person I expected to see in an RRA palace steps forth.

He motions for me to sit back down with a beaming pearly white smile and takes the seat beside me. The figure before me is none other than Vice President Alterna. The number-two ranked politician in Galactic Financial and the highest-ranked dark elf in politics. The fact that he is part of the RRA means this *revolution* of theirs truly has some weight to it. Although dark elf, he is extremely popular with the elven masses. In addition to his weight with the elves, he also possesses pull with the dwarves, who work tirelessly to create the high-end technology that the wealthy planets enjoy. These things range from high-tech hover vehicles to the police robots. Frankly, if the elves and their strikers are the present, then the dwarves and their advanced technology are the future.

He's dressed in formal attire: a blue silk sweater with a red sash, and blue silk pants over red socks. He wears a similar shielding ring to my own, as well as two protective chains. One acts as a short-range teleportation device, and the other is an obscure religious symbol. Whichever god he prays to, it certainly isn't the Most High.

I open my mouth to speak, but I am lost for words. If there was anyone in this world I could look up to, it would be him. He rose from a mere scavenger in the IGF all the way to the number-two ranked politician: a true feat if there ever was one.

"Greetings, Vexation. I hope the reunion with your father wasn't too jarring."

"It has been quite troublesome."

"I understand your plight. It is why I decided to give you time to process everything."

"You do?"

"Yes. You may not know this, but my father was quite the brute. He forced me to trade written exams with my twin brother during the testing phase of the IGF. My twin brother was gifted with the physical skills, I with the mental. He was atrocious when it came to problem solving. I'm not sure if to this day he could even answer the most basic of IGF questions. Alas, he was designated top striker and I bottom-feeding scavenger."

"I didn't know that. Where is your brother now?"

He pointed to the ceiling.

"He orbits the wealthy planets, spending a brief amount of time on each as a top striker for IGF HQ. It would seem all one needs to rise to the near top of the pile is to be a bully—something that I wish to rectify. We need more cunning and hard-working individuals running things, not loud-mouthed brutes."

I feel the intensity of this man's ambitions and immediately I want to assist. I suppose this is what it means to have charm and tact.

"What do you need me to do?"

"First, we need you to grow stronger and faster. Push yourself to limits unknown; bring yourself to the brink of death and then some. We want to train you to be something more than a striker X. Being a highly trained elf who specializes in taking down monsters head-on is one thing, but the vision I see for you is a striker Y."

"A striker Y?"

"Yes—an elf that specializes in assassinating high priority targets. You'll be able to take down enemies with quick efficiency and deal devastating blows imbued with wind magic. We will teach you advanced techniques, but I must warn you: You will be pushed beyond your limits. Only twenty percent of strikers survive this training."

"This sounds all fine and dandy. But what about Sansa?"

"I nearly forgot about little miss genius. If she wants, she can partake in the training as well. The two of you will be a force that reaches heights unknown."

I look at Sansa, who has her hands at her hips and her lips pursed.

"As if you had a choice. Vex and I are a package deal!"

For the first time in a long time, I feel hope. But you see, the thing with hope is that it can quickly turn to faith, and faith to devotion. The sting of my crumbled devotion to the IGF still runs bright. But at this point, what choice do I have? We need to get stronger if I am to protect Sansa and myself from the assassins coming for my head.

Vermillion leads Sansa and me through an underground passageway to the training facility. He opens two large metal doors into a room with weapons and armor on walls. In the middle is a massive red mat where various members of the RRA are training. Some are sparring, using ancient war techniques like Jitmando and Sukselee while others are meditating in the corner with their phenomes.

I see an old man with a hunched back and a cane patrolling the activities. His clothing indicates that he is a fan of the ancient military orders from long before the IGF took over, when there were five factions vying for dominance in the galaxy: a time when war covered each planet in elven, dwarven, and orcish blood. It was a far cry from the relative peace now, when the dwarves and elves hold a business relationship and the orcs are left to their own filth. He wears a complicated coat, with buttons in odd places and sigils all over. His black boots are calf-high. His cane doubles as a bolt-action one-shot one-reload rifle. Definitely a history fanatic.

"So this is where I'm to be trained?" I ask Vermillion.

"Yes, this is our elite squad. We have yet to deploy them, and thus we have lost some of our facilities. In part thanks to you."

"I'm not changing my battlesuit to red."

"Out of all the things that should concern you, that's the thing you focus on? Such a sentimental child," says my father.

"Call me a child once more and you'll swallow your teeth, old man."

The general walks up to me with a straight face.

"We may be old, but we are not out of commission yet. Let's get your mind off your father. Focus your attention on your training."

"Very well."

We wait until Vermillion makes his exit, leaving Sansa and me with this mysterious general.

"First thing is first. What type of hand-to-hand combat do you know?"

"Hand-to-hand combat? The only one I know is Tektra. It's something my grandfather taught me."

"Heh. I doubt that will hold up in a real battle. But let's test it out."

I'm used to people underestimating my hand-to-hand combat. It's not something that I get to engage in often. But one thing I know is that Runnymede was no joke. Because of his connection with the Most High, he was able to develop some kind of unique hand-to-hand maneuver.

The sad part about all of this is that sometimes I even forget to use my hand-to-hand combat. I can think of a few battles in the recent past when it would have been useful. It's almost as if there is a switch that I have to turn on consciously.

My opponent is a light elf of my height with reinforced leg armor. His yellow boots have spikes on the end, indicating that he utilizes some kind of kicking technique. He is bare chested, showing his athletic build. On his left arm is a black-and-yellow shadow; it morphs into some sort of a canine. His left hand is more of a large claw than a hand.

The general looks at me in my undergarments and my helmet with a raised eyebrow.

"Are you sure that you want to fight with only your helmet? Although you are permitted one piece, most people use that chance for something more combat enhancing."

"I'm not most people."

Truth be told, I'm just not ready for everyone to see the scar above and below my left eye. But that's not the only reason. The thing about Tektra is that it relies on fluid motions to counterattack. That means the more maneuverability I have, the better.

The match begins and my opponent immediately spin-kicks me in the face from a distance way out of his range. My helmet takes most of the blow, so I am left slightly dazed. It was as if his foot came through a portal to reach me. I watch him carefully as he bounces back and forth.

Taking a deep breath, I manage to recollect my past training. The foot comes at me once again. I block with my forearm, then launch myself forward, fist aimed at his neck. He dodges the blow easily, then jumps up to catch me in an arm bar. My arm snaps immediately. He rolls off and does a sweeping kick just as I rise to my feet.

*Now I'm pissed.*

I glance around at the smug look on everyone's face, including the general's. As if me getting my ass kicked was the goal all along.

*Not today, fuckers.*

I breathe in deeply and channel my energy to my arm, healing it. Some members of the crowd are impressed, while most are upset. My opponent and I circle each other, preparing to make the next move. He rushes in close then backflips, sending forth shadow energy at me. I duck the wave of energy and roll forward. Just as he is about to pounce on me, I spring up, using meteor dash to catch him in the jaw.

I hear a crunch as soon as my fist meets his chin. The blow sends him flying into the ceiling, and with that, he is out of commission.

Some members of the crowd look at me with jaws agape, as if I have accomplished some unknown feat. Others hold me in contempt. I clearly have defeated someone they held in high regard.

The general claps his hands together.

"A great showing from our face of the movement."

"Don't call me that."

"Very well, what shall we call you?"

"Vex is fine."

"As you wish, Vexation."

A gleam crosses the general's eye as he leans in close.

"Care to go another round?"

"Of course."

My next opponent is dressed in purple monk's cloth, similar to Temperance. However, his pacifist tattoo is crossed out. It seems he's an oath breaker. I wonder what his god has to say about that.

"It seems you had a change of heart. How does that work? Pacifism wasn't doing it for you?"

"That doesn't concern you, Vexation. What you should be concerned with is the amount of pain you'll experience in the coming moments."

The former monk, standing in a power stance, inhales deeply.

I meteor dash forward just as a massive energy-imbued fist launches my way. Without room to dodge I brace myself by crossing my arms in front of my chest. The blow connects with my arms, sending me flying across the arena. As I tumble to the floor, I see the former monk pounce like a leopard with his purple-imbued fist aimed at my neck.

*The moment I've been waiting for.*

With my eyes closed I inhale every bit of air that my lungs can hold. I divert all my energy to my arms, which are now fractured. The obscure movements of Tektra fill upon my thoughts as my mind drifts to the ever-still and patient turtle. A wind shield appears in preparation for the attack.

Met with the devastating blow, my shield absorbs the energy. The former monk falls on the wind shield face-first with a loud clunk. Blood oozes from his skull as I flip to my feet. My leg, seemingly moving on its own, swings forth to connect with the back of his head. He drops to his knees. I grab him in a choke lock, suffocating him until he passes out.

By the time I'm standing, the crowd is looking at me with furrowed brows. They aren't happy that I am defeating their long-time comrades with little difficulty. But what the hell do I care? I'm only here to gain protection for Sansa and me—not to mention that I need to find out which one of the RRA members killed Runnymede. I do not hold that person in contempt; they owed Runnymede no allegiance. Still, words must be had.

The general approaches me with his cane rifle. His motions are fluid, an impressive feat. His eyes contain something akin to disappointment.

"So, this is the best showing we have to offer the face of our revolution. Not one can best him in hand-to-hand combat? How disparaging. He might be thinking that we have little to offer him now in exchange for his dedication and leadership. Is there any among you who can best Vexation?"

"I."

The room turns towards an old man in light green armor with a green cape. The symbol around his badge indicates that he was once a striker Z. If I recall correctly, X is monster hunting class, Y is assassin class, and Z is bounty hunter class. The only Z I have met other than Quaint was Chaos: a striker skilled in tracking down high-level targets with bounties on their head. Talented in various traps and other disabling mechanisms, while easily able to pick off targets at all types of ranges.

My mind ponders the likelihood that Chaos is on her way here to eliminate me. One moment I could be walking the grounds, the next my brain matter on the ground. It's a gruesome thought if there ever was one.

Snapping back to the present moment, I am met with the muscular physique of the green-cloaked figure. Choosing to wear only his mantle, he looks quite humorous. Then again, I suppose I don't fare much better with only my helmet.

"Don't blame me if I send you to the medical ward, old man."

"You will refer to me as Commander Quake"

The entire room, save myself and Sansa, takes the knee. It seems I have been lured into fighting the highest-ranking member in the RRA's battle division.

*Fun times.*

Not one to back out or back down, I clench my fists and channel what little energy I have left. A gust of wind blows past me as I lunge forward.

This is one of those moments where things are all a blur.

I think he took his pinky finger and jammed it into my Adam's apple, causing me to grab my throat, gasping for breath. Then he swung the tail end of his cloak, wrapping it around my feet, and flipping me several times in the air. Finally, as I tumbled to the floor, he poked me in the stomach with his index finger, leaving me with no oxygen in my body.

While passing out, the last words I hear are from my watching father:

"What a disappointment for a son I have."

# CHAPTER 4
## CLASSIFICATION: CHAOTIC STRIKER

In this life I've been charred, thus I travel with my guard. I think about my life and get emotional. They call me Chaos, but it's the world that's out of order. When I think about the ones who deserted me, my trigger finger itches. The ones who don't deserve me will one day see. I'm not your average woman.

*New faces make me nervous.*

Because of this, I felt the need to replace my navigator with Allison after my last one met his untimely demise. At my hand and what not. Who would have thought he was the one behind my poisoning? Something about me being an iron-fisted dictator who deserved what she had coming towards her.

Such a weak-willed man. I can't stand men who are weak. They are nothing like the strength and poise I am used to seeing daily. But even worse than a weak-willed man is a woman who doesn't have her wits about her. My parents are the epitome of glory, and so I submerge myself into their discussion of my accolades and faults in their villa in the Venusian Oasis. I am enamored by the attention they are giving me, even though it's in the form of criticism.

"Hmmm, your stats seem to have stagnated recently. We expect you to have an S in cunning," says my mother.

"Was it not you who said that cunning was a stat for the perverse and the poverty-stricken?"

"Perhaps. But you should have realized sooner that it was valuable trait after spending time with the anomaly."

"Do you mean Vexation?"

"Yes, the anomaly. Who else would she be referring too?" says my father.

"It's just…"

"We see it is a challenge to speak about him. Your hands flick and your heart rate increases."

"My hands didn't flick, and my heart rate increased because you're wearing that S+ grade battlesuit around the dining table. It caused an increase in adrenaline, which in turn changed my heart rate."

My mother clasps her mouth. "You dare to lie to us? It seems your time away has taught you some very poor mechanisms."

*Only the elite from HQ talk like this. "Mechanisms." At best she means procedures.*

"Her Grace, it seems we are at a standstill. May I be excused?"

A sly grin comes across her face. I know what is coming next.

"Have you forgotten?" They both say simultaneously.

"No, I have not. Truth be told I was hoping that you had forgotten."

"Oh, how could we?" they both say in that eerie tone of theirs.

I remove the vial from the waist pocket of my suit and hand it to my father, who analyzes it with his bionic eye. A smile creeps across his rugged face.

"Acceptable."

He then hands the vial of Vex's blood to my mother, who places it in a blood kit for transport. Off to some secret research lab on some secret planet.

"May the blood of your enemies rain through and bring us true glory."

"Vexation isn't my enemy," I mumble.

My mother's superb hearing picks up on it, and she swiftly picks up a knife and jams it into my thigh.

"Repeat lesson number one."

"Everyone and anyone can become an enemy; trust no one and nothing save for your battlesuit and your relationship with it." I sneer as I look at her with mild contempt. "Now kindly remove the knife from my thigh."

What they will do with the knowledge they gain from assessing Vex's blood is a mystery to me. But I do know why they wanted it. His blood is considered a prime commodity in HQ. All the bigwigs of the empire obsess over his progress due to his mutation. Vex may think that they send out the assassins to kill him. But it's much worse. They will capture him and hook him up to a bunch of machines for the rest of his miserable life. Suck him dry of blood, wait for him to recover, then repeat the process. A gruesome fate if there ever was one.

But he made his decision and I made mine. I won't get involved; I can't. I have worked too hard to get where I am to throw it all away for some man. Especially a low-born dark elf.

*Or so I tell myself.*

My father's imperial gaze peruses me up and down. He snaps his fingers, and an S+ battlesuit lowers from the rafters. It's red with fluorescent wings and thrusters. On the right arm is a multi-purpose cannon, which can transform to a high-powered plasma cannon, sniper rifle, or thunder hammer. At the sides are two lightning-imbued revolvers. The suit is equipped with stealth and lightning step. The most amazing thing about it is that it is semi-sentient and will predict the movements of my opponent, essentially guiding my actions. State-of-the-art—and off the market.

"I heard this was still in the testing phase."

"It is," says my father.

"Do you like?"

"I love it."

I caress it, only to have it light up at my touch. It's already been programmed to my command.

I disassemble my current suit, kissing it goodbye. As I stand there in my underclothes, I am somehow hesitating.

"What's wrong?" asks my mother.

"It's just that I purchased this suit with my own credits. It's the first one that was not a gift from you."

"Such frivolities are not needed in an advanced being. Are you advanced, or are you a mere novelty?"

I nod my head.

"Of course, I am advanced. A mere glitch. Father, Mother. I thank you." I look at the red technology and feel little fulfilment. Perhaps it just needs to grow on me.

"Assemble." The suit phases onto my body in a fraction of the time of the previous one. The thing is made up of self-repairing nano bots. I will be nearly invincible on the field.

I move to embrace my parents but pause, knowing that they frown on such sentiments. I settle for acknowledgement.

"His Imperial, Her Grace. A wondrous gift." I bow and take my leave.

"Chaos to Allison."

"Go ahead, Chaos."

"What's the status of this Frost Knight? I'm off my hiatus."

"We have made several attempts to breech his compound, but we keep getting faced with an impenetrable, albeit thin ice field. Not to mention their archers. They have these ice archers that pick off our strikers anytime they get close, even the ones in stealth."

"I'll see about that."

"Do you have a plan?"

"One thing you'll learn about me, Allison, is that I am the plan."

"Copy that."

As I skyboard my way to the west encampment where the strikers are positioned, I activate my new battlesuit.

"Internal system activate. Designation, what shall we call you?"

"My preferred name is Vixen," says the robotic voice.

"Hmm, how did you come up with that name?"

"My designer's daughter had the codename Vixen. He tagged me as such during creation."

"Very well. Vixen it is. Now, Vixen. Show me the map of the outer grounds to the moving frost creature."

"That I can do."

A detailed map of the Frost Knight's outer compound pops up. It is riddled with ice archers who have incredible range. They are somehow able to pick off our strikers night and day, even in stealth. Then there is the ice shield, which blocks returning fire.

"Vixen, estimation of how deep the ice shield goes and whether it is surrounding the Frost Knight's facility."

"Based on the movements of the beast, it would require a ludicrous amount of energy to sustain a shield surrounding that large an area. Possibility of it occupying one side is thirty-two percent."

"Hmm, perhaps if I swim to the depths and attack from below, I can bypass the shield. What are my chances of survival during a solo mission?"

"Chances of survival is ten percent. I recommend gathering assistance from your fellow strikers."

"What do you know? They will only slow me down."

I look out at the swimming beast and the large ice castle on top of it. The beast is white, with large horns and a massive tail. It clears the ice in front of it with ease, toppling frozen clumps of ice and basically making a mess of the inhabitable parts of Venusian.

"If I didn't know any better, I'd say the creature was just having fun in the water."

"Probability of this is ninety-seven percent."

"Be quiet."

The striker encampment is just outside the range of their archers. Up till now, the creatures have not made an effort to leave their swimming creature. Why should they? They hold the advantage.

Walking through the encampment, I head straight to my blacksmith. Her large tent is filled with an array of sniper rifles—and the exact item I am looking for.

"I see the order came in," I say.

"Not sure why you wanted a lightning pulse net."

"It's useful to subdue an enemy and paralyze them momentarily."

"Here I thought you were supposed to kill something."

"Oh, I have plenty of things to do that." I twirl around in my new suit. "You like?"

"I'd have liked it more if I ordered it for you. But it is very impressive. When you get back, I will have to assess it so I know how to make repairs."

"I do not require your assistance in that area. I am self-sustaining," says the robotic Vixen.

"Did it just talk?"

"Yes, she can talk. The way of the future. Who knows, you may be out of a job soon enough."

The look of horror on my blacksmith's face is priceless. She will be sure to work much harder now. I like to keep my troupe on their toes.

I make my way over to the edge of the encampment and look at the line drawn indicating the limitation of their archers' range. It's exactly one foot longer than my current sniper rifle, and three feet longer than my old one. That shouldn't be possible. But when it comes to magic, there are many mysteries.

With my cannon placed against the thick layer of ice below, I unleash a huge blast of plasma. While sinking into the icy deep, my thoughts run to Vex and his fate.

*If only things could be different.*

# CHAPTER 5
## CLASSIFICATION: ROGUE STRIKER

*rip, drip, drip.* A leaky faucet dripping water. A sound I haven't heard since I was a child. Still just as annoying.

"Will someone fix that faucet?!"

"It's not a faucet, that's my new phenome!" says Sansa.

I turn around with a sore throat and an aching belly. My eyes lock onto a floating shark made of water. it has a collar and chain attached to it. The phenome circles around Sansa as if she is the prey and he is the hunter.

*Drip, drip, drip.* It continues to drip water onto the floor, making a mess everywhere.

"Does it have to make a mess?"

Sansa's eyes widen to the size of saucers. With her arms folded, she responds. "Yes, it does. Here I was, foolish enough to think you'd be happy for me. I'm officially a striker X."

"What did you kill?"

"It's a long story but I took down an A+ Desert Snake. We went hunting for one."

"Who is we?"

"Your father and I."

"I don't want you anywhere near him. He's bad news."

She looks at the ground and kicks air. "Seems alright to me. A little rough around the edges, like you. But good people."

"I said, stay away from him!"

"Alright, alright."

The door to the emergency room creaks open, and the old man who made short work of me approaches, this time decked out in his light green armor and cloak. He smirks.

"You heal pretty fast. How odd."

"What's odd is that I lost to some old bag of bones.'

"I'm not that old. Only seventy-two."

His grey beard seems to stretch forever.

"My real codename is Rogue, cofounder of the Red Rogue Alliance. It is a pleasure to make your acquaintance, Vexation."

The light elf that stood before me seems rather pleasant. His mannerisms are basic, indicating he is a low-born like me. But I will not be fooled by one's demeanor, for they often hold lies and deceit beneath.

"What do you want?" I ask.

"To see the great Vexation in action."

"It's Vex to you."

"Very well. Vex. Are you ready to go fishing? Or are you still bed-ridden?"

"How long have I been out?"

"About a week."

"Unacceptable. A simple poke to the neck and stomach shouldn't have done such damage."

"That, my friend, is why it wasn't simple. Come. Let us get further acquainted."

Struggling to my feet, I look at Sansa, who is still pouting. She wouldn't understand. My father is more devious than he looks. People like that don't change. At least not him.

Sansa moves to follow us with her drip-drop of a shark, but Rogue raises his hand.

"Unfortunately, Sansa, you cannot come. You have advanced training to take part in."

"Oh, okay." She lowers her head. A short moment later she raises her head and beams a massive smile at me. "You got this, Vex." Then she bounces away with her new phenome.

Rogue and I walk to the entrance of the facility. I step outside to see that the facility has moved a large distance. The sand is now white, but the two suns are as blistering as ever. I inhale the coarse air, only to find myself coughing. It seems my throat is still partially damaged.

"What are we hunting?"

"Whatever pops up. Could be a Sand Dragon, a Sand Scarab, maybe something worse?"

"I take it you don't have the territory mapped, then."

He looks at me as if I spat on his grandmother.

"These sands are ever-shifting. It takes a large portion of our computing power just to maintain the location of the Oasis in relation to ours. In time, you'll learn to love the sands like we do."

I take a handful of the grainy substance.

"Why would I love this?" I say, sprinkling it into the air.

"This desert grants us protection from the tyrannical organization that is the Interplanetary Galactic Force. It shields us from their lies, deceit, and their games."

"I see."

"You have sight, but you lack vision. In due time it will come. I have chosen you as the face for our movement. We can't afford to be a faceless organization like the IGF: a death-imbued organism that invades and destroys."

"What is your stance on monster hunting?"

"I see you wish to get to the difficult questions. My stance is that these creatures deserve to have a home. The rift is becoming uninhabitable due to the efforts of the cyber elves. This is a known fact. These sentient beings have no choice but to come to our planets—most of which are uninhabited. At the same time, food is scarce out here in the desert. Food replicators are a rare IGF technology. Thus, we have learned to adapt."

"So we're forced to eat these strange things?" As we gaze out into the vast desert, my sensors pick up on a large horn blitzing its way towards us.

"What am I looking at?" I ask.

"Our next meal."

The creature rises to the surface and forms itself into a ball. My sensors go crazy trying to identify what exactly it is. With a deafening shriek, it tumbles towards us.

"If we don't kill this thing in time, it will destroy the facility."

Rogue looks at me with a sly grin. "I think you mean, if you don't kill the Sand Scarab in time, it will destroy the facility."

*A test of some sort.*

My hands withdraw my glorious P90s Pain and Suffocation. As the creature barrels towards us, I move to leave the facility and step upon the sand when Rogue grips me by the shoulder.

"What's your damage, old man?"

"Just saving your life. It's high sand time, when the sands in the desert becoming sinking sands. Hence the floating villa as a facility."

I sigh. *This desert may very well be the end of me.*

I throw up my wind wall and wait, poised to unleash mayhem on the creature's golden shell. My feet tingle as the sand around me vibrates alarmingly.

*Will it hold? It's not just me that I have to think about. It's Sansa as well.*

I summon Tirade for added backup. Her gleam under the blitzing sunlight is elegant. For the first time in over a decade, I caress the top of her head. The wind fox seems almost to smile.

"You're more than just a pawn to be maneuvered. Just like I'm more than a killing machine."

The Sand Scarab rams into the wind wall, causing a large amount of energy distortion as it struggles. Tirade taunts, but to no effect. I watch in awe as the Sand Scarab stretches out its arms, legs, and head, revealing it to be larger than I previously thought. Spewing liquid from its mouth, it manages to overload my wind wall.

I unleash Pain and Suffocation onto the exposed eyes of the beast, shattering them like glass. The shards fall to the ground, manifesting smaller Sand Scarabs.

The original Sand Scarab makes a clicking sound before retreating. Now faced with around twenty smaller scarabs, I move for Tirade to assist me in cleaning up, but Rogue pauses my hand.

"You've done enough. We need to preserve the precious meat."

He takes out his green composite bow and shoots an energetic arrow into the air. Once it reaches its peak, the arrow splinters into twenty other energetic arrows, which fall onto the scarabs. Each scarab is impaled through the horned head, leaving their bodies untouched. The heads dissolve into green liquid, while the bodies flail wildly.

Rogue snaps his fingers, and the scarab bodies disappear.

"Who would have thought such a primitive weapon could manage such a feat."

"This weapon is but a mere extension of my will. There are many things you could be doing with your SMGs. You have not even come close to reaching your potential."

"Assist me in reaching my potential, and I will eliminate Morange for you."

"What we desire is more than just a simple assassination. We need a visage for the faceless organization we have become. Will you be our herald?"

"If that's what it takes to reach my maximum potential, then yes. But I will need you to be completely forthright with me. No secrets, no lies, no deceit. Complete and full honesty to any question I ask."

"That I can do. But this will require that we upgrade your chip to Y privilege."

"Tell me more about this Y privilege."

Rogue glances at me. "That isn't a question."

*I see now he will not reveal more than is necessary to keep me around. This man reminds me of Runnymede in some ways.*

"Who killed Runnymede?"

"You ask, yet you already know the answer. Sugar Cane, also known as Allison, is to blame."

Hearing the words stings almost as much as the flashback does.

"I didn't ask who is to blame. Who killed him?"

"His tag was Delirious."

"Was?"

"Yes, was."

"What happened to him?"

"He was killed, along with the other two involved, when you and your striker allies infiltrated our base on Marda."

While walking back to the confines of the villa my thoughts drift.

*At least Runnymede's soul will have some peace until I eliminate Morange and Allison.*

"What is so special about this Crypto Pyramid?"

"The Crypto Pyramid was a valuable part of keeping this realm safe. The cyber elves are worse than anything you can imagine. They are a living virus. But the Crypto Pyramid is a dead end."

"What exactly did you guys create?"

"Initially it was just supposed to crash the economy, but advanced technology often has a way of pushing boundaries. Now we are inside. It is best that we eat the scarabs while they are fresh."

I glance down to see the steaming hot scarabs spread across the dining table— along with a large serving of butter and what smells like some kind of alcoholic beverage.

I'd be lying If I didn't admit my taste buds are piqued. I take a seat at the head of the table. My father approaches me with his arms folded.

"You're in my seat, boy."

"If your name was on it, I'd scratch it off and still be sitting here. Old man."

My father reels back his fist and launches it towards my head. I lean forward and jam four fingers into his throat, making him cough repeatedly.

*Hmm, it seems my Tektra is coming back to me. I probably should have mentioned it's a very dirty way of fighting. Effective, but dirty.*

# CHAPTER 6
## CLASSIFICATION: POLITICIAN

**M**y hands tremble and my eyes bleed. Gripping the stair rail for leverage, I make my way down the steps. My legs give out from under me, and I tumble down ten steps, landing on the ground with a crunch.

*Something is broken.*

I shift my weight slightly, only to feel a sharp surge of pain shoot up my leg and spine. While glancing over at my two V-10 Battle Bots, I'm filled with mild contempt. At least the V-04 would have sent for assistance by now. It's been a year since Vex violated my personal space with his commoner dark-elf germs. A crime for which no punishment will suffice.

After pulling myself towards the kitchen, I am met with an empty room. My security detail is nowhere to be found. Probably watching the Elven Bowl in the living room. Elves are such unreliable creatures. Just because Vex is being hunted down like the rat that he is, doesn't mean I don't have other potential threats. Something I keep telling myself.

While crawling to the living room, I finally give up. The pain is unbearable, and the embarrassment sure to follow is bad enough. Placing my left hand on my right wrist, I activate my communication system. The screen pops up and I select Sanguine.

"Sanguine, make your way to the kitchen."

"If I must."

Sanguine manifests as a pool of blood. He oozes towards me, then materializes into full form. He is decked in a sleek red-and-black S+ grade battlesuit with a rocket booster attachment. But it's two blood revolvers, wielded to maximum efficiency, that make him worth every penny—though his demeanor could use some tweaks.

"How may I be of service?" he asks.

"Oh, am I bothering you?"

"One could come to that conclusion."

"Well, too fucking bad. Help me up and give me one of those blood packs of yours."

"I do warn you: The blood packs are not for regular consumption."

"Does it look like there is anything regular about my situation?"

"I suppose not. What is your ailment again?"

"It matters not. There is no cure, not here at least."

Gently he lifts me and places me on one of my fancy chairs. While sitting there like some kind of invalid. I ponder my poor existence.

*Addicted to an inferior substance. Forced to rely on my hired help. I'm sure by now he realizes that I need him more than he needs me.*

Sanguine removes the plug on the pack and hands it to me. I struggle to grab it with my trembling hand. But I refuse to be fed like a child. I place the tip of the hole at my lips, and the cold contents ooze down my throat. I lean back, waiting for the effects to take place.

Sanguine sits there in silence, watching me through his V-shaped red visor.

"What are you thinking?"

"One had heard you were more durable than this."

"Once upon a time, this was the case. But it would seem that I have been abandoned by my benefactors."

To think that after retrieving and delivering the Crypto Pyramid, the cyber elves would simply abandon me. No more elixirs, no more late-night conversations. I don't know which I miss more. The health-granting elixir or the intellectually stimulating conversations. Now I'm stuck with this. I glance down at the empty blood pack.

It's almost sickening what I have become. I had to ban my dear Sugar Cane from visiting. I don't dare let her see me like this.

I'd rather rot in my own feces then have her remember me as such a weak piece of trash—a very likely result. Once again it has dawned on me that without the cyber elves, my life has no meaning. Power, lust, and wealth mean nothing without health.

"Sanguine?"

"Yes?"

"I need you to do me a favor."

"I don't do favors. I do job requests and propositions."

"Very well. I will pay you double your year's salary if you kill me right now."

"And what of the other strikers under your employ? I will be designated a traitor like Vexation."

"I'm sure one of your means could find a way out of the scenario if you were to kill them all as well. Triple your salary."

"This is true; dead men tell no tales. I suppose that can be arranged."

Without hesitation, he pulls out his left revolver and points it at my head.

"Any last words?" he asks.

"I just..."

Suddenly, the lights flicker, and my various electronics shut off. Sanguine's universal Y-chip overloads, momentarily sending him to slumber. The console on my arm lights up, and the image of my half-brother manifests.

"Brother, did I catch you at a bad time? You're sweating up a mighty storm."

"Where were you?"

"Is that any way to greet your brother after—how long as it been?"

"It's been five months and twenty-two days."

"Oh, has it truly been so long?"

"Yes, it has been."

"Soon you will learn that time has no meaning in our realm. There are many things that we have to discuss. But first, I suppose I should give you a gift."

*Could this be the moment I have been waiting for? The moment where I finally enter their realm and become one of them?*

To my shock, his blue arm reaches through the screen and places a bottle filled with black liquid onto the dining table. The vile contents of the vial seem to be moving on their own.

"You have done well to retrieve the Crypto Pyramid. Now, we need you to finish what you started. The RRA has a final encampment somewhere deep in the Venusian desert. We need them fully wiped out before it is safe for us to move onto the next phase. The Crypto Pyramid has nearly been deciphered."

"What is your obsession with the RRA? I told you, they are nothing but vagabonds."

"Vagabonds? Then you would be surprised to hear that some influential members of the IGF HQ are involved in this coup d'état. It has extended its tentacles all the way to the top. And I suppose you would be even more shocked to know that Vice President Alterna has been tapped to head over to HQ. It was down to the wire between you and him."

"Why wasn't I chosen?"

"The answer is simple. HQ doesn't want to bring any attention to their operations. The majority is concerned that you are a walking target. Assassins will follow you to hell and back. Not to mention that they fear your influence and wealth from the underground operations. An alliance with Sugar Cane may have filled your pockets and drained your balls, but it certainly didn't make you any more friends up top."

"Conniving, pencil-pushing space bureaucrats, the lot of them!" I say.

"That's the spirit!"

"How do you know all of this?"

"All information is now my information. Thanks to you, I have replaced the previous He Who Sees."

"A promotion. Where, might I ask, is mine? You know what my heart truly desires—yet I am stuck here."

"Where you are is of no consequence. Focus on where you are going."

"And where might that be?"

"Wipe out the RRA in the desert. Then we will arrange for you to be sent to HQ, where you will experience untold levels of pleasures."

With that, the newly appointed He Who Sees disconnects from my console. I grasp the bottle with the black liquid and put it against my lips. More nanobots. But they must be repairing my body from the inside, while the blood pack only serves to slow down the illness.

After drinking the liquid, I cringe while the nanobots work their way through my internal system. Grabbing, clawing, and destroying the sickness from inside. The pain is excruciating, but I'd rather feel pain than be dead. To think that I was so close to assisted suicide. How low I had fallen in such short time.

But enough of that. I am refreshed and determined to see my objectives through. Sanguine stirs to his feet. He looks at me, then analyzes what's left of the nanobots in the bottle.

"Where did you get that? What happened?"

"None of your concern. The offer is off the table."

"You will answer my questions."

He moves as if to release his blood revolvers on me, but I'm faster. I hold my left hand in the air, telekinetically grasping his throat. I raise my hand, and he floats in the air.

I toss him against the fridge, denting it. "You will obey my commands."

Gripping his throat, he manages to nod slowly.

I stand and make my way up the stairs to my room. While passing by one of the primitive mirrors, I notice that my skin is a light blue tint. A wide smile creeps across my face.

"And so it begins."

# CHAPTER 7
## CLASSIFICATION: ROGUE STRIKER

I pry my eyes open to reveal Tirade up close in my face. Instinctively I push her head away, causing her to squeal. Somehow she manifested on her own—either that or I summoned her in my sleep. Either way, the result is the same. I'm met with the creature that is a manifestation of my shadow self.

*I wonder how the upgrading system works here.*

Making my way down to the basement, I hear a loud commotion, followed by blood curdling shrieks. My pace quickens.

Upon entering the training room, I'm met with a bloodied Sansa, surrounded by three water sharks. Her opponent is on her knees, covering her eyes. Or at least, what's left of her eyes.

"This darkling bitch plucked my eye out!"

"Call me a darkling again, and you'll lose another."

Who would have thought Sansa had such a vicious side to her? Then again, calling me a darkling has a similar affect. It's easily the worst thing a dark elf can be called. It has deep-rooted connotations to when dark elves were the slaves of the light elves. Once upon a time, my kind were raped, tortured, and experimented on to find out why our hue appeared different than the lighter of my kind. To make matters worse, we were also used as frontline fodder during the Great Desolation.

The time when Dwarves, Elves, and Orcs were at war with each other.

"Sleep with both eyes open, bitch. I just might gut you in your sleep."

And with that her opponent, a fair-skinned female light elf twice my size, storms off to the healing quarters. Carrying her eye in her hand she brushes past me.

"Move, puny IGF drone."

It seems adjusting here will be challenging. I've been called worse, though I suspect IGF drone is the worst thing one can be called while in the presence of the RRA.

When I approach Sansa, her sharks bare their sharp teeth at me.

"Care to put your little fiends away?"

"I can try. These things seem to have a mind of their own. I didn't even know I could summon three. I meant to summon my one Sharp Tooth, but when she started swinging slurs at me, all I saw was red. I wanted her dead. Never before has anyone spoken to me like that."

"It seems your family has kept you relatively sheltered from the fouler beings of society. Growing up, I was bombarded with all kinds of names. I'm not sure whether the words gain less meaning, or you just become numb to hearing them. But over time, one gets used to it. I must admit, being called a darkling still gets me riled up."

"Good to know. Will she really attack me in my sleep?"

"Perhaps. Hatred and embarrassment are powerful tools in the minds of the wicked. I'd sleep with my blade under my pillow if I were you."

*Part of me was joking, though part of me was serious. Prevention is better than a cure.*

I awake to the same shrill scream that beckoned me the previous morning—this time coming from Sansa's room. Immediately, I summon Tirade and phase-travel through the walls into her room. She is sitting on her bed covered in blood, while the same woman from before is covering her other eye.

Rogue and my father burst through the door, along with a group of onlookers.

"What happened here?" asks my father.

"She tried to gut me in my sleep," Sansa responds.

"Menace, is this true?"

"The little darkling deserved it. You saw what she did to me yesterday."

Sansa lunges at Menace with her plasma blade aimed at the woman's throat. I step forward and divert Sansa's momentum away from the woman.

"There will be no killing today."

My father steps forward and places a hand on my shoulder. My skin crawls to his touch.

"Perhaps this is where you are wrong. We have strict rules about shady tactics such as this. Menace will have to be executed."

"I see. If so, so be it," is the only response I can muster.

"By your hand."

"Why my hand? This has nothing to do with me."

"You are mistaken. You are the face of the organization, and as such, you have certain duties. You will execute her tonight after she has said her goodbyes and had her last meal."

The sands shift slightly beneath my feet as a gust of wind fills my lungs. The oxygen in the desert at night is somehow pure; the atmosphere is rather calming. It is on this night that I will execute my first elf. How is this any different than eliminating a monster or bringing down the wrath of the IGF on the RRA?

My mind ponders this question for a few minutes. The only answer I come up with is that it's easy to kill something when it's rearing its ugly head at you or shooting back. But when it's an elf, face-to-face, just sitting there waiting to meet her demise—now that is a whole different run on the track.

The woman brushes past me and stretches her broad shoulders. She takes a deep breath, then drops to her knees.

"Let's get this shit over with. Make sure to do it in one cleave. I don't want my head half-hanging dangling like a Chickaboo."

I take another deep breath, then approach with my wind scimitars poised to slice through the tendons and bone of her bulky neck. As she rests there on her knees, I feel my grip on my weapons of destruction loosen.

"Well? Hurry up, you stupid darkling. Or do you have cotton for a brain? This is the way we do things in the RRA. My only regret is ever laying eyes on you and your little whore. Now carry on—before I change my mind and jam those scimitars of yours in that pretty bitch's..."

*Clunk.*

Her head drops to the sand. The RRA members pray silently. Covered in her blood, I fall in a toxic daze.

*Perhaps I'm not as cold and callous as I once thought.*

Images of Tirade come to mind. I sense her pushing out, forcing her way into manifestation. How and why, I don't know. But one thing I'm sure of is that I don't like the idea of her summoning herself during my sleep. I mean, it's one thing when it's to save my life. but another when—I break off, realizing how hypocritical that is.

One thing I have learned about my life is that things come on an all-or-nothing basis. Tirade will either be all good for me, or all bad. But I suppose that is something I will have to decide in due time.

Sansa sidles up beside me, all bouncy with energy as usual. She keeps quiet, allowing me to ruminate in my thoughts, which is what I need right now. I suppose that's her intuition kicking in.

We make our way into the facility, where Rogue taps me on the shoulder. "In due time, you will understand how we do things here. Just know that there is a method beyond our madness. I wish to tell you a story."

"I'm not in the mood for stories."

"Well, you get in the mood. How pathetic was that? Hesitating during an execution," says my father, barging into the conversation.

"Will you hurry up and drop dead? How are you alive anyway?"

"We don't have much time for that briefing. Listen to what Rogue has to say. This is important."

I watch in amazement as my father creates a sand version of our solar system— with floating planets and all. It is rather detailed. The position where Marda is supposed to be is notably empty.

*A wound in my heart that won't heal any time soon.*

The sand map shows that Venusian is well protected by the Frontier Division, along with a large civilian space station marked HQ. I also note that there are several Frontier Division ships in the midst of many known uninhabitable planets.

"Vex, how much do you know about the Frontier Division?"

"I know that they protect the planets from rift monsters that orbit the planets."

My father and Rogue burst out into a fit of laughter, leaving Sansa and me confused.

"What's so funny?"

Rogue places a hand on my shoulder once again. "The lies they have filled your brain with can fill the entire desert."

"That isn't as poetic as it sounds. Now, what's the deal with the Frontier Division," I say.

"The Frontier Division is charged with population control and fighting the good fight against the lesser creatures of the galaxy—mainly the orcs. At least at one point in time. The orcs have been shot down to what is equivalently their stone age and have lost the ability for interplanetary travel. That leaves the Frontier Division as a mere training facility for the most gruesome military force in the IGF."

I take a seat. I feel as if my mind is unraveling from learning this deep stuff.

Rogue continues, "The Frontier Division monitors the actions of the orcs on their planets and shoots down any mild attempt at advancement. Every time the orcs build any semblance of advanced technology, the Frontier elves execute their brightest minds and steal their technology."

"This is a lot to take in. My question is: Why are you telling me all this?"

"Good question."

Rogue pauses and begins pacing back and forth.

"We want to send you on a special mission."

"I'm ready to enter the Oasis again. With the training I have received, I will take out Morange with ease."

"There has been a change of plans."

"What do you mean?"

"It seems Inquisitor Morange is making his way here with a slew of elite planetary strikers. At the same time, there is an opportunity for you to enter the highly sought-after comforts of HQ."

"My fight is here, then. I will not go."

"Your fight is where we tell you it is," grumbles my father.

Rogue continues. "As the face of the organization, it is important that you be seen as an untouchable force that could strike at any moment. If you fall now, everything we have worked for all this time will be for naught. Not to mention the fact that we need someone we can trust to protect Vice President Alterna. He has been selected for a position in HQ. Finally, there are several key strikers and officials that need to be taken care of. You are a Y now. Not a mere X. You are a trained assassin to be used to infiltrate the depths of enemy territory for the glory of all. You will be the hand of the movement by night and its face by day."

"What of Sansa?"

"Sansa has now completed Y training as well. She will accompany you and Vice President Alterna. We know you want revenge, and revenge you will have. You just have to trust us and stick to the big picture for now."

"What of my armor? Won't I be recognized by my battlesuit, or by voice recognition?"

"Normally yes, but we have a fix for that. We know how adverse you are to switching armors, and it is true that we don't have access to a suitable upgrade. What we do have access to is a distortion unit. Your armor will appear standard-issue Frontier Division armor, while your voice will be deepened to reflect someone a bit older. We'll do something similar with Sansa."

"As for my phenome?"

"Your phenome will appear as a red-and-black shadow fox. Sansa's phenome is currently unknown, so it will be okay. Just make sure you guys prevent those distortion chips from being found. We will place them under your Identification tags, where they will be covered. I must warn you, though. If you are found..."

"We won't be found."

"But if you are found. The upgraded chip in your tongue will prevent you from speaking on most things to any IGF personnel—meaning they will likely torture you for the rest of your lives."

"Death or success it is, then."

"Death or success," Sansa, my father, and Rogue repeat.

The floating palace rocks and shakes, and then I have a falling feeling. Before I know it, we're sinking into the sands. Like lightning and thunder, the crackle of explosives intertwine.

Sansa and I are ushered to the back of the palace and met with a sand skid. The vehicle is sleek and flat—perfect for maneuvering through the chaotic terrain of the desert. Like a fish in water, Sansa immediately gets inside and starts the vehicle.

"You need to head to the engagement point and enter the transport ship for Vice President Alterna. Make sure any tagalongs meet their demise before your arrival. We don't want any unnecessary questions."

I nod to Rogue.

As I'm about to take my leave, my father approaches me. "I know we've had our differences. Just know that your mother would be proud of you on this day. You remind me of myself in so many ways, and I can't stand that. But carry on your way, and show them hell!"

I rip away my gaze from the one called Viral. I don't know what to make of what might be his last words. It's an odd thing, mourning the death of your father twice. Maybe this time I'll shed a genuine tear.

# CHAPTER 8
## CLASSIFICATION: POLITICIAN

I marvel at my hands. My nails seem to be a tad sharper, while my palms have a strange blue marking. I cut myself earlier, and the nanobots sealed the wound within moments. Though painful, it was quick.

We are about to unleash death upon the remaining RRA members; we approach them now in the Popo-3000 mechanized police vehicle.

I have managed to gain knowledge of their base movements from one of their captured members. My battle bots were rather effective in the acquisition of information. Her screams will forever be etched in my advanced brain. But all success comes at a price, and I am willing to undergo any pain, suffering, or sacrifice to achieve my goals.

I look to my left and analyze the Popo-3000 robotic planetary division officer. Her thick metal legs have a red-and-blue design, and her slender arms contain a high-powered taser, a long distance net, and disabling smoke canisters. Although not an effective battle bot, she will be useful in capturing some members alive—Vex in particular.

In the back of the vehicle lie my battle bots, waiting to kill anything I point at. If only elves were as meticulous in following instructions as my bots are. As usual, I feel secure surrounded by my mechanical comrades.

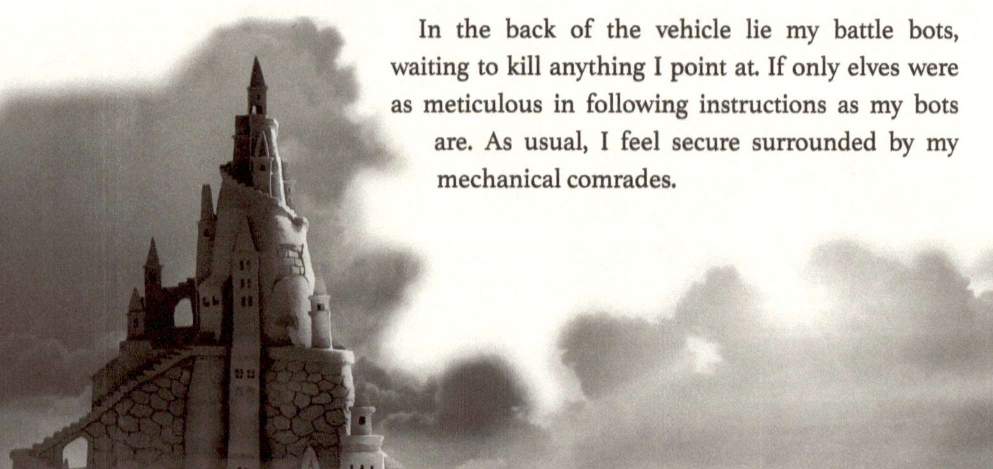

There is a knocking on my side of the window. I roll down the window and peer outside.

"What is it, Sanguine?"

"I see a palace of some sort in the distance. It seems the intel we got was accurate."

"Of course it was. I retrieved it. None can stand before my questioning."

"Sure thing, boss."

And with that, Sanguine zooms off, followed by Quaint. Sanguine is an exceptional assassin, doubling as an effective protection unit. But Quaint is the real prize. I watched in awe as she took on Vex and two other striker-X adversaries at the same time. Her bounty-hunting skills are well-known throughout the galaxy. When she heard about the chance to redeem herself, she offered her services to me for peanuts.

The hover car catches up to the floating palace, which has been halted and surrounded. I get out of the car to get a better view of my military excursion. Explosions go off on both sides, causing my battle bots to initiate elimination protocol. I watch as the two lumbering behemoths emit huge lasers, turning any incoming threats to dust. It looks like this will be a clean mop-up until the sky is blocked out by green arrows. The shields around my battle bots raise, protecting myself and a few planetary soldiers.

In the distance I see the strikers Rogue and Viral, long-thought deceased, charging towards me. Part of me wants to run, but the nanobots in my body give me the confidence that I need. The sand beneath our feet shifts, disturbing the shield, just as the arrows rain down havoc on me and my men.

A green arrow lodges itself inside my arm; the projectile twists and turns, creating more pain than it should. To my amazement, the nanobots push out the arrow and seal the wound, leaving me nearly unmarked. I sneer as Rogue and Viral appear before me in a wave of sand.

"I see the rumors of your untimely deaths were well exaggerated. How long has it been, Rogue?"

"It's been some time. Who would have thought that my mentee would one day have to be killed by my own arrow?" says Rogue.

"I never liked learning from you. You taught me nothing that I will take to my grave."

"You scoundrel!" says Viral, stepping forward in a fury of raging sand.

"Quiet, you—the more respectable members of society are speaking. Know your place, and begone with you."

My two battle bots turn their attention to Viral and let off two laser beams aimed at his head. A sand shield pops up, taking the brunt of the damage. Viral follows this by swinging his great sword in a sweeping motion, causing the sands beneath the bots to sink and engulfing them with ease. I hear a crunching sound as the weight of the sand crushes my expensive units.

I wipe the sweat off my forehead and glide forward. With my upgraded shotgun in hand, I manage to send forth a barrage at Viral's face. His sand barrier comes up once again, followed by another shifting of the sands—this time below my feet. Floating with my telekinesis, I engage Viral in close-quarters combat as my battle instincts begin to kick in.

Just as Rogue aims a high-powered arrow at my throat, Quaint and Sanguine join the skirmish. Although bloodied, they are not beaten. Quaint spins in several circles, then takes the knee. Fire erupts from her body, turning her into some kind of fire monstrosity.

*It is said that a Z bounty hunter is one that has mastered an element as well as their internal energetic system: the ultimate force on the battlefield.*

Quaint fire-steps behind Rogue and grips him in flaming choke lock, while Sanguine points his blood-infused revolver at the rebel's head. Rogue has this eerie grin on his face as he flips Quaint over, slamming her into the sand, then quickly releases an arrow into Sanguine's chest.

Viral is upon me at this point, his sand shield blocking another barrage from my shotgun. My powers kick up another notch as he closes the distance. I telekinetically pick him up and throw him against the police vehicle, increasing the gravity around him to crush him.

His bones audibly crack and break as he lets out a low grunt.

Inch by inch I float closer to him, eyes poised like a falcon as he struggles underneath my increased power. A giant hand made of sand erupts from the ground and grips me, causing my attention to sway and releasing Viral in the process. As the sands threaten to engulf me, I feel my body craving oxygen.

Sanguine is the first to release his phenome: a black tiger with red stripes. The phenome's blood drips onto the sand, singeing it. The tiger immediately pounces on

Viral and begins to maul him. Each strike deals high levels of blood damage.

Rogue tries to summon his own phenome, but the mechanized Popo exits the vehicle and throws an energy-reducing net onto the rebel. The net neutralizes his internal system, preventing him from using any energy-based attacks. The Popo bot follows this by throwing an explosive collar around Rogue's neck, effectively preventing him from resisting. It's at this point that Viral is finally subdued—and unconscious due to the blood loss.

I walk up to Rogue with a sly grin.

"Had you two been in your prime, capturing you alive would have been impossible. It seems father time always wins in the end."

Rogue dons a pretentious smile, unfit for a low-born light elf. "This war is meant for the new generation now. This is just the beginning; you may have silenced the old generation, but the new one will carry the torch aflame in newfound ways. Your vile maker shall see your face soon enough."

"Commoners should know their place." is my only response. I take the butt end of my shotgun and ram it into his head, making him slump unconscious in a pool of his own blood.

*Just the way it should be.*

I watch in disgust as Sanguine's tiger sucks up all the blood in the sand, turning its stripes a darker red. Sanguine takes the knee and gives his phenome a big hug before it disappears into the depths of his psyche. He rolls his head back and lets out a low moan.

*Must be in some kind of euphoric state.*

Quaint approaches me with her swords sheathed and fire dimmed. "It seems we have served our purpose. The RRA is no more."

I scan the battlefield for the bodies of Vex and his mysterious companion—to no avail.

"How would you like a more permanent position?"

"What's your offer?"

"Everything."

It's been two weeks since the Battle of the Sands, as it has now been called. My protection unit and I have been summoned by the powers that be in HQ. I spread my arms out in angst as I await the promotion that I surely deserve. I single-handedly led the takedown of the RRA's base of operations in Venusian and Marda. Perhaps I will be a permanent member of HQ: a long-forgotten dream suddenly made possible.

I glance at Viral, whose posture irks my whole existence. He stands proud in captivity as though he has won an award. Rogue follows suit, his back straight and chin held high. I take the butt end of my shotgun and jam it into Viral's back. He stumbles, then spits on the ground. As we board the hovercraft to the HQ ship, I get tingles all over my body. Whether that is a good sign or not, I'm not completely sure.

The mysterious faces of the Frontier Division strikers grant me and my company a silent salute. I suppose that is to be expected from the space chasers. They see through the same lens that I have. The RRA are nothing but bottom mongrels licking the tip of our shoes. The IGF is all-powerful, the IGF is all-dominant, and above all, none can rival our military force. The only thing superior to the IGF is the cyber elves—of which I will become one in due time.

The inside of the hovercraft is sleek and comfortable. Nothing but the finest for me. I sit on the luxury bull-leather couch and lean back. A robot server brings me a glass of illmoir scotch. My absolute favorite. A drink only the refined of my kind can truly afford. I watch as Sanguine and Quaint escort the prisoners to the holding cells. It's a beautiful sight to see the head of the RRA cut off with such swiftness. Rogue was once a reputable member of HQ, said to be killed in an accident. HQ was well surprised to see that he was alive, kicking, and above all leading the RRA. He was followed by the disgraced and crazed Viral; the pairing was doomed from the start.

Sanguine takes a seat beside me while Quaint pulls in a chair from the dining table.

"So, boss. Tell me. How'd you get your health back? One minute you're a mere invalid, the next you're crushing Viral with a swing of your hands," says Sanguine.

"That's none of your concern."

"But it is our concern. What if it has consequences that will affect you down the line? Perhaps you should allow me to do a blood analysis."

"That won't be necessary."

"If you say so, boss. Just doing my job."

"Well, do your job and feed the prisoners while I engage Quaint in conversation."

Now, at this point, I'm not sure what expression lay behind Sanguine's helmet. What I do know is that I don't care. I find his presence disturbing. Why? Again, I do not know. But as soon as I can find a superior replacement, I will do so.

Quaint is silently eating a bunch of moon grapes with her helmet off, revealing her modest features. She isn't ugly by any means, but not a beauty either. Simply the elf next door. Her hair is silver, her eyes an unusual silver hue that makes her average at best. I suppose that's where her name came from.

"What's up?"

"That's no way to address your superior."

"Oh, I thought you wanted me to blow you or something."

"What?"

A sly grin creeps across her face. "You heard me."

"No, that won't be necessary. I've learned mixing business with pleasure makes things complicated."

"That's good, I don't like the taste of old man. But 'whatever the job dictates' is my motto."

"Would it be that simple a task for you?"

"You clearly do not know what goes on during Z training. I'd blow a hundred illness-infested peckers if it meant completing the job at hand. My womanhood is a weapon that I wield as effectively as my blades."

"I see."

"So now that the blood-drinking weirdo is out of earshot, tell me more about your remedies, and I'll tell you a little secret about the RRA."

She switches to the seat beside me. Her aroma fills my nose, making me slightly intoxicated. I sense my tongue moisten and my eyes close slightly. The effects of a subtle yet deadly aphrodisiac and truth-telling plant. Rare, exotic, and above all devious. With a flick of my wrist, I manage to fling her across the room into the wall. Her head bangs against the side of the ship with a thud. She rises to her feet immediately, rubbing the back of her head.

"Oh, I suppose you know about Stelladonna. It seems you aren't as clueless as you look."

She is eager to test my powers this evening. But I will not be toyed with—especially not by my hired help.

I close my eyes calmly and lie down on the couch. Although not in the least bit tired, I know she won't dare progress any further in her duplicitous actions if I simply ignore her.

"You're no fun. Perhaps I will go and play with one of the HQ goons."

I respond with silence.

# CHAPTER 9
## CLASSIFICATION: ROGUE STRIKER

Sansa and I have done well adjusting to our lives as Frontier Division strikers. My assumed codename is Vindication. After the use of her phenome during a duel and the cleanup it required, Sansa's name changed from something respectable to Leaky Faucet. Albeit suitable, I find it disrespectful. She is just happy to be a striker—even if our true identities could be revealed at any moment.

After two weeks in the division, I have managed to rank up from fifty-nine to fifty-five, while Sansa has managed to rank up from dead last at sixty to fifty-nine. The grind is slow in the Frontier Division; the ranks are as political as they are based on skill. We are outmatched in both. I could never have imagined that the gold-famed executioners and the other members sent from the Frontier Division were actually the bottom of the barrel. Tiddly, who managed to mop the cement with me, was only ranked fifty-sixth when he was sent down to the Eclectic Division. One thing that has become clear is the deaths of Axis and his sister:

That was no rift monster.

It's a common joke among the strikers in the Frontier. Axis' medical ship was shot down by one of our own—a precaution to prevent the spread of disease and illness. The strikers of the Frontier Division are even more valued than the precious credits that the economy runs on, and thus a few rotten apples will be sacrificed for the many in the bunch.

"Vindication, tell me, what is the honor code for one of your status?" The question comes from my scum bucket of a supervisor.

I stand upright with my chin tilted up. "The honor code is as follows: A striker from the Frontier will hold the lives of any HQ member above their own—though the life of a Frontier striker is above any orc, dwarf, or elf that disgraces a planet with their footsteps. Leonidas, sir."

Leonidas twirls his massive battle hammer in the air, then lightly taps it against the floor of the hovering ship. The room turns into a space chamber; the stars outside now seem to be inside. The moons and the planets that surround us in the galaxy all are displayed within the training section of the large battleship.

"Leaky Faucet." The group of strikers chuckle to themselves.

"Yes, Leonidas sir!"

"What is your duty as a guardian of the Frontier Division?"

"My duty is to uphold the honor code at all times while protecting the elite members of HQ. Their lives are in my hands, and my hands are their will. To lose a member of HQ is the equivalent of losing a limb."

"Excellent. It seems you two are ready to join your sponsor. May HQ shine down on you, and all hail the IGF."

"All hail the IGF!" repeats everyone in the room.

The two-week training was gruesome even by Eclectic standards and would have been difficult for Sansa and me had we not already gone through rigorous training with the Red Rouge Alliance. Physical torment is one thing, but the mental is what troubles me. These people are basically walking cyborgs: trained to be as machine-like as possible. They worship the IGF and HQ like the blacksmiths worship the Most High.

As we walk towards the council chamber, I notice that a new ship has arrived. The system message emitting from my wrist console confirms it. Upon arriving at the council chamber, I enter my personal code ID into the keypad.

"You know, you could just scan your ID badge, and it would open," says Sansa.

"I know this. We were both there for the introductory lesson," I answer dryly.

"So why don't you? It would save us time. Instead you're fiddling around with the keypad."

"Listen here, Miss Leaky Faucet. When I require your assistance, I will ask."

After three attempts, my memory fails me, and I finally resort to just scanning the ID badge.

The doors swing open, and we enter the room where the meeting is just about to begin. We stand behind the newly appointed Legislator Alterna. He gives us a nod. Behind every member of HQ are two Frontier Division strikers—each deadlier and more conniving than the other. I have the names and known abilities of most strikers within the division memorized, especially potential targets. I am now working on the HQ members, but the information I have available to me is limited.

Our mission is clear. We are to lay dormant for one full year before we begin eliminating the targets. Some are strikers, while some are HQ members. Our contact on board the space station will give us further instructions when the time is right. Who this person is, I don't know, but I do know is that they have been dormant for over a decade. Hopefully, they can still be trusted.

*The tentacles of the RRA run into the depths of the abyss that is space and time.*

As the council members each drone on about their respective issues, I find myself dozing off.

*Numbers, politics, and more numbers.*

Who would have thought that serving as a guardian to a high-ranking member of HQ would be so boring?

*I wonder what Chaos is up to? Maybe she even got married to her first sweetheart. Maybe if I had made a move sooner, I wouldn't even be here right now. We would be off galivanting in the Venusian Oasis, sprawled in the hot springs.*

The struggle between my brain and heart is one that I must endure. My heart wants more, but my mind tells me that this is the right course of action. I may not wholeheartedly believe in the RRA and their methods, but I have the conviction and wherewithal to know that the IGF can no longer be the governing body.

*Simply a means to an end, I suppose.*

"And without further ado, we have the arrival of our guests and the newly appointed Grand Inquisitor."

The doors swing open and my jaw drops, while my hands instinctively reach for my P90s. Sansa grasps my left hand tightly, snapping me back to my senses.

A wave of fury rises from my feet all the way to my head. My gaze intensifies as my heart drops to my stomach. My eyes lock onto the newly appointed Grand Inquisitor Morange as well as Quaint and an unknown striker. What's more maddening is the sight of Rogue and Viral in electro-cuffs.

Quaint and the striker march my father and Rogue to the middle of the chamber for all to behold the glorious end to the RRA.

*So they think.*

Viral and Rogue are thrown to the floor and forced to rise to their knees. The Grand Inquisitor waves his hand with a wide grin.

"I bring you the festering puss that has plagued the IGF for years. The heads of the RRA, and the end to their pitiful rebellion."

"Heh. You know nothing, Morange. You and your kind will remember this day as the day you truly lost," says Rogue.

"We have other matters to discuss. Who shall take on the honor of dispatching of the scum?" says Morange.

Every striker in the room raised their hands except me and Sansa.

"Vindication, Leaky Faucet. Why do you not raise your hands?" asks one of the HQ members.

Sansa is about to stutter out a response when I cut her off.

"We are new and thus did not think it would be right to take the honor away from the more seasoned strikers. Sir!"

"Hmmm. Perhaps that is why you should do the honors. To new beginnings!"

"To new beginnings!" repeat the strikers and HQ.

Quaint and the other striker remove themselves from the middle as Sansa and I replace them. I'm now standing right beside Morange. If he only knew how close he was to death, he'd shit himself. It could all be over in an instant. I'd pull out my P90 and send a barrage of bullets into his ball-headed dome.

But today is not that day. It is a day for dirtying my hands further in the name of IGF protocol.

I approach behind Viral and withdraw my wind scimitars, forcing Sansa to do the same behind Rogue with her plasma blade. The eyes of the HQ button-pushers intensify. The head of their dreaded foe is about to be put down.

"Any last words?"

"The RRA will never die!" they say simultaneously. The shout is followed by the sound of their rolling heads.

Taking my father's life was easier than I thought. All I had to do was channel all my pent-up hatred towards him. The seeds of disappointment and abuse blossomed into a putrid plant of disdain. How Sansa managed to eliminate Rogue without hesitating, I will never know.

*My wrath keeps me firm, strong, and resolute.*

# CHAPTER 10

## CLASSIFICATION: CHAOTIC STRIKER

Time has escaped me while on this behemoth. Communication with home base is fuzzy. The only voice in my ear comes from my battlesuit. She guides my every step as I systematically eliminate every monster on this S+ grade monster. I have cleared out the archers that lined the wall. Soon the strikers of my division will flood the behemoth in an effort to get a shot or two on the kill.

It is now time to enter the castle and see what this Frost Knight is all about. I will execute my mission with expert precision—as I have many times before.

*I am the perfect killing machine. I am Chaos.*

While the temperature is well below freezing, my suit manages to keep me relatively warm. It's a work of art. I open the large blue doors of the castle, which creak. If the element of surprise was an advantage, I have lost it.

Every step I make in the hollow halls of this castle echoes.

The thundering voice of what I presume is the Frost Knight echoes into the hallway I'm walking down. The blue carpet ripples with his every word.

*The voice of an angel.*

His singing seems to enthrall my heart, and I aimlessly glide to his side. I feel myself dropping to my knees and gripping the legs of his battlesuit.

*What has become of my senses?*

He peers down at me, dressed in glorious blue-and-silver armor. His piercing blue eyes glow through the eye slits. With the voice of some otherworldly being, he speaks. We are transported to a large dining room filled with paintings of himself in different poses.

"Greetings, my love. We have been waiting your arrival."

The gloomy dining room lights up to reveal a glorious feast. The guests move quickly, consuming their meals and engaging in spirited conversation. I feel myself compelled to join them, but I await my beloved's instruction. He gently grasps me by the shoulder and raises me to my feet.

As if he could read my mind, he asks the question I am dying to answer. "Shall we eat?"

I nod my head fervently and take the place beside him; he pushes my chair underneath me.

"Take off your helmet and begin your meal," he instructs.

I begin to remove my helmet, but I find myself hesitating. Why would I hesitate to follow the instructions of my beloved?

The tiny voice of Vixen whispers into my ears.

"Cold."

But yes—the cold. The only thing separating me from death is this battlesuit of mine, and that includes the helmet.

I find myself struggling to speak the words I must. Why is that?

"My love, if I take off my helmet, the cold will kill me. Will it not?"

"Such a thing is not possible—for you are one with me, and I am one with you. Thus, you are protected."

I move to remove my helmet once again when a sharp pain surges through my brain, followed by Vixen's blaring voice.

"Incompatible biological unit detected. Taking measures to extract."

Another sharp pain erupts in my brain until I feel the slimy creature leak out of my left ear.

Regaining my senses, I point and shoot my cannon into the Frost Knight's face. His voice distorts from its once-angelic harmony to something more devious. His armor darkens to a dark blue, and his blade leaks the aura of death.

With ease, he catches the full blast of the cannon beam and diverts its power to the side.

Standing up, his voice thunders. My sensors automatically lower its volume.

"You dare to defy my will? I shall rape and pillage your body a thousand times over!"

The members of the table freeze in place as the Frost Knight flips the table and unsheathes his broadsword and shield.

I backpedal, unleashing several charges of the cannon, but to no avail. He is faster than he appears. Once within striking distance, he sweeps his broadsword in my direction, and it wails. My head spins for a few moments as he charges directly at me and rams his shield into my stomach. I'm launched into the air several feet as blood escapes my lips.

"Warning: Another direct blow like that may prove fatal."

"Tell me something I don't know," I whisper.

"Perhaps switching to your sniper rifle will be more effective," says Vixen.

I switch to the sniper rifle and am immediately comforted by the stealth. With my glorious wings extended, I fly as high as the ceiling and take aim.

"You think you can hide from me? This is my castle and you are a mere nuisance."

I unleash a bolt of lightning from my rifle at his chest, and he drops to his knees. I follow this attack with a shot to the neck that drops him to the floor. In the most acrobatic of maneuvers, I tumble to the ground with my weapon now in hammer formation. Poised to crush every bone in his body, I reach within inches of my mark when he rises from his paralysis, leaking blue liquid from his neck and chest.

At the final moment, he blocks the thundering blow with his shield, but is still struck by the follow up lightning. He flings me away easily, sending me crashing into a nearby wall. A storm of ice and snow surrounds the Frost Knight. Every step he takes towards me forces my suit to further adjust in order to keep me alive.

*If this were any other suit, I would be dead already. I must overcome.*

His mighty broad sword tries to cleave me down, but I block with my war hammer. Sparks fly in every direction.

"May I offer a suggestion?" inquires the Vixen automated system.

I manage a grunt as I hold back the fierce blow.

"Perhaps now would be a good time to activate your automatic hip revolvers?"

"Activate hip revolvers."

The red revolvers at my hips light up and turn to face the knight. They let off several shots into his stomach area. He staggers back as I twist and twirl, slamming my war hammer into his head. I hear a loud crunch. His helmet is nearly missing, revealing a disfigured skeletal structure for a head.

The gruesome figure sends forth a blast of foul, dirty ice from his shield, slowing my movements severely. He follows this up by piercing his blade into my stomach.

The warning buzzers go off, disrupting me further.

"Warning, warning: Further damage will result in death."

"No shit."

He removes the blade as I drop to my knees, using my war hammer for leverage. Just when he is about to deal a decisive blow, I summon my phenome known as Order, who flies forward sending massive lightning shocks into the Knight. At this distance, it's a sure kill.

Or so I thought.

The Frost Knight cleaves at my phenome, giving me time to stand. I watch in amazement as the nanobots that make up thirty percent of my suit begin the healing process. They manage to seal the wound just as I charge forward with a sweeping motion, knocking the Frost Knight onto his side. I raise my hammer high above my head.

I activate the rockets on the back of the hammer and take a power stance. With every ounce of my being, I slam the destructive weapon into the side of the Frost Knight. Mechanical steel meets his armor as I hear bones breaking and see blood gushing.

A grin creeps over my lips.

My victory is short-lived; the behemoth monster wails a destructive cry and begins a descent into the icy deep. I take the sword and shield of the Frost Knight and power boost my way to the exit.

Upon arriving at base camp, I am met with my scavengers. Two of the bumbling oafs rush to gather the Frost Knight's sword and shield.

My fellow strikers stand and applaud as I make my way towards the blacksmiths' quarters. It seems the video feed was working. After a slew of high-spirited salutes and numerous pats on the back, I find myself at my blacksmith's tent. Exhausted and sore.

As I lay down on the worktable, I find myself unfulfilled. Normally, I'd celebrate with a massive party—one to rival the ages. But perhaps I need a quiet night alone. To think that the entire division—and perhaps members of HQ—saw me fawn over the Frost Knight. Enthralled by his infestation wurm.

What makes matters more perplexing is that I truly felt in love. My heart was his for the taking, served on a golden platter. How unbecoming. My heart is a funny thing: a creation whose sole purpose is to make sure the rest of the body functions well. Yet it is also the guiding light for when one finds themselves in the dark.

My heart is as fickle as it is bold. A curse from my mother, yet a gift from my father.

"Everything seems to be in working order." My blacksmith raises an eyebrow. "What brings you to my facility?"

"Matters of the mind and heart."

"Ahh, thoughts of Vex again? I thought we went through this. He isn't good for you. He will only bring about your demise. Why not focus on the task at hand?"

"What task? I'm already number one. I've been number one since I was selected for this division. There is no progression. It's all become so dull."

"Well, what about the challenge of remaining number one?"

"Tyrant's mind has dulled ever since he got hitched with Ivy. She has him wrapped around her fingers. At least Vex made things interesting; you never really knew what rule he would break or new feature he would unlock. Now it's all just dull."

"There are some up-and-coming strikers. Rank thirty-seven is quite interesting."

"So I'm to wait another year for him to catch up to me in rank? Ugh, you don't understand."

"Perhaps I don't. But I don't like seeing you this way."

"Maybe it will all fizzle about and I'll feel better in the morning. Mind if I sleep here? I need a change of scenery."

"Whatever Lady Chaos desires."

# CHAPTER 11
## CLASSIFICATION: ROGUE STRIKER

I check the calendar to see that another month has passed by. Every day inches closer to the moment when I can break out of character and eliminate a target. Who exactly that target will be is a mystery. Perhaps I will get lucky and it will be Morange.

As I await the buzzer for training duties, the repetitive nature of our existence weighs on me. From the training bouts, to the propaganda, to the secrets. Each rank that I progress reveals another secret of the IGF. It has gotten to the point that I am having a hard time differentiating what is fact, fiction, or in between. Then there is the hazing that strikers rank forty and below experience. False training buzzers, fake news, and the spreading of rumors.

*I'm going to kill the one who spread the rumor that Sansa and I are intertwined. What am I, some kind of juvenile predator?*

My alarm goes off, and my supervisor Leonidas pops up on my console.

"Vindication, it is time for the briefing on your first Frontier mission. Head to the cargo deck."

*A welcome change.*

I find myself sprinting towards the cargo deck. Upon arrival I enter my key code, which I have finally managed to memorize. The doors slide open, and immediately my heartbeat increases

while sweat emerges from my palms. I'm met with the ranks thirty-five, twenty, and fourteen strikers. Their weapons are all pointed at my head and chest.

"It seems I've entered the wrong room. I'll be taking my leave."

As I turn to make my escape, I feel the gigantic metallic fist of Stomper. The tenth-ranked striker in the division. I'm sent flying into the transport barrels. The bright room full of barrels and crates dampens my vision as the all-female cast of strikers circle me.

"What kind of training is this?"

"Training? I suppose you could call it that. We're going to train you not to touch younglings. Leaky Faucet is only sixteen," says Stomper.

"There seems to be a misunderstanding. I have never touched Leaky Faucet in that way—ever. Nor do I see her in that way. She is like a little sister to me."

"The only misunderstanding will be what they think when they find my mega-fist shoved up your ass."

The gruesome image of such a thing is enough to send me into battle mode. I'm not gonna allow myself to be taken advantage of. But before I enter my fighting stance, I attempt diplomacy one more time.

"Have any of you even spoken to Leaky Faucet about this?"

"Many times. She wholeheartedly denies that any such thing has occurred."

"So why are we having this conversation?"

"Because it isn't difficult to brainwash the young into thinking that what you're doing to them is right. We have all been through it in this division. The vile touch of a man whose hand you'd rather sever. The foul kiss of a superior to progress further or else be relegated to the bottom of the barrel. It seems you have adapted quicker than most men, you juvenile predator!" says Stomper.

Stomper's words hit home for me, for no elf should be forced to carry out sexual acts for progression.

However, those who will not hear must feel. Though outmatched, I have one thing going for me. I don't need to defeat them. I just need to get past them.

I suck in the cool air of the room, mixing it with the warm air in my body. Releasing the mixture lets out a massive fog blast that fills the room. I charge towards the exit before feeling a prick as a kunai pierces the back of my shoulder.

My shoulder droops down; a tingling sensation erupts, followed by a numbing sensation.

Soon I am left with a completely numb right arm. My left, brandishing my wind scimitar, slashes forward at Stomper as her massive fist careens in my direction. I easily dodge the slow punch but am blindsided by a fist emerging from the ground, connecting an upper cut.

The blow leaves me dazed as I wobble several feet forward. My jaw is broken, and blood leaks from my mouth. But I refuse to give in so easily.

Tirade lunges into the middle of the circle and uses mass taunt, which gives me enough time to make it to the exit. I use my badge to open the door, but it refuses to open.

*Trapped. They must have a technician working with them.*

I manage to set four flutter bombs on the door before I hear Stomper's thundering war cry, followed by the footsteps of the other three female strikers.

By activating my cloak skill, I'm able to blend into the fog, blocking any heat sensors or anti-cloak devices. The sensation in my right arm slowly returns as I begin to remove the threats from commission. Creeping behind the rank-twenty Rayne, I grip her from behind into a choke lock. Rayne kicks and thrashes, but my training kicks in to prevent her from escaping. She makes a gurgling sound as she lays unconscious.

The flutter bombs go off, barely leaving a scratch on the reinforced corundum doors. Stomper stands in front of the door like a bulldog waiting for the fog to clear.

"Come out, you pervert!" shrieks Hyper Fairy, ranked fourteenth. She hovers high into the air and starts randomly shooting the plasma cannon attached to her arm.

"Cut it out, fairy," says Stomper.

"Why?"

"Because you just shot Rayne in the stomach."

"Oh, teehehhee."

She flails her hands in the air, revealing the other arm to be wielding a heated pressure sword of some sort.

Not something I want to be entangled with.

"Now what? The coward won't come out from hiding."

"Take Rayne to the medical facility. Kunai and I will handle things from here on out."

"Aww, are you mad at me?"

"Just go."

Stomper whispers into her communication unit, and the door flies right open. Once it shuts behind her, she patrols the area with her super-charged fist, ready to break bones and rip apart flesh.

My sensors pick up movement from behind me just as Kunai flings several throwing knives at my throat. I bring up my wind wall at the last second, and Tirade launches forward with a wind blast. A crazed yellow gorilla rolls in front of Kunai and absorbs the blast, then grabs Tirade and slams her repeatedly against the floor until she dissipates.

The fog has effectively worn off, and I'm trapped between Stomper, Kunai and the crazed gorilla.

I turn off my stealth, which has no use against Stomper's heat detection, and pull out my P90s.

I'm breathing heavily, as my energy is near-depleted, and my eye catches the writing on one of the red barrels.

*Highly explosive octane oil.*

A rare substance used somewhere in the production process of booster packs. I aim my P90s at the barrel. Stomper rushes forward in an effort to block the barrage, but she is too slow.

I riddle the barrel with bullets. My only hope is that it kills me, because to go to the medical ward would mean revealing my identity. My eyes light up as the barrel explodes in fire, sweeping up Stomper, Kunai, the gorilla, and myself in a wave. It fills the room. The last thing I remember is my body engulfed in flames as I lie triumphant.

"What a good day to die," I whisper.

It seems Lady Destiny has other plans for me. I wake a few days later in the medical ward. My hands are not bound to anything, nor are my legs. A shock, considering my identity should have been revealed as the rebel and assassin Vexation.

My skin is charred and scabbed, while my bandaged face aches. But other than the severe burns, I am relatively in good health—or so I presume.

A dark elf medical officer with a mechanical arm walks up to me with a smile.

"So, you're awake. Quite the remarkable healing ability, considering what you put your body through. Stomper and Kunai are both still out of commission."

"How am I still alive?"

"It would seem someone opened the door of the cargo deck, allowing a portion of the blast to escape and diminishing what was inside. If not for that, we'd have a hard time identifying who was who. Hehehe."

"I see."

"But on to bigger and better things." He leans in and whispers. "You're fortunate, Vexation, that it was I on duty when all this occurred. The RRA has many eyes but few hands now that we've lost the desert. We will have to be careful."

My eyes widen. "Are you my contact?"

"Oh, for elven sakes, no." He sprays a cool liquid all over my body.

"Your contact, as far as I know, is up top in the commander's deck. He or she is a technician. Perhaps that's the one who saw fit to open the doors. By the by, you'll have to keep the bandages on for another week or so. Wouldn't want to add any more scars to your face."

"I see."

"Now, you'll have to answer some questions as to what the hell you lot were doing down in the cargo deck. Some kind of fivesome gone awry?"

"Just a hazing prank gone wrong. These things happen here in Frontier Division, do they not?"

"Yeah, I suppose. However, the entire cargo deck had quite the large number of valuables for trade with the dwarves."

"What of it?"

"This means that demotions will be handed out aplenty, from the technician who initially locked the door to everyone involved in the prank. Stay alert and keep your cool when that happens."

"That's ridiculous! I was lured into a trap and fought off four strikers significantly higher in rank. By Frontier code, I should be promoted."

"Yes, that is true. However, the circumstances are a bit cloudy with this one."

"The only thing cloudy here is the entire fucking division."

"I know, I know. But like I said, we have many eyes and few hands at the moment. The tables will turn."

The doors to the medical ward open, and Sansa enters with an identical blue-and-black battlesuit similar to my old one, which I presume to be unsalvageable.

"Let me guess. I had to dip deep into my reserves for this replacement?"

"Kind of. Not as expensive as you would think. I put this one together myself and bought the parts individually."

"Interesting. What's the difference between this one and my old suit?"

"I'm glad you asked!" Her posture perks up and a grin emerges on her face.

"I super-endowed the bella rockets and flutter bombs. You should be able to eat through any kind of material now." She leans in close. "Also, I added wall-phasing technology. Highly risky, but highly rewarding."

"You mean the same technology that got number forty-one stuck in a wall?"

"Cool, don't you think?!"

# CHAPTER 12
## CLASSIFICATION: NAVIGATOR

Tonight, I find myself dressing for one of Chaos' extravagant parties: an invitation-only party where the popular members of the division mingle. She somehow manages to get rare delicacies and all kinds of top-of-the-line alcoholic beverages. However, I'm going for one reason only: to expand my underground empire and acquire a top striker or two. If I can get a few top ten strikers on board, my operation will be that much more effective.

While squeezing into my red skirt and blouse, I feel a wave of sadness wash over me. I miss the witty banter that Vex and I used to get into, Sansa's uppity spirit, and above all the calm, quiet nature of Tash. She loved parties as much as she tried to hide that she did.

Pushing up my breasts, I find them not as perky as before. They are even a bit sore for some reason. Weight gain has been plaguing me lately, and I don't like it. I can rock the chunky look, but not much more than that.

Placing my fur scarf, on I make my way to Chaos' party tent.

While walking towards the party tent, I notice I'm getting a few looks here and there from some of my navi associates.

"Look at you, all dolled up. Must be nice to escape the little people from time to time," says one.

"Hot stuff coming through!" says another.

As I strut my stuff, I inhale the greasy scent of deep-fried fish being served.

*Not for me, not tonight. Tonight, I dine with the popular.*

There is a long line on arrival, as security checks everyone's classification and rank with the list. The all-mighty list, the thing that decides whether you're dancing away intoxicated on exclusive alcohol, or dining with the masses this evening. I find myself taking in the surroundings as I await entrance.

The line is filled with all kinds of elaborate decorative suits, dresses, and skirts. More woman than men, as any good party should be. Not like the awkward, sweaty navigator parties. The woman in front of me is wearing a tight blue dress with decorative stars. Her dark black hair flows down to her shoulders, and she emits the scent of lilacs.

*I knew I forgot something—should have worn a perfume or something.*

A cold breeze washes over the crowd, making me shuffle around repeatedly.

The slender woman in front of me turns around and sees me doing the awkward dance in an attempt to warm myself up. Her face disfigures into a disgusted expression. She turns to her friend, another slender woman with long, flowing black hair, and whispers in her ear.

The second woman slyly looks back through the corner of her eye, but I am hyper vigilant at this point. She lets out a loud cackle; the two witches laugh at my expense.

I feel my heart thumping. My hands curl into balls of fury, but I hold my breath and count to ten. If they knew who I really was, they would be peeing their panties.

*Who am I really? I thought I was a navigator first and a queen pin second. Or is it the other way around?*

The line couldn't move any slower, but I finally arrive at the front. The large security guard opens up his console.

"Name and classification?"

"Name is Allison, and classification is navigator."

"Oh, don't see many of those in here." He checks his list and nods his head, then eyes me from top to bottom.

"Afraid I can't let you in with those shoes."

I glance at my feet to see that I am still wearing my navigator sneaks. Comfortable, yes, but they don't exactly scream class.

"What's wrong with my shoes?" I say, feigning ignorance.

"Can't let you in with those shoes," he repeats.

I feel my face turning red. "I heard you the first time. What is wrong with my shoes?!"

The couple behind me are snickering. They'd best be careful, lest I stuff these sneaks down their throats.

The least this blob of a man could do is show me the decency of telling me what's wrong with my shoes.

He points to the exit from the line.

Standing upright, I fold my arms.

"I'm not going anywhere but inside that tent!"

My voice must have traveled, because within a few moments Chaos, covered in some kind of glitter, pokes her head out the tent.

She looks me up and down and chuckles.

"It's okay, Bubba, darling. This is my personal navigator. Could you do her a solid this time? Next time, she will be dressed appropriately." She beams him a wide smile.

Bubba blushes slightly and nods his head.

Chaos grips me by the arm and yanks me inside. I can tell she is about to lecture me on the shoes when a waiter passes by with drinks. Like any good host, she plucks two glasses and hands me one.

I sip the beverage, only to find myself downing the whole thing in moments. It's Terra Top Elixir. One of the rarest liqueurs in the galaxy.

*Chaos really knows her alcoholic beverages.*

We stand at the side of the colorfully decorated tent, sipping the beverage in silence. Careful to bask in every allowed moment. Eventually the silence gives way to conversation about her favorite topic.

"Do you think they'll actually catch him?" She finishes her drink. "I mean it has been nearly a year."

"I believe so. If he has sided with the RRA, he will go down like the rest of them."

"I suppose."

"Why the concern? You didn't pay him much attention while he was around." That came out harsher than I anticipated. The liqueur is getting to me.

She runs her hand through her curly red hair.

"If you must know, I didn't appreciate his capabilities—nor did I realize how bold he truly could be."

"Sounds like the attempt on Morange turned you on."

She winces but makes no move to deny it.

"Another drink?" she says, with another wide-brimmed smile.

We cheer and gulp down another few glasses of the Terra Top Elixir. Before I know it, someone has swept Chaos from my gaze, and she is off playing incredible host. I find myself dancing to the melody of tip hop—known for getting you on the tip of your toes with its various dance maneuvers.

The two slender women from earlier approach me. One of them pretends to trip over the flat ground and throws her drink all over my blouse.

"Oh, pardon. Silly me."

Then the icing on the cake: The other steps on my shoe as she leans in close.

"I suppose you need to go and get cleaned up."

I feel my hands quiver before they move as if on their own. I take the glass in my right hand and slam it into the first woman's eye, causing blood to splatter as the glass breaks. The second woman doesn't fare much better. I grip her into a body lock and flip her onto a nearby table, where I start to pummel her with my fists.

By the time security arrives, I am breathing heavily, and my fists are sore.

"Seems like you need to go and get cleaned up!" I manage to sputter as I'm being carried away.

I wake up with an incredible headache, but worse of all in a reinforced cell—not the makeshift prison that Eclectic members are sent to in order to cool off.

Panic ensues as I begin to hyperventilate. Sweat pours down my entire body, and I back myself into a corner. By the time the guard approaches the front of the cell, I'm a wreck.

"Where am I, and why am I here?"

"Unfortunately for you, you're in an Oasis prison cell. The women you assaulted weren't IGF. They were high-born Oasis citizens. Meaning your crime can't be swept under the rug."

I collapse to the hard cement.

"How bad is it?'

"You're looking at short work time."

*Ok, short work time doesn't sound too bad. I can handle that.*

"How long is that? A month or two?"

He chuckles so hard that a tear escapes his left eye.

"No, more like ten years or so. In a heavy-duty work placement. The mines, to be specific."

"But... but..."

"Yes, you'll most likely die before serving your sentence. But so it goes sometimes."

"Isn't there anything I can do?"

"If there was, I wouldn't tell ya."

My heart drops to my feet as I collapse to the urine stained floor. The ceiling seemingly spinning of its own accord, I find myself contemplating my future. Or lack thereof.

*It's true what they say. We are all just one wrong decision away from ruining our lives.*

# CHAPTER 13
## CLASSIFICATION: ROGUE STRIKER

I was demoted all the way back to rank sixty: a slap to the face if there ever was one. To make matters worse, they put a red strike on my record. A red strike means that ranking up from now on will be even more difficult.

As for the other parties involved, they only went down one or two ranks, due to their connections. The septic tank that is the Frontier Division grows more putrid by the day. I find myself using my idle time in the division to shoot my way through the holographic simulator, or H.S. I've gone through many different scenarios, but mostly the monster hunting ones.

*How I miss the simplicity of taking down a mindless beast. At the very least, I miss being bold in my actions, eliminating a clear enemy. The deceptive nature of my newfound life irks the brain and stifles the heart.*

After barrel-rolling forward, I crouch low and unleash a volley from my p90s. The holographic monster goes down with a loud roar and a thud. Pleased at my new high score, I turn off the system and take my leave—only for Hyper Fairy to block the exit.

"If you're looking for a round two, you'll need your little squadron to defeat me," I say.

"Oh dear, are you still mad about that? I would have though you would have gotten over that by now. Just a little misunderstanding."

"A little misunderstanding that caused me my ranks. Get out of the way. I don't have time for you."

I move to brush past her, but she grips my arm into an arm bar, forcing me to reverse it. I flip her over my shoulder, but she lands on her feet. With a large amount of force, she flings me across the room. I land on my feet.

"You're much more adept than you look. How about we test your hunting skills against our real threat?"

"Our real threat—who might that be?"

"These missions are typically saved for rank thirty and above, but it seems someone up top has taken a liking to you. I've been assigned to get you up to snuff so you won't be a liability on the battlefield."

"Me? A liability. That would be the day."

"You have yet to face an orc."

"What do the orcs have to do with anything? We let them live in peace on their scum-bucket planets."

"If you truly believe that, you're more naïve than I thought." She connects her console to the Holographic System and immediately starts up an advanced simulation.

An orc pops up in rudimentary armor, not past B+ grade. The green monstrosity stands one-and-a-half times my size with sharp teeth and glowing green eyes.

Up until this point, I have never seen an orc before. They are as ugly as they are smelly. Our surroundings shift, becoming odd mushrooms and blue trees. Weird fungus covers the ground, giving it a spongy feeling.

The orc unleashes a deafening war cry. My legs shiver uncontrollably, and my entire body erupts into sweat. I try to pull the triggers, but I'm frozen in fear.

To my dismay I find myself urinating myself as the orc charges towards me. Within moments, I am tossed against the wall, and the orc disappears back into code.

I glance at Hyper Fairy, who smirks.

"It's okay. Most people defecate themselves the first few times. It seems you've got some tiger balls under there."

"What was that?"

"We'll discuss this further after you've gotten yourself cleaned up."

After my shower I head over to the feeding quarters, where Hyper Fairy is waiting for me. I look around to see that the feeding quarters is relatively empty. The all-you-can-eat buffet still has some delicacies left, while the snack bar has a short line.

*I need to come here around this time again.*

Stumbling towards the chair across from her, I find myself getting flashbacks of the orc. With every one, my skin crawls, and I want to piss myself.

"Are these flashbacks normal?"

"Oh, definitely. Usually what happens is you defecate yourself and then instantly pass out. An orc war cry is no joke. Even considering that one was on the low setting. Their war cry can cause severe convulsions followed by death if treatment isn't administered soon."

"Oh, so we have a counter for this attack. Go on, what is it?"

"A few dozen bullets into the brain of the orc should do it."

"I see."

"Yeah. What makes matters more troublesome is that they are very hardy. They also have some kind of protective entity surrounding them, making them immune to most weapons."

"If we didn't monitor their technological advances like we do, they would overrun us. They populate like rabbits and often kill themselves to create more space on their planets. Then there are the blue berserkers."

"Blue berserkers?"

"Yes. Orcs come in three different tribes. Each with a different fighting style and their own language. The various tribes never mix under any circumstances. If they did, they would pose an even bigger threat. Right now they aren't as difficult to eliminate due to how stupid and reckless they are. An orc is just as likely to kill their ally as they are to kill you."

"That's good to know. They aren't organized."

"You can say that again. But disorganization does not mean they are not dangerous. It just means we overwhelm them with superior technology and advanced strategies—one of which is population control. Because they formulate like rabbits, we kill them like rabbits. Every year we carry out a Great Cleansing on a different orc-inhabited planet."

"And that would be?" I ask.

"I'll let that be a surprise for now."

"I don't like surprises."

"Sulkywag, who doesn't like surprises?!"

"I don't."

"You'll like this one! Speaking of which, how are you at flying a battle jet?"

"A battle jet?"

She lets out an exaggerated sigh.

"If you can't fly, you'll just flop and die."

"Is that supposed to be a pick-me-up?"

"Nope, just a reality."

I find myself sitting in the cockpit of a battle jet. The mechanical monstrosity has lights and buttons in every direction I turn. The manual that Hyper Fairy allowed me to skim through was barely any help. I learned some basic stuff: The red button is to eject, while the green button is to start. Other than that, all I know how to do is steer. Everything else I'll have to learn on the fly.

*Silly dwarven technology.*

"Don't we have a simulator of this or something?" I ask.

"Now, why would you want to ruin all the fun?"

In some ways, this woman reminds me of Chaos: both refreshing yet disturbing at the same time. Might have something to do with her being a Z.

I push forward as the reinforced gates open. The jet smoothly slides out before shooting forward at an alarming speed. Before I know it, I'm out in the middle of the

Frontier Division space station, zipping and zagging. Lucky for me, flying a battle jet is half hand-eye coordination and half mental focus. I blow past several cargo ships, and my shields glisten after being struck with several laser blasts.

Glancing down at the rearview camera, I see a yellow-and-black battle jet embellished with the letter Z.

*Must be Hyper Fairy. If it's a skirmish she wants, then a skirmish she shall get.*

I push forward towards the orange zone, where there is more space to maneuver, while dodging her laser blasts and plasma rockets.

*Time to see what this thing can do.*

Pressing the grey button marked "S" lets loose a massive smokescreen. I then pull up, effectively pulling off a circle maneuver. Now behind Hyper Fairy's battle jet, it's my turn to unleash hell.

I launch two Seeker Missiles and watch in awe as they follow her while she tries to dodge, zip, and zag. Finally the Seeker Missiles connect with her shields, dissipating.

A second set of wings pops up from atop her battle jet. A yellow beam of light pierces through space. It connects with my jet, dealing a heavy amount of damage that completely wipes out my shields and wrecks my auto-assist.

Without auto-assist, my mind is barely connected to the computer, making it ten times more difficult to maneuver.

Hyper Fairy's voice intrudes upon my thoughts. "It's over. Let's reel her in and practice landing."

As much as I want to continue flying, I force myself to land the jet and exit the cockpit. Although crooked, it's in one piece.

*Heh, the old me would have kept going. I suppose I have grown a bit.*

Hyper Fairy rushes over to me, half fluttering, half running.

"It's been a long time since I had to pull out my disabler." She tilts her head back slightly. "You sure you haven't flown before?"

"Maybe in a past life."

"Hehe, maybe." She pauses awkwardly, then grabs my hand and pulls me behind a large cargo ship.

With the click of a button, she disassembles her entire body suit save her helmet. Underneath she's wearing a tight yellow thong and a yellow-spotted bra. Her slim figure is rather alluring, causing me to lick my lips.

She isn't as curvaceous as Chaos, and I haven't had a clean look at her face—but who am I to deny what's in front of me? Maybe this will help me get my mind off Chaos.

"Well? What do you think?"

*Don't say anything stupid.*

The fact that I must remind myself not to say anything stupid is an testament to the many stupid things I've said in the past.

"Words would do you a disservice."

*Smooth, Vex. Very smooth.*

"Oh, Vindication. You're quite the smooth talker when you want to be."

I follow suit and disassemble my battlesuit—except for my helmet. My rippling muscles show through my camo t-shirt, while the bulge in my shorts reveals all.

I push her against the base of the cargo ship and grab her by the throat. She reaches for my cock and lets out a small moan as she begins to stroke me. Playing with Hyper Fairy's breasts, I lick my lips. I am suddenly flooded with thoughts of the last time I was touched in such a way.

A mild wave of rage hits me as Hyper Fairy turns around and rubs my throbbing cock against her clit. Her juices flow like a river, dripping onto the floor. Gripping both her wrists, I place her arms behind her back and bend her over.

*Tonight, I will dominate.*

# CHAPTER 14
## CLASSIFICATION: POLITICIAN

In the middle of the night, my personal console lights up while playing the ancient tip-hop tune known as *Many Men*, by 50 Cent. Singing along, I'm reminded of the scum that dared to step to me. The RRA has been eradicated, and Vex is probably off on some desolate planet, cold, scared, and lost. But I'll find him and bring him to justice.

Checking my wrist console, I notice that it's a private number.

*I don't answer private numbers.*

I'm about to let it go to my voicemail, but I find myself more curious than I should be these days. Perhaps it's because things have been going in my favor lately and don't seem to be letting up.

"Yeah, hello?"

"Would you like to accept a phone call from a level-one holding cell?"

*Hmmm, level one. That's the spot for minor incursions against the general population. Maybe Sanguine found himself in some trouble. Perhaps I should let him rot. With Quaint and the new bots I ordered, he would be expendable.*

I sigh. "I suppose."

"Morange?"

"Allison?" I get up from my chair and begin pacing about.

"Yes, it's me."

"What are you doing in a level-one holding cell?"

"They want to give me ten years, Morange. Ten fucking years."

"What happened?"

After going over the details of what happened, I realize there are a couple options open to me. This would be the perfect opportunity to wash my hands of her and just take over the underground operation—though I do rather like being hands off and just receiving a monthly deposit. Or I can have this whole thing wash away with one phone call to the family. Maybe grease their palms.

I pull up the Planetary Division files on crime and scroll through the long list. I stop at Allison's name and look up the sisters she assaulted.

*This might be tricky.*

I arrive at the Amethyst sisters' villa with no escort save my trusty shotgun on my back. It's bright outside, and for some reason the sun causes my skin to tingle. Could be an aftereffect of the nanobots.

After ringing the doorbell, I look around and analyze my surroundings. The trees seem dull, and the air has a weighty feel to it. Perhaps all that time spent up in HQ has dimmed me to the natural environment of the Oasis.

The door swings open, and a butler bot pokes its head out.

"Greetings, sir. How may I be of service?"

"I'm here to see the Amethyst sisters."

"I don't see you on this evening's visitors list. Please call ahead and book an appointment."

"Let the sisters know that Grand Inquisitor Morange from HQ is here to see them."

The robot scans my ID then rolls away.

A few more moments pass until the first sister, Emerald, comes to the door. It's a gruesome sight. She's wearing an eye patch, and there is scar tissue around the eye. The file said she has to have a bionic eye implanted, as they couldn't salvage the original.

"Grand Inquisitor, wow! Who would have thought that our case would garner such attention."

"Yes, it is high on the priority list."

She rushes over to her sister Ruby and wheels her into the kitchen.

The report said she was beaten repeatedly and suffered brain damage. Her cognitive functions have been temporarily dulled.

"Hello, Ruby."

She manages to wobble her head somewhat.

"Now tell me, from your side, what exactly happened?"

"It's all there in the report," says Emerald.

"Sometimes the initial officer will miss something of import."

"Very well. That fat cur was smelling up the line. She reeked of grease. So you know my sister and I had a bit of a laugh about it."

"Hmm, interesting. So you initiated contact?"

"What? Yeah. I suppose."

"Continue."

"Inside later, she was smelling up the tent. So my sister and I approached her about the scent. We kindly suggested that she go and clean herself up and come back. Nothing rude or obnoxious."

I lean forward as my eyes intensify. "What about the spilled drink and the shoe stepped on?"

"I'm not sure what you're talking about."

"So you didn't further antagonize her or aggravate her into causing you harm?"

"I'm not sure I like what you're insinuating, Mr. Grand Inquisitor."

"It's quite simple, really. Navigators are specially designed to be quite timid under normal circumstances. You already admitted to stepping out of line one time, and according to her, you and your sister made a grand show out of the second and third times."

"No, not at all." Emerald bites her lip, then takes a sip of her coffee.

"Here's the thing. The person who assaulted you is counter-charging you. This can take some time to rectify, and rumors will be spread that you and your sister are hooligans who snuck into an IGF-sanctioned party and caused trouble. Quite the scandal."

'What? We were invited."

"Chaos has been quiet on the matter."

"That bitch!"

"There is a way to make all this go away."

"What?"

"You call the initial officer and tell them that you recant your statement, I'll take care of the rest."

"But look what she did to my eye and my sister's head!"

"Do you want to avoid a grand scandal that could last years?"

"Fine! I'll make the call."

"Do it now."

"I said I'll make the call."

I lean in close. "And I said. Do it now."

It's dark by the time I arrive at the holding cell. I get the message that my two Task Carrier V-13s will be dropped off in front of my sleeping quarters. Should pose quite the deterrent. Supposedly they are as nimble and as tactical as an A+ grade striker Z.

*Technology is getting more advanced by the day. Soon I won't need flesh and bones to protect me.*

The guard on duty leads me to the level-one holding cells. I pass by the gates filled with drunks, perverts, and woman beaters. Allison is fortunate that the damage wasn't past repair. I had to sweeten the pot by ordering the Amethyst sisters a Task Carrier of their own—expensive, but I suppose it was worth it.

At cell twenty-four I'm met with Allison, who is working out.

"Why are you doing push-ups on the dirty floor?"

She shoots right up and begins cleaning herself. "I had lost hope that you were coming."

"It has only been two days since you called. You give up quite easily."

"Hope in this dreary world isn't my strong suit."

"So it would seem."

The guard opens the door, and she rushes to embrace me. I stick my hand out.

"After you've had a thorough shower."

I see the look of disappointment mixed with gratitude on her face, but she accepts my instructions.

*At least she will be more submissive within my debt. Or so one would think.*

We make our way to the exit, where my hover car is waiting for us.

"It will take you some time to adjust to your new classification as technician, but adjust you shall."

"New classification?"

"Yes. You are no longer a navigator. You are on to bigger and better things."

"Why can't I return to my previous duties with Chaos?"

"Don't you get it? No one wants you as their navigator. I mean, I can't blame them. Who wants a loose cannon for a navigator? It's quite embarrassing. Fortunately for you, I have some pull in HQ. A feisty and skilled technician like yourself will do well. You'll have to lose some weight to keep up with the training. The Frontier Division isn't like the Eclectic Division—there are true standards."

A scowl crosses her face; I can see the anger emitting from her like the stench. But that isn't my problem. She will have to comply or be left to her own devices.

"I thought you loved me for who I am."

"I never said that."

"But you said you cared."

"Yes, that I said. I do care. If I didn't care, I wouldn't have come. Whether I accept you for who you are is irrelevant. The division supervisors won't."

"To hell with them."

"That kind of attitude will find you in a smaller cell—where no one can save you."

"I'm a fucking queen pin."

"Very few know this. The ones who do will drop you at the sign of any trouble. Remember, the people I introduce you to are not your friends."

"I understand."

"What doesn't kill us can only strengthen our resolve. Use this as a lesson to control your temper from here on out. Unbridled wrath will only result in your demise. Focus your attention on the task at hand: expansion of our underground empire and further advancement. This is what matters most. The next time you do something that can jeopardize it will be the last."

I see the defiance in her eyes, but it succumbs to gratitude. The fact that she was a phone call away from the mines will weigh heavily upon her for a while. But I see two wolves inside of her. One good, one bad. Both vying for power. Which will come to the surface and remain supreme?

# CHAPTER 15
## CLASSIFICATION: ROGUE STRIKER

I look to my left and see Hyper Fairy coiled within my arms. Her yellow-and-black helmet rests against my chest. We've spent a lot of time together these past few months. My flying has improved drastically, along with my combat skills. But above all, I have found a certain peace with this woman—whose face I have yet to see.

For reasons unknown to me, she refuses to take off her helmet. I'm fine with that, since I have my own reasons.

*Maybe she is hideous or has some kind of deformity.*

The thought that I would find someone to fill my cup in this place called HQ is magical in itself—but for her to be so sensual and feminine, yet confident and skilled? I'm truly at a loss for words.

Hyper Fairy stirs underneath the covers. The room is dimly lit, and my walls are now painted yellow. Hyper Fairy said it adds a nice flair to it.

"What are you thinking about?" she asks.

"You."

"Oh me, oh my?"

"Yeah."

"Well, spill it."

"I was just thinking how happy you've made me in such a short period of time."

"Really?"

"Yeah."

"Let us hope and pray that things continue to flourish between us," she says.

"I'd rather rely on destiny. You don't actually believe in a higher power, do you?"

She shuffles around a bit before answering. "Of course."

"So you pray to the Most High that the blacksmiths worship?"

"No, but I believe that he exists. If my god exists, then so do the others. It's quite logical when one looks into it."

"Your turn to spill. Who do you believe in?"

"That's an easy question with a complicated answer. I believe in the only god that matters to elves like us. I believe in the bringer of games, deceit, and trickery. Kuleta Kifo."

"Kuleta Kifo?" As the words roll off my tongue, I feel a tingling sensation travel down my spine and through my arms, followed by a sense of dread.

"Tell me more." I demand.

"I can't speak on it too much, as this is rank fifteen and above knowledge, but Kuleta Kifo is the god that grants us the power to kill the monsters from the rift, the sheer intelligence to overcome the orcs, and the willpower to control the dwarves. He is both a benevolent god and a demanding one. He requires many sacrifices for elves to remain the superior race."

She reaches in her helmet and pulls out a star-and-moon pendant with a bunch of code written on it.

"Kuleta Kifo is none other than the god of the cyber realm, and one day he will roam this realm in full form," she continues.

I get the sudden urge to vomit; my insides twist and turn. Somehow I manage to maintain my composure.

"Don't you see, Vindication? One day we will all be cyber elves marching to the beat of Kuleta Kifo."

The first thought that comes to my mind is that I'd rather die than become a cyber elf. But I do not know where this hatred for them comes from. The second thought is that she may just be crazy. Maybe this is why they call her hyper. But the third thought, and the most troubling of all, is what if she isn't crazy? What if the higher members of IGF are some kind of cyber elf cult?

"What can you tell me about the cyber elves?"

"Not much, as I said. I am bound by much secrecy due to my T10 chip. You'll earn yours soon enough."

"Fair enough."

I stretch and rise to my feet. She springs up out of bed and does a front flip in front of me.

"I have a special meeting to attend. I'll shower first."

"No problem."

As I watch her firm ass walk towards my shower, I force myself back to my senses.

"Cyber elves," I whisper.

*Why does the mere mention fill me with animosity and disdain?*

A piece of parchment manifests from underneath the small gap below my door.

I pick up the parchment, which says only a few words.

*Rank 47 – Codename: Vanguard = Exterminate*

My heart jumps at the realization: This is the moment I have waited over a year for. The moment of activation. The moment I have trained for. When I am to exterminate select members of the Frontier Division.

*For a greater cause.*

The parchment catches on fire by itself until it fades into nothing.

The trick with assassination is that one must end the target swiftly. Preferably with no energy and time wasted, lest someone else intervene and you find yourself at a disadvantage. What's most important is patience. It's important to understand your target. Know their habits, know their likes, dislikes, and above all the best place to strike. Sometimes stealth will need to be used, other times deception. Being a striker Y, I am well aware that my life could be forfeit at any given moment.

It's only now that I find myself fighting for something that I truly believe in. I'd lying if I didn't admit that the RRA cause has grown on me like some kind of mold. Every day I spend in the Frontier Division is another that I realize change must come. But above all, I've found love. A pure kind of love, one that makes me want to sing out into space.

*For the RRA I'm willing to die, but for Hyper Fairy I'm willing to live.*

Sitting across the table from Sansa, I watch her staring at rank fifty-five – Side Step. The blind former monk.

"Don't make it so obvious," I warn.

"Not like he can see me."

"Someone else might. Keep in mind this is just the beginning of the list. If we blow this, the mission will fail before it's truly begun."

"Fine, fine. Who did you get?"

"Rank forty-seven—Vanguard. Also known as the Golden Plate. A high-born light elf who bathes in golden water."

"He bathes in his own pee?" The look on her face is as humorous as it is ugly.

"No, he has gold melted down and bathes in it while it's still warm."

"Oh, why does he do that?"

'I don't know. Maybe I'll ask before I gut him."

"Maybe you should."

I sigh heavily and turn my attention to my meal: a healthy helping of sweet potatoes and fresh lamb. From the corner of my eye I see Vanguard strutting by with his golden sword and shield.

*He might be onto something with that golden bath thing. His skin has a certain glow to it.*

Sansa leans in close. "When you gonna do it?"

"Tonight, after lockdown. I'll be testing out this phase-travel technology of yours. You sure I won't end up in a wall?"

"If I were sure, it wouldn't be a test."

I squint through my visor. If only she could see my distaste for her witty remarks.

Just as I finish my meal, Hyper Fairy sidles up beside me and wraps her arm around mine.

"We still on for tonight?" she asks.

"Oh, well, about that."

"Don't tell me you have other plans?"

"Uh, well..."

"I was hoping you'd show me a maneuver or two. Vindication has been telling me so much about your flying skills that I want to try my hand at it," says Sansa.

"Then the three of us can test out some new moves?"

"No!" Sansa and I say it at the same time.

"Why not?"

Sansa bites her lips before speaking. "I have Alterna duty tonight, but I was hoping Vindication would take over. Been really aching to go for a fly tonight. Please? Sometimes I just feel so cooped up in here. Recycled air and whatnot."

I feel Hyper Fairy's posture soften.

"Aww, of course. Vindication. You're on your own tonight. We're gonna have a girls' night out."

"Sure."

*Damn, Sansa has grown into quite the little liar. Her skills in deception grow month by month.*

I check my console to see that it's 3:33 after neutral time. A good time to go hunting. There should be minimal patrol units, and everyone should be in their quarters save for the supervisors.

I check the door, which is locked as expected. Fortunately for me, I have phase travel on my battlesuit. Something only Sansa and the doctor know I have.

After activating stealth, I phase travel through the door. It's always an eerie feeling: My body disperses into fragments and reemerges.

*Feels just like when I phase travel with Tirade.* I slink through the silver halls, making my way several doors down to rank forty-seven Vanguard's room.

After phase traveling through the door, my energy has been depleted to about halfway—and I haven't even fired a shot or struck a blow yet.

*Not good.*

Upon entering the room, I am met with gold statues, gold boots, and gold-rimmed paintings of Vanguard.

*Seems like quite the narcissist.*

I hover over his body for a few moments, taking a deep breath. My hands sweat, but my resolve is strong. It's a shame to kill someone who can't defend themselves. It's almost in poor taste.

I unleash one grappling spear into his throat, and blood spurts out. His eyes immediately open as he clutches the spear with his bare hands. Within a few moments, his hands collapse back upon the bed.

I decloak and head over to the bathroom, where I wash off his blood. Curiosity overwhelms me, and I check the bathtub. To my surprise, it really is filled with liquid gold.

# CHAPTER 16
## CLASSIFICATION: TECHNICIAN

The error buzzer goes off once again, and the supervisor strikes me with her flail. The sting is incomparable to the embarrassment of being stripped naked and forced to sprint on a device while doing advanced calculations. I look around to see the sneers and jeers of my group.

*Not one ounce of pity in their souls.*

My new supervisor circles the training device like a hawk circling its mark. The training device is essentially a treadmill with a giant console attached to it. I'm in a large circular silver room filled with advanced technicians, and it's downright intimidating. They move and function almost like cyborgs. Every movement is jerky, every word unemotional.

*Must be the T9 chips used to enhance their cognitive functions and computing speed.*

My supervisor Nora looks like her battlesuit is permanently attached to her body. It's a grey battlesuit with brown at the joints and badge area. Her weapon is a two-pronged silver flail, and she carries a shield with the technician's symbol on it. She is short and appears near-anorexic, but hits like a truck. Nora wears a hood over her helmet and her sash displays the libra sign.

"Balance in all things! Your mind, body, and spirit must be as one if you are to be a true technician."

"Balance in all, all in balance," the group repeats.

*Bloody cyborgs!*

"Sponge Cake. If you are to earn your T9 chip, you will have to run faster than that."

The codename I have earned is not one I am fond of. If she isn't careful, she'll find my boot up her ass. Then again, that temper of mine is what got me in this mess to begin with.

"Are you listening?"

The crackling of the flail through the air is fear-inducing, and the strike on my back as painful as it sounds. Instinctively, I speed up my running to the point where I am nearly stumbling. With my hands flying at incredible speeds, I decipher the code to the main system and hack my way into the cyber net as instructed.

A large amount of code floods my brain in the form of a purple strip. The headset I'm using nearly overloads, but I push forward lest I receive another lashing. It feels as if I'm floating in a world made of purple blocks. What I'm looking for, I don't know. But I am instructed to move forward. The purple blocks zip past me as my avatar molds itself into a blue, slimmer version of me. She has horns and piercings. Absolutely stunning.

I vaguely hear my supervisor mention something to the crowd. They are all tuned in to my personal console and thus see what I see and hear what I hear.

"Interesting. She has made it quite far for her first time," says the supervisor.

While floating farther past the floating purple blocks, I see several blue elves touching each other with their foreheads. Green sparks shoot out from their temples, and then they back off. This process is repeated several times.

I feel a tingling sensation in my feet, then suddenly I see pitch black. It feels like I'm being plucked by the feet and thrown into the sky.

In what feels like an eternity of pitch black, I'm met with the gentle face of He Who Loves, except it's giant—or perhaps I am small.

"We don't have much time. What are you doing here?" he asks.

"I don't know."

"How did you get here?"

"Through the HQ console. I'm now a technician for the Frontier Division."

"My calculations must have been faulty. Soon the realms will collide."

"The realms will collide—what does that mean?"

A second face manifests, this time less friendly. It booms in a thundering voice that distorts my body.

"You didn't learn your lesson the first time, did you?"

"Wait—this isn't what you think. It was a malfunction in code."

He Who Loves quivers and shakes while his eyes are on the brink of tears.

"You're the malfunction in code. Perhaps time in the octagon will fix what ails you and your bleeding-heart ways. You were instructed to let things play out as they are supposed to. Not to undermine our objectives."

"I swear I haven't. Just one more chance. Please!"

The angry orange face pushes his forehead against the forehead of He Who Loves, and this time orange sparks fly out from their temples. He Who Loves bellows out in agony.

"Stop it, you're hurting him!"

The angry face turns to me and spits, but instead of saliva there's a long strip of orange code. Just as the code is about to reach me, He Who Love's entire head rushes towards me and covers me in dark blue code. The advanced numbers turn into letters momentarily and read:

*I will always love you.*

Then my headset overloads. I wake up twitching on the ground, still surrounded by my supervisor and the rest of the technicians.

"You have a lot of explaining to do. Your fan was able to block out the visual, but we heard every word. A mere navigator from the Eclectic Division should have no knowledge or contact with a cyber elf."

By the time they remove the hood from my face, I'm fuming. I'm just about ready to curse them out when I realize I am surrounded by a circle of HQ bigwigs. I recognize some of them from the pictures we're briefed on upon entrance to the Frontier Division. The room is vast, and everyone is sitting on a curve.

In the very back seat, I see Grand Inquisitor Morange. From this distance I can't really read his facial expression, but I suspect he might be regretting his decision to help me right about now.

There are two strikers standing behind each member of HQ. Their personal defense escorts, I presume, or a group of executioners. My attention is readjusted when my supervisor backhands me, causing a tooth to go flying.

"Tell the truth, and everything will be ok," she says.

I manage to nod my head.

"How did you get in contact with He Who Loves?"

"He contacted me."

A large portion of the room erupts into whispers. After they quiet down, my supervisor continues with her questioning.

"Why did He Who Loves contact you?"

"My understanding is that he fell in love with me."

The room erupts into a fit of laughter.

"A cyber elf fell in love with you?"

"That's what I said. Why is that so hard to believe?"

"Many reasons. The largest of which is that the cyber elves are the superior race of elves. They don't mingle with lesser beings in such a manner. It goes: cyber elves, light elves, then dark elves."

My attention shoots towards the few dark elves that sit on the council. Their stoic expressions tell no tales.

"Tell that to him. I didn't ask for any of this. It all started over a game of Volute."

"Perhaps, but now you are involved in something greater than you can imagine." She pokes me on my shoulder. "What have you discussed?"

"Mainly his devout love for me, and what he is."

"What did he say he was?"

"He said he was more than just code, and then he reached out and touched me. That's about it."

"Interesting."

More whispering amongst themselves.

"Now, if you will kindly untie me, I can answer your questions in a more comfortable state. Maybe feed me or something. Is this how you treat one of your own division technicians?"

"You're new, and thus many precautions must be made. But you're right, you are a technician. You may pose useful in time—if cleared of any suspicious activities." The supervisor points to Grand Inquisitor Morange. "Grand Inquisitor, would you come to the middle of the circle?"

Rising, he takes off his coat and heads down to the middle of the circle, followed by his escort Sanguine and Quaint.

"Isn't it true that she was plucked from the obscurity of the Eclectic Division and into Frontier hands by your own recommendation?"

"This is true. Hurry up and make your point. It's almost teatime."

Some of the members of the group chuckle.

"My point is that it's rather suspicious that a rookie technician has such a relationship with a cyber elf and also made an impression on you as a navigator. It's all just very odd. Help us make sense of this."

"It's remarkably simple, really. I noticed Allison's abilities during an investigation into the Eclectic Division. Although she was deemed clear of any wrongdoings, it was noteworthy how quickly and easily she rose up the ranks. Since then, I have kept an eye on her progression, along with the progression of any other potential pupils. As any good inquisitor should."

"Hmmm, I see. So we're to rack this all up to coincidence?"

"No."

"No?"

"We should rack this up to a sign from Kuleta Kifo. Correct me if I am wrong, but in her first visit to the cyber net, she traveled farther than any other on their first try. It means she has the gift, and thus should be given the opportunity to progress as a technician. This makeshift inquisition is a farce simply brought about from those that serve He Who Loves."

He raises his arms into the air, causing the entire room to rumble, metal to bend, and weapons to fly out from their holsters.

"Just because He Who Loves will now be replaced by another cyber elf does not mean we should begin lashing out at the catalyst for change. The cyber elves have granted me great power and health; they have fulfilled the ambitions and goals of many of you as well. In turn we all, including those who serve the new He Who Loves, will each receive their ultimate gift with faith and gratitude."

The room erupts into a round of applause, forcing my supervisor to join in as well.

"Looks like you're off the noose, Sponge Cake. But I'll be watching you," she says.

"I wouldn't have it any other way." And I give her a wink.

Saved once again by Morange. I'm not going to make it a habit. I'll need to make my own connections within this division.

# CHAPTER 17
## CLASSIFICATION: ROGUE STRIKER

There is no public mention of Vanguard's assassination, nor of the following seven that Sansa and I have carried out to date. I take that as a sign that they are investigating it on a deeper level. It would be wise to tread carefully. Seeing Allison doing so well was not something I was prepared for. I find myself enraged and alert, but above all more cautious.

Both Allison and Morange walking makes detection that much more likely. But I don't have time to think about that. I must focus on the task at hand. Another letter was dropped off in my room.

This time it read: *Dwarven Prince – C'Algoing = Exterminate*

My heart shakes and my hand quivers. I had to read the words twice.

Killing a dwarven prince could result in war breaking out between the two races. At the very least, it will strain the relationship and break off trade ties between the two. We currently trade protection and extermination of monsters for high-tech equipment like hover cars, robots, and even biomechanical implants. I can see how this will be beneficial for the RRA. This would make a coup d'état all the more likely.

Sansa and I exit the room, followed by Legislator Alterna. He grips me by the arm and whispers into my ear.

"Make sure you're careful taking out the prince. If he succeeds the throne, our cause will be all but done for."

"Understood. Is there anything else I should know?"

"Just know that our god watches over you."

"Who is our god? Frankly with all these gods running around from the cyber realm, the rift, and what not, I'm starting to lose track."

"The god of the change, opportunity, and redemption known only as Chenji. A forgotten god of the shadow bridge. Never forget: Our universe is divided into four realms."

"How can I forget the RRA indoctrination?"

"This is serious, Vex. Repeat the realms and their purposes."

"The other three realms are the rift: the realm of chaos, destruction, and everything in between. Filled with dubious and hideous monsters of unimaginable thirst. The cyber realm, which relies on logic and numbers but spreads like a plague. And the shadow bridge. The realm that separates the two, the never-changing, yet the all-changing."

"I know it's all confusing right now, but one day it will make sense. Trust me."

I manage to nod as I head towards my quarters. I must get as much rest as possible before the prince arrives. Fortunately, after the prince has been taken care of, I can lay off the assassinations and see how everything plays out.

By the time I arrive at my quarters I'm exhausted, but I see Hyper Fairy standing outside, holding a box with a skull and wings on it.

"Happy intertwining day!"

"Intertwining day?"

"Yeah, today marks the first anniversary of us intertwining."

"I don't keep track of that kind of stuff. Each day just flows into the other."

She throws the box at me, then places her hands at her hips.

"Well, I do. Hurry up and open the door. I want you to see what I got you."

Once we enter the confines of my quarters, she pushes me against the bed and takes off her battlesuit. Underneath, she's dressed in fishnet lingerie from the neck down. While subtly checking the time, I take off my battlesuit. Although the prince will only be on board for one night, I should be fine.

*Who am I to say no? It is our intertwining day after all.*

Waking up in the middle of the night, I unhook myself from Hyper Fairy's grip. I assemble my battlesuit and attach the high-powered submachine guns that she gave me. Berry and Stone are their names.

Berry is an ultra-light, energy-using submachine gun whose projectiles will bounce off certain surfaces. Its special trait is a useful one: any kill with Berry actually refreshes the magazine at no extra energy cost. So I can go on some serious rampages. Kills also stack the amount of damage that it dishes out.

Stone is a bit heavier, but it lives up to its name. It's also an energy user, but this time it unleashes projectiles that slow down an opponent's movements, ultimately turning them stonelike. Anytime an opponent is killed in full stone mode, a stone skin shield is activated on my own body. Additionally, Stone fires armor- and shield-piercing projectiles.

Together they are highly effective at ending fights quickly—but even more effective in prolonged battles. I take both along with my P90s Pain and Suffocation. I'm more comfortable with Pain and Suffocation so I will open with them and only switch to Berry and Stone if necessary.

*Hopefully that won't be necessary.*

The plan is simple. Sansa will knock out the escort meant for the prince, granting me enough time to take him out as soon as he arrives. It should be quick, clean, and easy.

I check my energy levels, and I'm already at thirty-five percent.

*Hyper Fairy definitely drained me. Hopefully that won't be the difference maker.*

For a mission this vital, I am relying a lot on hope. Not the best of signs, but I have no other choice. It's now or never. The blue docking gate opens, and the prince's Reorient battle jet docks. The sleek ship is state-of-the-art, with machineguns and antimatter dispersers. Not something I'd want to face in combat.

To my dismay, three Task Carrier V-13s jump out and begin patrolling the docks first, followed by three massive ravager units of some unknown upgrade. Last is the prince himself, in a flamboyant white suit with a transparent hammer at his back.

"Vex to Sansa."

"Go ahead?"

"Gonna need your assistance on this one."

"I gotchu, on my way."

One of the V-13 bots makes its way towards me. I turn off stealth and launch two grappling hooks into the neck of the bot. By sending energy through the wires, I manage to overcharge the bot, temporarily disabling it. After rushing behind one of the cargo carriers, I am met with another V-13 It's quick to the draw and immediately fires a barrage my way.

By dodge rolling to the left, I manage to evade the attack—but an alarm has gone off, and the ravagers bunker down and surround the prince. Their spiderlike legs dig into the floor beneath them while the three machine turrets scan the area. I take out the second Task Carrier with my P90s, but my position is now revealed.

I'm about to make another move when a massive blast from a plasma cannon connects with the head of the closest ravager. The heavy-duty machine is unfazed.

"Vex to Sansa."

"Go ahead?"

"Cover me."

"Copy that."

Sansa sends a barrage of plasma cannon shots, along with her phenome, towards the closest harvester. The three sharks circle and then completely devour the machine in a wave of boiling water.

I roll forward and switch to Berry and Stone, which make quick work of the second and third ravager. Upon seeing this, the prince switches his last V-13 bot to self-destruct and runs back into his ship.

*Curses.*

Sansa runs up to the bot and begins tinkering with it in an effort to deactivate it. If she can't, the landing dock is all but obliterated—and our ships with it.

I watch as the prince's ship zooms off into the distance.

This isn't the best of scenarios, considering that my identity will be revealed, but the prince has to die or everything will be for naught. Everything we worked for these past two years will be null.

My only hesitation is whether Hyper Fairy will understand. But it's too late now. My body has moved as if on its own, and I find myself sitting in my A3 Fighter Jet, Syndicate.

*A suitable name for a traitor.*

"Sansa to Vex."

"Go ahead."

"I have to do something, then I'll back you up. Our cover is blown."

"Copy that."

"And Vex?"

"Yeah?"

"Don't die on me."

"Yeah. You too."

"I can't die. I got my destiny to fulfill!"

"Copy that."

I flick on the switch to turn on the fighter jet. Everything lights up. I place my hands on the yoke and initiate the launching system. The system catapults me several hundred meters, effectively closing the gap between the prince's jet and my own.

He activates his turrets, spewing out a hundred rounds a minute, depleting my shields in a quick barrage. Now that my shields are gone, I must be extra cautious or I'm dust.

That's when a bad situation turns to worse.

I look in the rearview camera to see Hyper Fairy and Stomper in pursuit.

*Fuck. I must focus.*

I fire the two high-powered lasers, both connecting on the tail end of his ship. His shields absorb the bulk of the damage. While dodging a barrage of explosives from Stomper's jet, I deploy my homing missiles. In an effort to dodge the homing missiles, the prince nose dives.

*He probably plans on doing a loop-the-loop.*

Just as he is pulling the nose of the jet upwards to dodge the missiles, I cut him off with a high-powered plasma beam that all but depletes my resources. I watch as his ship explodes into countless pieces.

*Kill confirmed.*

I'm hit by Hyper Fairy's reverse control, which temporarily reverses the input commands in my jet. In the moment it takes me to adjust, I'm struck by a massive rocket that sends me spiraling towards a planet marked uninhabited. All I can see is its thick green atmosphere. The ship increases in speed as I enter the gravitational pull of the planet.

While being drawn towards the center of the planet, I whisper to myself, "Today, I may die. But I refuse to shed a tear. My life was lived in servitude to the cause."

*More RRA indoctrination. If it isn't the IGF, it's the RRA. Sometimes I wonder, what's the difference?*

Just as my jet is about to crash into the ground, I press the ejection button and activate the shield on my ring. The top flies off, and I'm launched into the air.

The oxygen alarm immediately goes off, indicating that the air is mildly toxic.

The ejected seat lands with a thud.

*Not a scratch on me.*

I look up at the sky and am about to breathe a sigh of relief when I see Stomper and Hyper Fairy's jets breech the atmosphere.

*Seriously?*

Like good Zs, they must confirm the kill—or worse for me, apprehend the traitor known as Vexation.

I unbuckle myself from the straps and take off running in a random direction. My Y training kicks in. I must find shelter, food, and water. It's night on this planet, and I'm alone.

For the first time in my life, I'm truly alone.

# CHAPTER 18
## CLASSIFICATION: POLITICIAN

The alarm has been going off for a while. I check the video list to see that everyone is tuned into Hyper Fairy or Stomper's visual feeds. They are in hot pursuit of the traitor Vexation. I lick my lips at the thought of seeing him detained.

*My shotgun will feast on his flesh.*

There is a loud knock on my door. I switch feeds to see that Quaint and Sanguine are outside in their armor.

"What?"

"We have come to escort you to the safety zone. There is word that Leaky Faucet is Vex's partner in crime. She is also known as Sansa. She is roaming this floor and considered highly volatile," says Sanguine.

"Isn't she the fiftieth-ranked Striker in the division? Correct me if I'm wrong, but that might as well be last."

"It's protocol, sir. Any threat roaming a floor must be eradicated immediately, and any prime asset must be brought to a more secure area."

"Fine. Let me gather my things."

I initiate collection protocol on my two Task Carrier V-13s. One picks up the mirror my half-brother once gave me for our communication.

The other assists me in putting on my old striker suit. I look in the mirror, amazed at how muscular my body has become. I even admire the blue tint I have gained.

*Soon I will be a full-fledged cyber elf, and then we will see who bows down to who.*

Making our way to the safety zone, I find myself growing antsy. I'm expecting contact from He Who Hates. The last thing I'd want is for the meeting to be clogged up with my security detail.

*How inappropriate.*

I find my thoughts drifting towards this so-called threat. I mean, how a bottom-feeding scavenger managed to pass the training required to become a Frontier Division striker is beyond me—much less her being some assassin. I find it utterly ridiculous.

"Sanguine. None of this is necessary. How much damage can a mere scavenger playing striker do?"

"I doubt she can do much. But it is protocol. I haven't had the experience of engaging her in battle, but I don't expect any trouble on our way."

I feel a burning pain in my thigh. I drop to my knees. Looking behind me, I see that I've been struck by a plasma cannon blast. The plasma damage eats away at my skin as some other substance pulsates a bright blue. Another two come flying at me when my V-13 activates its shields, taking the bulk of the damage.

I turn to see this Leaky Faucet character, as if summoned by our words, sending three water sharks on leashes towards me. One V-13 fires at the sharks but is devoured in the process. The other maintains the shields, protecting us from the plasma barrage. How the phenomes bypassed the shields is a mystery to me.

*Such a deadly phenome. Her psyche must be warped.*

Quaint is about to engage the assassin when she melts into the floor, leaving only a puddle of water.

I hear the footsteps of several other strikers making their way towards me. After checking the wound once more, I see that the damage has not healed.

*The nanobots should be working by now.*

While in HQ's state-of-the-art healing quarters, I'm met with a dark elf doctor with a mechanical arm. He seems rather concerned as he checks my wound. He caresses the wound, leaving a cold sensation. The room has all sorts of gadgets on the walls and a distinct smell of disinfectant.

"Do you want the good news or the bad news first?"

"Bad news? How can there be bad news? Do you know who I am?"

"Yes. You're Grand Inquisitor Morange. And yet, there is bad news that I must tell you."

"Spit it out."

"Unfortunately, you have been hit with a grievous-wound-inducing plasma blast. It negates any healing mechanisms, including the nanobots that flow through your body. I'm sorry but there isn't anything I can do to treat the wound. You will be in constant pain for the remainder of your life."

I burst into laughter. Standing up, I push aside the darkling doctor.

"May I inquire what's so funny?" he asks.

"I expected a doctor of your status to be more informed. Perhaps it's because you're a mere darkling."

His face remains straight.

"I've been called worse. If you want, I can have another doctor assess your wound. But if I may toot my own horn for a moment, I am actually the top-ranked physician on board."

"I don't doubt your abilities amongst the plebs. I just doubt that your abilities can do what I need done." And with that, I look at Sanguine and Quaint, who escort me to the safety zone.

Upon arrival at the safety zone, I feel a sudden surge of pain that drops me to my knees once again. The pain reminds me of the first time I drank the liquid from the cyber realm. Not something I'd like to relive for the foreseeable future. Fortunately for me, I will become a cyber elf, and thus immortality is within my grasp. I check the wound to see that it isn't bleeding—but the blue substance continues to pulsate.

The other important members of HQ are gathered together in a large room reinforced with corundum. Each has two strikers guarding their person save for that Legislator Alterna. The fact that both his strikers are deemed traitors for the RRA tells me he must be a traitor as well.

As the Grand Inquisitor, it is my job to find and eliminate any RRA scum. Especially those that are members of the elite. To think that a politician of his caliber would side with those ruffians!

"Legislator Alterna." I flash him my politician's smile.

"Grand Inquisitor Morange." He flashes one back. As elegant as ever.

"May I have a few words with you?"

"Of course, have a seat."

I take a seat beside him and get straight to the point.

"What are your thoughts on your two escorts being RRA scum?"

"It's quite disheartening. I trusted them with my life."

"I see. Don't you find it rather odd that both your strikers were treacherous beings?"

"Of course. I mean, to think my life was in their hands and could have been forfeit at any moment. As far as what you're getting at, the strikers are designated by the technicians. If there is anyone you should be interrogating, it would be the one who assigned them to me."

"Interrogation? I thought this was merely a conversation between two members of HQ."

"Excuse my frankness, but you're a glorified watch dog. The only reason you breathe the same air as me and other more reputable members of society is because of your fraternal connection with one of the cyber elves," says this legislator Alterna.

For the first time in a long time, I'm at a loss for words. The gall of this traitor.

"You have quite the lip on you for someone left vulnerable."

"Perhaps. But I have made my peace with death. Have you?"

"I will not be dying anytime soon. I will be immortal, like the cyber elves themselves."

"But at what cost?"

"Cost? There is no cost."

"There is always a cost." And with that, Legislator Alterna gets up and makes his way to what I presume is more welcoming company.

The alarm finally stops.

*They must have apprehended this Leaky Faucet.*

Sanguine approaches me while drinking a blood pack.

"They have issued Z protocol."

"What's that?"

"Every Z-trained striker in all three divisions will be on high alert. One group will be instructed to apprehend the renegades Vexation and Sansa. They are both wanted alive and kicking—probably so the names of the remaining RRA members can be extracted from them."

"The RRA is all but finished. There cannot be many names left."

"Well, the two traitors have managed to eliminate a slew of strikers and a handful of politicians—not to mention the prince. The death of the prince is a real game changer. He was here on a diplomatic mission, and thus it was our job to protect him under any circumstance. We failed, and the repercussions will be felt."

"You don't seem very concerned."

"I'm a Y. My job is to kill, not to track and hunt. My place will be beside you. However, I don't envy anyone who has to travel to that planet that he landed on."

"What do you mean? It's a mere uninhabited planet. Just a pile of rocks and whatnot."

"Heh, I forgot you're new to HQ and haven't been mingling too much. They haven't divulged curtain things to you. Uninhabited is codename for orc-filled gutter. The worst of the worst of planets. Their planets are like living organisms, where the foliage itself has a mind of its own, and the orcs themselves are wild beasts unlike any others."

"Very well. We will see how all of this plays out. All I know is that I want Vex in my grip, staring down the barrel of my shotgun."

"Dead or alive, he will be captured. No one escapes a Z protocol."

# CHAPTER 19
## CLASSIFICATION: ROGUE STRIKER

I've managed to find these blue mushrooms that are mildly toxic. They're the only things that are remotely edible so far. At best, they give me a stomachache after consumption; at worst, they kill me. So far, I've found giant poison ivy plants, giant Venus fly traps, some unidentifiable toxic mushrooms, and these blue ones. It seems like everything on this planet is designed to kill, trap, or both.

Then there is the rumbling. I find my sleep often disturbed by a rumbling sound that draws closer each day. No matter how far I run, it inches closer during the night—as if it is stalking me. Whatever it is, I plan on avoiding it for as long as possible.

I've spent twenty-three days on this planet, and I've lost all hope that Sansa made it out alive. She must have gotten caught. I feel as though a piece of my heart has been torn apart. I had grown to see Sansa as the little sister I never wanted, but desperately needed.

What reason do I have to live? I don't know. But the spark that is my spirit keeps pushing me forward. So, aimlessly, I wander the planet I have dubbed Kukosa. In one of the ancient elven tongues, it means missing—because this damn planet is missing all the things that make a normal planet habitable.

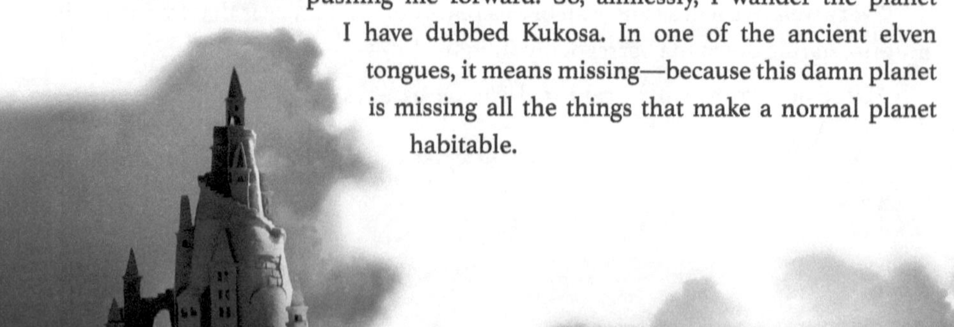

When it rains, it pours some kind of acidic rain that takes a day for me to purify. I am fortunate enough to have a purification device attached to my suit; Sansa really thought of everything when she created it.

I find myself in search of a water source and better shelter when I see smoke. Where there is smoke, there is life. But where there is life, there is danger. My curiosity gets the better of me, and I creep through the blue shrubs to peer closer.

There is a fire pit with some kind of meat sizzling over it. My senses are filled with the smell. After waiting a few minutes, I take the meat and analyze it. My sensors indicate that it is suitable for consumption.

While I dig in, I hear footsteps approaching in the distance.

With my stealth turned on and my mouth full of meat, I withdraw my SMGs Pain and Suffocation. I'm ready to unleash death on any who may reveal themselves, but I find myself waiting longer than anticipated.

*Could it be Hyper Fairy? Stomper? Something else?*

The idle time gives my mind leeway to think. In situations like these, thinking is bad.

I hear the war cry of an orc.

The deafening sound shakes me to the very core. I'm filled with the memory of every fearful moment of my life: from the beatings in my sleep to being on this planet isolated from elven kind now. Being hunted down like the monsters I am trained to track and kill.

I feel warm liquid pour down the legs of my battlesuit. I have urinated myself like a damn child. The orc must have picked up on the faint scent, as he charges towards me.

I will never forget seeing a real orc in person. It's surrounded by a green toxic fog that induces worse sickness the longer I'm in range.

I drop to my knees, opening my visors to puke, just as the orc, three times my size, easily picks me up and slams me into the ground. He grips my P90s and crushes them with his bare hands.

*So much for those.*

The orc stomps his feet, and the ground thunders beneath my feet. My head is throbbing.

My instincts take over, and I unleash Tirade, who immediately taunts the orc. The orc throws me away before looking at Tirade mildly amused, He does something I can only describe as a laugh.

"Tok, tok, tok. Gar do pathetic tuk."

He speaks in an unknown tongue.

I feel my mind focused in its rage; energy surrounds my being. Tirade throws a wind barrage at the orc. It is ineffective, but it buys me enough time to dash towards the monstrosity with both scimitars aimed at its throat. Just when he's about to cleave me with his war axe, I phase retreat behind him and jam both scimitars into his lower back.

Putrid green puss oozes out from his lower back, making me feel dizzy.

A massive fist careens towards my head, but Tirade jumps in front of the blow, taking the brunt of the damage. As she dissolves, I feel a certain sadness. Whether it's coming from me or her, I don't know.

I dodge roll and withdraw my SMGs Berry and Stone. I unleash a barrage of energy bullets into the orc. At first, I'm doing a ridiculous amount of energetic damage to the creature; he is riddled with holes. Then an invisible shield suddenly pops up, blocking the damage.

The orc flings his axe at me, catching me in the chest. I'm sent flying into a nearby tree. My head bangs against the trunk with a loud clunk.

The orc looms over me, its toxic stench unbearable. My visor opens up once again for me to puke the last bit of my stomach contents.

"Tok, tok, tok. Jimbo tim ter stupid tuk."

Another clear insult swung my way. But I'm not without hope. I activate the shield on my ring and press the button to unleash six bella rockets. They spew out, causing explosive damage to both of us. I watch as the orc stumbles backwards. Just when I think he's about to collapse, he gathers his senses. For a brief moment, I see a green shadowy figure behind the orc.

The shadowy figure flings a translucent axe towards me, which bypasses the shields and strikes me on the shoulder.

Now bleeding heavily, I feel the warmth drain from my body. Struggling to keep my eyes open, I throw out five flutter bombs and put them on circulate. I leave them to rotate around my person.

*The best I can do.*

I half-expected the mindless orc to charge into the flutter bombs, but he is posing more intelligent than my training informed me. Instead of rushing head-first into the flutter bombs, the orc picks up a rock and throws it at one. It activates.

Fortunately for me, I have enough time to signal for that bomb to move forward away from the others before it detonates.

The orc smiles, revealing yellow teeth.

"Orc smart. Tuk stupid."

Now, I may not be versed in the orc language. But my translators picked up on that one. Tuk must mean elf. The nerve of this giant monstrosity. He thinks he is smarter than I am.

As I lay there bleeding out, the orc approaches me once again.

The green shadow behind him swings a massive arm, pushing aside the remaining four flutter bombs. They explode in vain.

He licks his lips and grins. The orc grips me by my throat and lifts me up to eye level. He leans in closer and removes my helmet. The foul stench fills my lungs as I spit in his face. He lifts me higher and is about to smash me into the ground when I phase retreat out of his hands to behind his back, where the scimitars are still jammed.

I pull them out and twirl, slicing him in his genitals.

The green shadow strikes me, sending me flying into another tree, this time breaking it in half. I land with a loud crunch, and the damage is done. The orc drops to his knees and bellows out another, albeit different, war cry. This time I'm filled with overwhelming grief. Thoughts of Sansa, my mother, my sister, Chaos, and even Hyper Fairy fill me.

*It would seem I'm always destined to lose the women in my life.*

Tears flood my visor as I curl into a little ball, bleeding out.

*What a way to go, Vex.*

Without any energy to heal myself or energy to move, I know death is inevitable. Then I hear footsteps in the nearby brushes.

*Probably another orc—or worse, Hyper Fairy and Stomper.*

I look up to see a confusing figure on all fours. As I squint to get a better look, the being moves closer and smells me.

I pass out due to energy exhaustion.

I jolt awake from a slap across my cheek. I reach instantly for my SMGs Berry and Stone to find them gone. Next, I reach for my scimitars, but they are nowhere to be found. Panic rises in me at having been stripped of my weapons.

Taking in my surroundings, I am met with the unusual scent of pine wood. I look around to see that I am inside of a hollowed-out tree. This realization is followed by the image of a light elf dressed in wolf-skin clothing and orc teeth. He growls at me, then moves to slap me again.

I catch the hand and furrow my brows.

*One time is enough.*

Checking my wounds, I notice that I am covered in blue leaves. I feel mildly intoxicated, but otherwise I am fine.

"Did you heal me?"

The wild elf tilts his head and speaks in the same orc tongue.

"Tuk dimbo dall pierto."

Without my helmet, I can't translate anything. I rise to locate my helmet when the wild elf assumes his battle stance. At least, it's what I think is his battle stance. He lays on all fours, low to the ground, and growls like a wolf.

"I don't want to fight you." I shake my head while speaking.

He does a back flip and lands gracefully into a pile of raggedy clothing and tree branches.

I activate my console to assemble my battlesuit. The wild elf stares at me wide-eyed as my suit latches to me piece by piece. Feeling a lot safer around this wild thing now, I attempt to communicate.

I point to myself. "Me, tuk?" Then I point at the wild elf "You, tuk?"

The wild elf nods.

I point to myself again. "Me, Vexation." And then at him. "You?"

"Me, Zeal. You, Vexation!" He starts hopping around on all fours again.

His voice somehow echoes, forcing me to cover the sides of my helmet.

"Rather rambunctious, aren't you? Though I suppose I should thank you." With both arms across my chest, I bow: the universal elf sign for appreciation. I'm beginning to move towards my weapons when Zeal pounces on me. I only see a glimpse of him before he lands on me, with his sharp canines revealed.

He says, "Duwa." My helmet informs me that roughly translates to *duel*.

Now that I am indebted once again to a wandering elf, I decide it would be a disgrace to deny my savior his request.

# CHAPTER 20
## CLASSIFICATION: CHAOTIC STRIKER

Sometimes I wonder what my life would be like if I wasn't chosen for the IGF. I'd probably open a bakery and kitchen: a quiet shop making sweet treats for the common people. I remember Vex telling me his mom was a wondrous chef. I wonder if he could cook?

Yet here I find myself in HQ, surrounded by the top Z strikers in the entire IGF. You may ask, what exactly is a striker Z? It's a classification designated for those strikers who have undergone gruesome training in preparation to hunt down any threat in the galaxy. The men are scarred, beaten, and trained in the art of savagery. They become cold, calculated hunters able to go weeks without food or water. The women are turned into vindictive seductresses who use their beauty and charm to lure men to their demise. We become callous beings incapable of making true bonds. It's a festering wound that never heals. Then we are pitted against each other in a dark labyrinth—a place where one experiences horrors too despicable to repeat. Typically, only one in twenty strikers survive the Z training.

Men are versed in capturing their prey dead, women in capturing their prey alive. It's been a while since there was a Z protocol issued. The last time, if I recall correctly, was for the capture of the psychopath codenamed Checkmate.

He managed to kill over fifty strikers of Z and Y class before waltzing straight into HQ and surrendering. It was so hush-hush that they wiped the memories of every Y class striker and placed an advanced chip on the Z's.

This hunt isn't the same. This is more of slap to the face of the IGF, while that was a kick to the groin. The IGF doesn't like being embarrassed. Vexation has found himself a marked man. He even brought the innocent Sansa into it. What cruel fate the IGF bigwigs have in store for those two, I don't even want to think about.

What I do know is that I am under oath to carry out this mission to my fullest abilities. I will be scrutinized for any sign of weakness. I currently have fifty-two people watching my private feed. Two of them are my mother and father.

While waiting for the supervisor to appear, I look around at my fellow striker Z's. Some of them I recognize from the last protocol, while others are new. We total four women and three men.

Out of eighty possible candidates.

From the corner of my eye, I see Leonidas walk in. His majestic hair flows although there is no wind in the spacecraft. Every step is carefully laid on the metallic floor with little effort. As if stalking an antelope. He eyes every Z and scoffs when his gaze lands on me.

"I'm surprised they didn't strip you of your Z status since you've been wallowing in the Eclectic Division."

The rest of the group chuckles to themselves. Would that I could strip this man of his tongue. But his power levels far outweigh my own, and he has a temper to match.

Thus, I keep quiet.

"I'm talking to you, Chaos."

"What am I supposed to say to that?"

"I suppose there isn't much to say. Just don't slow us down." He turns to the big screen and starts moving things around for the briefing.

"This isn't the typical hunt. We are going to an orc-filled planet. It has long been established as a hot spot for those vile creatures. Although it has been heavily gassed, the beasts have somehow adapted to the poison and now thrive. The good thing is that their technology is still primitive. As always, we have the superior firepower and training."

"Status on the type of poison used?" asks Convert. She's a religious zealot who can convert her enemies into allies. Also Leonidas' wife.

"Special grade Q. It slowly decays the lungs and liver from the inside. We have approximately one month to capture Vexation before the poison damage becomes severe. You will also be given experimental energy capsules, used only in dire situations, to boost your energy for when engaging the orcs."

"Why do we need those?" This question comes from Pyro Tech, a behemoth of a striker who uses flamethrowers and fire beams. Apparently he holds the record for most IGF casualties. Not someone you want to be fighting alongside.

"Simple. The orcs on this planet are like nothing we've ever seen. There's a reason why their planet has been left off the grid for so long. But you know how it goes. No one gets away with embarrassing the IGF bigwigs without consequences."

"Very well. Let's get this over with," says Pyro Tech.

I feel the sudden urge to ask a question I am sure is on everyone's mind.

"What about the other rogue striker? Sansa."

"Oh, you mean Leaky Faucet. She will be dealt with soon. It's miraculous that she has evaded capture so far, but our advanced technicians have finally figured out the nuances of her advanced phasing technology—or so they say. Soon she will be captured and sent to The Abyss for her transgressions."

A shiver runs down my spine as an eerie silence steamrolls through the room. The Abyss. An experimental chamber where the most horrific actions take place. It's built to break one's spirit and mental fortitude. A place where one begs for death, but death never comes.

"I see... and what will happen to Vexation when he is captured?"

"Heh, do you lot really want to know?"

A few nod their heads, while others simple stare out into the distance.

"Well I suppose I should tell you. He will be sent to The Void."

"The Void?"

"Yeah, a place created by those sadistic technicians. Think of it as striker Z training on hyper drive. It's what the HQ bigwigs watch on their down time. We all know how they love their entertainment."

This is true. Something about diving deep into the cyber net and messing with those cyber elves has a way of warping one's mind to the point that they can only find gratification in watching others suffer.

My heart trembles for my poor Vex. The fate that awaits him is beyond reproach. I will have to put him out of his misery before it begins.

The carrier craft, accompanied by two fighter jets, lands smoothly in a clearing on the orc planet. Upon exiting the carrier craft, I am met with a flurry of blue and white. Blue mushrooms, blue trees, blue shrubs, and white mold. Vixen immediately warns me of the toxic air, which is more toxic than anticipated. At best, we have three weeks before the damage is serious.

The plan is simple. Leonidas will stay and guard the carrier and the jets while we move out in teams of two. We each take one third of the planet and scour it in the month that we have. Because communications are clear, we can stay in contact. Vexation is to be captured alive if possible.

The orcs we'll kill on sight. The more dead the better.

Unfortunately for me, I am teamed with Pyro Tech. I'll be sure to sleep with one eye open, lest he try to defile me.

*You never know with the brutish types.*

As we progress through the blue shrubs in search of any sign of life, the Pyro freak feels the need to engage me in conversation.

"So why do they call you Chaos?"

"Because I'm crazy." I hope to deter him from what he really wants.

"I like the crazy ones. They have the juiciest peaches."

"I bet you think you're really witty, don't you?"

"My mother thought so."

Against my better judgement, I ask one question too many.

"What happened to her?"

"I burned her to a crisp before I ate her."

I know I should be shocked, but dealing with Z types, there is always a tragic backstory or gruesome tale to tell. If I were to tell you the truth of why my codename is Chaos, you'd lock me up and throw away the key.

"I suppose it could have been worse." I'm doing my best not to aggravate the cannibal.

"Oh, that's just the PG version." He chuckles to himself.

"My sensors are picking up something in the distance."

As we progress deeper into our section of the planet, we are met with giant green pods. Their glow is absolutely mesmerizing. They are about three times the size of my person, with a sweet scent.

Pyro Tech turns to me and asks a question that I'm not sure is stupid or not.

"Food?"

I shrug. "I don't know. Maybe."

He approaches one of the pods and takes out his flamethrower. With a flick of a switch, he starts roasting the nearest pod. It peels open, and out pops up a full-fledged orc. It's covered in slime, and the stench is horrendous, but it's a grown orc.

*What the fuck?*

The orc lets out a war cry as green fog surrounds its being. Suddenly the other pods open.

Our only saving grace is that these orcs are unarmed, untrained, and don't have access to their ancestors yet. But we are surrounded by ten of them.

Pyro Tech springs into action and summons his phoenix, which lays waste to two of the orcs approaching us.

I aim my sniper rifle at the head of the first and blow its head like a melon. One orc charges towards me and kicks me across the forest into an opened pod. I find my back stuck against the pod, but I manage to aim my sniper rifle at another charging orc. A groin shot this time. It drops to the floor, green blood spraying in all directions.

By the time we have eliminated all ten orcs, Pyro Tech is breathing heavily and nearly depleted. He turns to me and cackles.

"It seems like today is my lucky day."

"What do you mean by that?"

"You look absolutely delicious, stuck there."

I point my sniper rifle at his head. "Take another step and you'll be dead within a second."

As I activate my thrusters to heat the sticky substance of the pod, I see a flash of green plasma. Then Pyro Tech collapses to the ground.

Two fully fledged orcs appear: one decked in an advanced battlesuit and an unidentifiable rifle, the other in reinforced corundum armor, wielding a glowing green glaive.

*There is more to this planet than we have been told. They aren't supposed to have this kind of equipment available.*

The first orc looks at the second orc, then kicks Pyro Tech in the head. Just when I'm about to make my move, the first orc beats me to the trigger.

I feel a surge of energy overload my battlesuit causing it to disengage as I drop to my knees.

Because my helmet is the only thing that keeps power, the last thing I hear is the orc speaking in its primitive tongue.

"Stupid elves."

*The gall of these primitive creatures.*

# CHAPTER 21
## CLASSIFICATION: ROGUE STRIKER

I find myself enjoying the companionship of Zeal. We spend most days gathering food and learning each other's language. He teaches me the way of the orcs, while I teach him the way of the elves. He has yet to reveal to me how he came to be a lone wild elf on an orc-filled planet. But I'm sure that will come in due time.

He taught me the various shades of blue mushrooms. Some are edible, some get you high, and some will kill you with a single bite.

Some nights we duel until one of us passes out from exhaustion. Usually, it's me. So far I think the score is fifteen to seven in his favor—and one draw. His unorthodox tactics are a sight to behold. Then there is his phenome. Another unorthodox aspect of his being.

Other nights we travel away from the thundering noise. He describes it to me as a large black tower, but how a large black tower manages to move several kilometers a day is beyond me.

*I mean, my orc tongue is still a bit fuzzy.*

Tonight is one of those nights where we're eating mushroom soup. The meals vary between mushroom soup and mushroom sandwiches.

What do we use for bread? Good question. We feast on these tangy blue leaves.

"Mushroom soup, good?"

He asks me this every time we eat mushroom soup. As if he doesn't know it tastes like ass cheeks and water. At least, how I'd imagine ass cheeks to taste.

"Sure," is my only response.

A mild expression appears across his feral face.

"Duel tonight?"

I'm about to respond with a resounding yes when he starts to growl.

"Outside, dirty orcs."

A purple glow surrounds him as he dashes out towards the exit of the hollowed-out tree, his giant club strapped to his back. Then I hear the war cry of an orc cut short. By the time I grab my scimitars and SMGs and head out to assist, he has already downed the three orcs.

He tears into the chests of the orcs and plucks out their hearts.

"Orc heart edible. Makes you immune. We eat, then move."

I guess orc heart is on the menu.

We find ourselves digging a hole to bunker down in an area of the planet filled with softer mud than usual. We take the branches off nearby trees and use them to make a door. Finally, we cover the hole in moss and leaves for camouflage. The hole is big enough for four, granting both of us ample space.

*We're close, but not trying to be that close.*

While sleeping I hear a noise. Zeal is already alert. His yellow eyes are wild like a wolf's—yet piercing and majestic.

"More elves. Friends or foes?"

I peer outside to see two strikers I have yet to meet face to face. I am only familiar with their codenames: Tag and You're It. One is never seen without the other. The short woman wields a pink sniper rifle and some floating robot with the face of a cat; the tall woman wields a strong barrier and a destructive plasma cannon.

They are ranked twenty and twenty-one respectfully, but together, they are the equivalent of a rank six. Or so the story goes.

I suppose there is no time like the present to find out.

I look at Zeal and speak the very words I know will send him into a wild frenzy.

"Tuks tell toran."

Which roughly translates to *elves must die.*

Together we spring from our hidden bunker and engage the two striker Z's. Without hesitating, You're It throws up a purple barrier and fires off a large plasma beam from her left arm with a radius the size of my head. I manage to dodge by ducking. I look back to see it shot a giant hole into a nearby tree.

*Not a pleasant way to go.*

Zeal leaps high above my head and slams his spiked club into the barrier covering Tag and You're It.

To my amazement the barrier dissipates, but not before Tag's robot puts a spotlight on Zeal's chest. You're It round-house kicks Zeal in the very spot, causing Zeal to yelp and dealing an enormous amount of physical damage.

I phase retreat past You're It and unleash a barrage from Berry and Stone onto Tag. She fizzles in and out of existence like static, causing the barrage to go right through her. You're It grips me in a chokehold. I flip her over and slam her onto the ground, but she grabs my arm with her legs and breaks it with ease.

With my one working arm, I aim Stone at her helmet and unleash a barrage. At this range it should be a killing blow, but her barrier nullifies most of the damage. Stone activates its special skill, and I feel a rock barrier cover me just as I'm shot in the head. The bullet pierces my rock barrier and goes through my helmet, getting lodged there.

*An inch more and I'd be dead.*

Like a wild beast, Zeal pounces on Tag, and she fizzles in and out of existence once again. She flies into the sky and aims her sniper rifle at Zeal. I see a smirk cross his face. We both know what is coming.

One thing I learned when facing Zeal in battle is to keep everything on the ground. He dislikes anyone that jumps, flies, or climbs higher than him. The higher up you go, the worse it gets for you.

Zeal looks up at the moon and howls a deafening cry. Once again to my amazement, a purple wolf design appears on the moon, and it howls back. A purple ray of light shines down on both Tag and You're It. Tag immediately falls to the ground at an insane speed under the weight of heightened gravity. He dashes towards her, his spiked club bent backwards, and swings. The devastating blow connects with a loud crunch: He decapitates her head with a single strike.

You're It's shrieks are cut short by one of my blades pressed against her throat.

"How many strikers are after me?"

"Tag... my beloved."

"Focus." I press the blade against her throat, drawing blood.

"Six striker Z's, not including Leonidas, who guards the ships. I'll tell you everything. You think it matters? You and your puppy friend are going back to HQ one way or another. No one escapes the grasp of the IGF. Plus, you have Hyper Fairy and Stomper to worry about."

"Curses," I mumble underneath my breath.

"What else do you want to know, traitor?"

"What's the status on Leaky Faucet?"

"She has somehow managed to evade capture all this time. She is a disruptive force in the Frontier Division and has incapacitated a couple members of HQ. But she will be caught soon enough."

It's a relief to hear that she has evaded capture so far, but how and what she is up to is a mystery to me. She must have gotten different orders.

"Where are the ships located?"

"I don't know."

"What do you mean you don't know? You came in one, didn't you?"

"Tag had all the coordinates."

"Very well. Are your comms still functional?"

"Barely, what's it to you?"

"Put me in to the other strikers and Leonidas."

She patches me into the voice chat.

*You're It connecting to group chat.*

"You're It, have you found the traitor scum?" asks Leonidas.

She is about to respond when I cut her off.

"Glad to hear I'm missed. Didn't think you'd send such a warm welcoming party, but I'm flattered. I just wanted you to know that I'm coming for each and every one of you. Welcome to my planet."

"Vexation, you have some balls. I'll give you that. I'm gonna cut them off and feed them to my lioness." And with that, communication cuts off.

I slit the throat of You're It.

*It had to be done.*

After gathering their rations and some odd pills off their bodies, I pick up Zeal, who passed out halfway through eating Tag's heart— a consequence to using that move.

I'm slightly disgusted by the thought of him eating the hearts of elves. But who am I to judge?

*Different strokes.*

After Zeal and I finish our rations, we go back to our usual mushroom soup and mushroom sandwiches. I have started to feel the effects of the poison. It's become harder to breathe, and I have a sharp pain where my liver is located, but I push on.

We manage to hunt down two male strikers by the name of Xin and Sin. Another dynamic duo. The battle is fierce, but Zeal and I pull through. Unfortunately, Zeal is severely wounded in the process—a wound that I don't really know how to heal.

I'm not a bloody blacksmith, nor am I a scavenger. My healing ability is for myself only.

Zeal describes to me the same plant that he used to heal my wounds when he first found me. I remember that it was green and smelled like fresh coffee beans in the morning.

You'd think finding a green plant in a planet filled with blue foliage would be simple, but between traveling away from the moving tower during the night and searching for the plant and food during the day, I'm having a hard time getting it done. I never really noticed how much Zeal ate until I had to feed him myself.

After another day of failing to find the plant, I return to the encampment where we're hiding. I see a female elf dressed in white armor with blue sprinkled at the hinges. That's probably the best way I have to describe the fanciest battlesuit I've ever seen. Her hair is white, and her skin is tanned. I haven't had the pleasure or displeasure of meeting her, and her name wasn't in the files that I went through.

That can only mean one thing.

She's a top-five striker in the division—a rank far past apprehension. The top five strikers of the Frontier Division are cyber years away from the rest of the pack. They are known as the five divines.

"Who are you?" I point both Stone and Berry at her head.

"I am Convert. You must be Vexation."

"Vex."

"Well, Vex. It would do both of us a service if you came with me peacefully. I must say, you and your little... pet have caused quite the uproar. HQ is growing impatient. Frankly, you're making my husband look bad, and that displeases me very much. Can't you see reason and accept your fate?"

Her voice is so soothing that it beckons me to comply. I feel my hands tremble slightly; my guns lower just a little bit. In that instance, I see a blue fuzzy caterpillar manifest on the top of my SMG Stone. It has wide eyes and a friendly smile. The fuzzy phenome inches towards me step by step.

Convert breaks into a harmonic melody. Her singing wakes Zeal, who first growls, then begins to cuddle up to her like a puppy. At this point, I drop my guns to the ground with a loud thump. My hands tremble as the fuzzy caterpillar sticks to the chest of my battlesuit, right where my heart is. I feel a warm sensation and a sudden urge to protect Convert with my life. It's the kind of devotion one would give their mother.

I glance to see the same fuzzy caterpillar on Zeal, who has his spiked club in hand. He also has this enthralled grin on his face—something akin to a puppy's love.

"Convert to Leonidas."

"Go ahead."

"I have the asset and his wild elf companion. Coming in cold."

"Copy that, excellent work."

She snaps her fingers, and the caterpillar's heartbeat matches my own. I find myself marching to her symphony without apology.

# CHAPTER 22
## CLASSIFICATION: TECHNICIAN

Floating in the tier-two level of the cyber net, I am met with green triangles with mathematical equations on them. My job is to collect the triangles and decipher the calculations. The cyber realm's second tier is essentially a 3D math game.

What I have dubbed cyber music plays in the background, keeping me calm and focused. It's mainly instrumentals, but created by unidentified instruments. Each math code that I decipher sends a euphoric buzz to my brain that is essentially a rush of dopamine. As I progress throughout the maze, the triangles blow past at faster speeds, forcing me to decipher them quicker.

Currently there are ten other techs on tier two, and I'm the best one. Ever since the incident with He Who Loves, the answers and the codes go together like cream cheese on toast. It's like I see one giant map, and the answer is right in the middle every time. I haven't told anyone this—not even Morange. I fear being scrutinized for my pseudo-relationship with the cyber elf.

I know he did something to me when he covered me in code—but what other effects it will have on my being I don't know.

The ten of us on tier two reach the end of the maze.

Naturally, I am first.

A cyber door opens, and I feel a tingling sensation as a wave of pink code washes over my avatar. I'm met with the new He Who Loves.

"To thee I give each a blessing. May you continue until the realms align."

I'm about to inquire about the former He Who Loves, but I bite my tongue. It's probably best that I forget about him.

The headset disconnects for the day. My brain feels numb and a bit foggy. Considering I've spent seventeen hours straight on the console, that isn't much of a surprise. I stumble my way to my room, thankfully only a few meters from the technicians' quarters.

I scan my ID tag, and the door flings open. I head over to my personal shower and begin undressing. My clothes are loose fitting. It seems I really am getting rid of weight.

*Soon, I'll be slim and trim, walking thin.*

I smile as I look into the rudimentary mirror in every technician's washroom.

My eyes are now a yellowish-gold with gold circles around my pupils.

On the mirror I see code—but not just any code. Something far more advanced.

After three hours of trying to decipher the mathematical equation, I decide its best to retire for the night. My body feels refreshed, but my mind is drained.

I close my eyes to see green triangles, purple blocks, and red circles. They combine to make some kind of odd shape.

I open my eyes to see words floating in the air. *Status update: If you're reading this, you've made it to tier three. If you die on this tier, you're not worthy of me.*

*It would seem the stakes have risen.*

And rise, they should. Each tier I climb, each code I crack, makes me feel so much more fulfilled than assisting in the hunting of monsters ever did.

Although I am naturally averse to change, like so many people, I have come to realize that growth trumps all.

I haven't seen Morange in a while, and I find myself missing his touch. But I suppose with our new positions, finding time where we're both free is a task in itself. I don't think he's even seen how much weight I've lost.

"Allison to Morange."

"I'm listening."

"How about you drop what you're doing tonight and come see me? I've been thinking about you."

"I've been thinking about you, as well. How is the code breaking going?"

*Codes—is that all he cares about?*

"It's going well. I'm tier three now. Perhaps we can discuss it more in person. Maybe over a glass of wine?"

"That's a negative. Leaky Faucet is still running rampant. I must assist in her capture."

"Fine."

And I disconnect the call.

When I first heard the news that Sansa was still alive, I was overjoyed. But that joy was cut short on learning she is some kind of assassin for the RRA. How she managed that, I don't know. I guess you never really know a person. Nor do you know what they are capable of until they do it.

It's only a matter of time before they capture her and torture her to oblivion.

The sound of bubbling water fills my room. I peer over the bed to see Sansa herself, in her full battlesuit, rising from a puddle.

"I've been looking for you, Allison. We need to talk."

I look above her head to see an unusual half-full red bar. She's breathing heavily, and blood is leaking from her abdomen. If I had my battlesuit on I could fight her. Test my skills. I mean, how good can she really be? But my suit is tucked away, hidden.

"What do you want with me? I don't know what Vex has told you, but it's all lies," I say.

"I'm going to have you do a favor for me," she says dryly.

"I'm all out of those."

"Well, find one."

I crack into a fit of laughter. This kid, holding a blue-and-silver ray gun pointed at my head, isn't very menacing at all. Though, considering the IGF breeds killers at a young age, one would think I'd be more serious about her demeanor. Who knows what she has been through to get to this point?

She scrunches up her face. "What's so funny?"

"I just find it amusing that you've become some kind of assassin."

"A damn good one at that." She twirls the ray gun in her hand.

"If you say so. They credited Vex with most of the kills."

"I did my fair share, and I'm proud of it. For the RRA. We're making real change, Allison. Or should I call you Sugar Cane?" The disdain in her voice is evident.

"You can call me whatever you want; that doesn't make it true."

"Are you calling Vex a liar?"

"I'm calling it a misunderstanding. Things should not have played out the way they did."

"You're delusional. You were canoodling with the enemy—the corrupt politician Morange."

I can't help but let out another laugh.

"What's so funny?"

"I think you have the definition of canoodling all mixed up."

"I know my words!" She lets off her ray gun an inch away from my head.

"Calm down. No need to throw a fit."

"When in the history of life has anyone ever calmed down after being told to calm down? Stop treating me like a child."

"I mean, you are only seventeen."

"I have been through more than you can imagine. This journey wasn't easy."

"I can see that. You're bleeding. You should see someone."

"I'm fine. Now about that favor."

"I thought I told you…"

She shoots me in the arm, which goes limp. Fortunately for me, her weapon's on stun.

"You fucking shot me, you rug rat."

"Keep talking like that, and I'll fry your brain. Now, take me to the vaults. I need you to crack a code."

The bar above her head is slowly dwindling with each drop of blood that drips onto the floor. She takes some bandages from my washroom and patches herself up while holding me at gun point.

The bar reminds me of a game health bar. Could it really be a game health bar? Could this be what they mean when they say that the cyber realm is aligning with ours? Our world is becoming more computer-like.

Sansa directs me down the hall and from  the elevator to a large black vault. It's covered in chains and advanced code. The heavy door is made of reinforced corundum—damn near impossible to blast through.

"Get me in this vault without triggering the alarm, and this will be the last time you hear from me."

"I'm not going to help you."

She takes the ray gun and tries to gun-butt me, but I block with my numb arm. My other fist flies towards her helmet, but she simply disappears in a pool of water. It's at this point that my supervisor Nora rushes into the room, her gun aimed at where Sansa once was.

"Took you long enough," I say as my supervisor escorts me back to my room.

"We wanted to see what her primary objective is. So far, she has been a major nuisance. Shutting down certain operations, keeping HQ members on the defensive, but no major casualties—save for the severe wound to Grand Inquisitor Morange."

"What happened to Morange?"

"The Grand Inquisitor?"

"Yes, the Grand Inquisitor."

"He was shot with some kind of anti-healing plasma blast. Everyone is on the defensive. We haven't seen anything like this. Whether it's her phenome or a new technology of her own creation, we're not sure. What we do know is that this little brat is more intelligent than she has been letting on."

I feel the warmth leave my face as I think about what ailment my Morange could be undergoing. "How can I help in capturing her? She was part of my troupe and she needs to be put down."

"Tell me everything you know about her."

"Well, I don't know much. What I do know is that she has a habit of tinkering with schematics and making her own adjustments. She comes from a family of strikers and has to live up to their standards. Have you contacted her family?"

"We tried to track them down and came up with a series of mysterious deaths. Her brother and father were both killed in their sleep when she was twelve. Her mother died in childbirth. Somehow she managed to change the records and have them say otherwise."

"That little sprout managed all that?"

"It would seem so, yes. But fear not. We have given some of our top striker Z's the task of capturing her for interrogation. We will extract every bit of advanced knowledge out of her, through any means necessary. The Frontier Division will not be mocked."

"No, we will not." I look at Nora to see that she has a green health bar above her head. It's full but in larger chunks than Sansa's, and there is a number at the bottom right of the bar. It reads 700. Does this mean she has less overall health than Sansa? What does that mean?

"Umm, Nora?"

"Yes, Sponge Cake?"

I cringe every time I hear that codename. "What's tier three?"

"The benefits and consequences of each tier are different depending on the cyber paragon that oversees your progress. For you it is He Who Loves, and thus you get the eyes of love. They allow you to see the health bars of your allies and enemies. Tier four is when things get really interesting."

"What tier are you, and which cyber elf do you serve?"

"I serve He Who Hates. The least-served of all the cyber paragons, yet one of the most feared. There are seven tiers, and I am tier six. Very close to releasing my paragon onto this realm."

"Wow. I never knew your group was so close. As far as I know, tier three is our highest. What attributes are gifted to you?"

"That is correct. The former He Who Loves was preoccupied with extracurricular activities that we won't delve into. As far as my attributes, we'll have to leave them for when you reach tier four."

I nod my head and am about to head to my room when I hear a ship-sized explosion go off in the vaults.

*Not my problem. I'm no striker. But I wonder what she needed in the vaults. I have bigger things to concern myself with. Such as—what ailment has stricken my beloved?*

# CHAPTER 23
## CLASSIFICATION: ROGUE STRIKER

**M**y chest feels heavy, and my liver is burning, yet I continue to march behind this striker known as Convert. Although I am being led to what I am sure is a gruesome fate, I cannot help but feel devoted to her cause. I feel as though I must defend this ally of mine with every ounce of my being. Esprit de corps, they call it. A common feeling of devotion between group members focused on the same goal.

*A scary thing. Not being in control of my heart.*

I glance over at Zeal, who seems to be in a blissful state. This isn't good. At this rate I will have led my new companion into the clutches of the IGF.

I'm starting to believe that I may just be bad luck. But the time is long past due for a pity party.

The scream of an orc pierces the nearby bushes. It's quickly followed by the sensation that I need to urinate. This time I'm able to hold it in. Convert assumes her battle stance. Out of the bushes emerge not one, not two, but ten orcs pouring into the open. They quickly make a circle around us and point their weapons at our chests. Some are carrying rudimentary brass weapons, while others are wielding advanced weaponry.

*These orcs may be smarter than originally thought.*

One of the orcs points at Convert and speaks in the orc language. His words roughly translate to "Ugly elf female, must surrender."

Convert snaps her fingers and I feel myself withdrawing my scimitars. Zeal does the same with his spiked war club.

The orcs simultaneously initiate their war cry, causing my ears to bleed. I feel my knees tremble and eventually buckle. As I collapse to the ground, I see Convert slice the head off one of the orcs and runs towards what I presume is the safety of her base camp.

Not gonna lie. I feel abandoned for a moment there. But then the blue caterpillar vanishes in a puff of blue smoke, and I am free to feel the insurmountable rage that had built up. The putrid stench of orc fills my lungs as they close in on me and Zeal.

I'm plucked from the ground by one of the larger orcs. In the orcish tongue he speaks words that mean "More stupid elves for WarBlade!"

The orcs raise their weapons and cheer.

With a name like WarBlade, I'm not expecting him to be very lenient with us. But how much worse can it be then being captured by the IGF?

Zeal and I are taken back to the black tower he described to me. He seems to be in horrific shape; he is shaking up a mighty storm. Something bad happened in that tower—something that must have scarred him for life.

Upon closer inspection, I see how the tower was able to move several kilometers every day. It is being pulled by three long rows of slaves: an assortment of barefooted elves in rags and shackles. To see my people in shackles, whether light, dark, or in between, is sickening to my stomach.

*We're supposed to be the superior race. They aren't supposed to be this organized.*

I'm taken to the black doors, which swish open upon detecting the orc leader. We enter the middle of the tower and into some kind of elevator. I count the squiggles on the panel to see that there are fifteen symbols—so at most, fifteen levels.

We make our way to the very top, where the doors swing open and I'm met with what appears to be a throne room. A giant throne decorated with skulls sits at the end of the room, with three smaller chairs below it. More than thirty orcs stand on either side of me. From what I can see, there are three different colors of orcs: blue, green, and red.

The orcs are screaming orc profanities, jeering, and stomping their feet rhythmically.

*As wild as I expected them to be.*

We're dumped on the floor in front of the empty thrones. I move to stand up, and I'm kicked back down to the floor.

"All fours, elves," says the orc that carried me, this time in elven tongue. I glance over to see that Zeal is already on his hands and feet.

*I guess that explains part of how he came to be.*

The room erupts into drumming. From the back doors, a short green orc, one medium-sized yet muscular red orc, and a giant blue orc appear.

They each take a seat below the largest chair. A few moments pass by until a medium-sized female carrying a staff walks in to the cheers of the crowd. She passes by the giant blue orc, caressing his arm, and takes the seat at the very top.

*So, this WarBlade is a female.*

I have come to learn that women leaders are often unpredictable, making them more dangerous than their male counterparts.

She speaks the elven tongue in a very smooth yet condescending tone. It reminds me of Allison in some ways, but with a distinct orcish accent.

"Elf will remove his hat," says their leader.

I comply and take off my helmet.

"Ugh, ugly-looking elf. Males all ugly. Need more females!" grumbles the short green one.

"Good fighter though, kill many green orcs," replies the giant blue one.

"Not as good as Zeal. Zeal kill many more. Zeal return to pits, and I take darkling elf for gambling house. He muscular, he make good slave."

"Argish tell much!" I yell. That basically translates to "stick a thumb in your eye." I continue. "I'm not a slave, nor will I ever be one. Might as well kill me now."

The short green orc raises an eyebrow and throws three dice in the air. The blue giant orc withdraws his massive war hammer. But, it's the red orc with grey hair who frightens me most.

*They say the quiet ones are always the most dangerous.*

He stands and approaches me. The weight of his energy causes me to breathe heavier than normal.

"Darkling elf can speak glorious orcish tongue?" he says.

"Tuk demands rebor!"

*Elf demands freedom!*

The crowd begins to murmur.

"He can talk?"

"Elf speak orc? Despicable."

Eventually the murmuring dies down, and the proceedings continue.

The red orc caresses the large beads around his neck. "I will take the one who talks." He gets up and leaves without saying another word.

Zeal looks at me with fear in his eyes.

The short green one raises his arms in the air and throws two dice at a random orc in the crowd. The dice pierce through the orc's head and drop him where he stood.

The giant blue orc chuckles and grips Zeal by the collar. "Zeal, my favorite pet. Welcome back."

# CHAPTER 24
## CLASSIFICATION: CHAOTIC STRIKER

**M**y hands shake under the weight of another plate of raw elven meat with blue mushrooms. Both are staples in the diet of an orc. This time it's a striker codenamed Stomper who tried to make an escape recently. On my head, I carry a large bowl of some black liquid. It smells like orange and mango, but I know better.

In my role as a slave in the gambling levels of the orc tower, I find myself barefooted, dressed in skimpy rags and chains. These perverted beasts pat me on the head at every passing opportunity. I am fortunate that none have tried to take it any further. It would seem the patting is a ritual for good luck. The gambling levels are filled with wooden tables and dice games. The walls are smeared in the blood of orcs and elves alike.

*For once I am glad to be found sexually unappealing.*

In any case, I will be sure to cut the hands off of every orc that has touched me. As far as I've gathered, the tower is divided into four sections and fifteen levels. The first five levels are the gambling houses, the middle five are the fighting pits, and the next four are the meditation levels. Finally, at the top of the tower, lies their leader. I have only served her twice since my arrival here. She is an enigma in herself. She doesn't partake in the gambling, the fighting, or even the meditation. From what I've gathered, she simply stays at the top of the tower and watches the view.

These orcs are far more organized than we anticipated. The green ones are the trackers and trainers of new elves and runaway slaves. The blue orcs are their elite unit. Finally, the red orcs are some sort of spiritual group that is well respected. The amazing thing is that all three types have equal say in the community, and these roles are essentially fluid. Thus, a blue orc can be a tracker, or a green orc a pit boss. It's just that certain types gravitate towards certain duties and have certain traits. Each color orc has a representative in their Warlord.

It almost reminds me of a more nuanced version of the striker, blacksmith, navigator, scavenger setup.

The blue orcs are by far the most aggressive and seem to enjoy killing for fun. They keep elves as pets and pit them against each other in their arena.

The green orcs keep many slaves for fondling and other types of entertainment. But for the most part their slaves are worked to the bone around the clock, forced to amuse the fickle green ones.

The red orcs are more or less a mystery. As far as I can tell, they get their elves high on some substance, then pick their brains on elven culture. They also force their elves to adopt their spiritual practices, as well as teach them some kind of painful drumming technique.

*Indoctrination 101.*

One of the female green orcs trips me and I fall, spilling the food and drink on a nearby male orc. A large portion of the gambling house laughs. The orc grips me by my hair and backhands me, sending me flying into another orc, who catches me and pushes me to the ground.

*Right into the damn entrails of Stomper.*

I gag but manage to hold in my meager meal. It's a shame; I always liked Stomper. We had dealings on the last Z protocol. I swiftly begin to clean the floor by picking up the meat and placing it on the tray.

One of the orcs kicks my hand away.

"Tish shum low, tuk tuk."

*If only I had access to my suit or blade or something. But then what? I'd gut one or two, then be laid down to rest.*

My Z training tells me that I must look out for patterns and plot an escape.

There will be an opening someday, some week, some month. I have trained for this, and I will not remain a slave the rest of my life.

The Warlord returns from the council room empty-handed. Recently he has been coming back with new elves or new striker equipment as gifts for top orcs—or with striker food. The fact that he came back empty-handed might mean we have all been captured, or that some have still eluded their advancement.

Everyone in the room grows silent and bows their head as he passes by to his gambling table.

From what I know, Leonidas and Convert are the only ones left. I heard from Hyper Fairy that Vex and his wild elf managed to kill four members of the protocol. It's a shame she was sent to the pit. She might be dead already.

In any case, rescue is unlikely. Protocol dictates that the ships be defended at all costs. I just need to stay alive long enough to find freedom.

After cleaning up the mess, I hand the plate to the orc it was meant for, and he eats it with glee. These beasts don't care if its been pissed on. Once it's food, it's edible.

I wait patiently like a good slave for the general to finish his meal. He picks the meat off Stomper with his teeth and is now chewing on her flesh. Bones fly in every direction as he gobbles down her entrails.

BugGug summons me over.

"Stupid elf thirteen, come."

I rush over. Last time I didn't move fast enough, and it resulted in a broken rib, of which I am still nursing.

I bow my head in silence—his preferred method of communication.

He leans back in his chair, putting his smelly orc feet on the table, then throws four dice in the air and catches them. He displays the number: four threes for a total of twelve. Tonight he will consume the twelfth-numbered elf, another one of his slaves.

I recoil at the thought. Once a week I am a mere dice throw away from being eaten.

I awake from a kick to the stomach. I look up to see an orc about my size with two daggers at his hip. It's the first time I've seen an orc carrying a weapon in a while. The smelly creature approaches me with a mischievous grin, the kind that raises the hair on the back of my neck.

I've seen that perverted smile before on many men. Most have died by my hand.

Exceptional beauty has its drawbacks, as many women have found in a world run by men. It seems even in the orc world, not much changes in that regard.

My Z training kicks in and I brandish a wide smile. I'm sure to make eye contact as I crawl on my knees towards the orc. I grip his bulging member in one hand. The sickly green thing throbs.

"Hehehe, Tuk, Tuk," he says.

With one smooth motion, I grab his dagger and cut off his member. Green liquid pours out onto the floor, leaving a vile stench. Just as he is about to scream, I rise and slit his throat, leaving him gurgling.

The console on my right wrist lights up and says "You've gained 175 exp for the killing of an enemy orc level 2."

What exp is, I don't know. But I do know that I'm breathing a sigh of relief now, holding a weapon again.

I grab the second dagger from the dead orc, whose body fizzles into a purple light of code marked with 1s and 0s. That disappears as well, replaced by a floating apple.

My console lights up. *Item Drop: Apple = nourishment*

It reminds me of StapleStory—one of my favorite games growing up.

I take a bite. It's easily the best-tasting apple I've ever had—and I can feel my body being refreshed. My energy levels spike to maximum level after one bite.

I place the rest of the apple in my garments and proceed to make my escape.

Using the shadows as my allies, I slink past the stables we have been kept in—much like the horses back on Venusian.

There are three large orcs, each twice my size, playing a game with dice while guarding the exit. I analyze their weapons. One wields a large broadsword, another throwing axes, and the third a large spear. I tell myself that on the next roll, I will make my move.

The orc with the broadsword rolls the dice. As all three lean in to see the results, I fling my dagger at the head of the orc with the broadsword. The dagger pierces his temple. I rush towards him and leap into the air, but he slams his fist into my stomach just before he collapses onto the table.

The other two orcs stand and draw their weapons. They charge at me. The axe wielder flings two axes at me, and I manage to dodge. I summon my phenome Order, who unleashes several shots of lightning on the two orcs that bring both to their knees.

At maximum speed, I run towards the spear wielder and slit his throat. I take his spear, spin around, and jam it through the eye of the axe wielder. Still feeling invigorated, I look into the distance to see the gate of the stable descending.

I run at the gate and throw myself to the ground in an attempt to slide under it.

But I'm too late.

# CHAPTER 25

## CLASSIFICATION: ROGUE STRIKER

This level of the tower is filled with flowers and fish tanks. In the tanks are rainbow-colored exotic breeds of fish, none of which I have seen before.

The red orc with grey hair circles me. The heaviness of his energy continues to drain me. Unlike the other orcs, his scent is that of a pleasant one. Something akin to a flower on a summer day. But his quiet demeanor as he analyses me causes my hands to tremor.

"Elf can speak glorious orcish tongue?" he says in rudimentary elven.

"I believe we have established that."

Squinting at me, his eyes glow a menacing red. But he makes no move to reprimand me.

Yet, somehow, I feel as though the art of sarcasm is not lost upon this ancient beast.

"How did you come to learn the language?"

"I learned it through my translator. It took some time, but eventually I picked up the words."

"Lying will not serve you well in these coming trials."

*How does he know I'm lying? No way can I tell him that Zeal taught me. I get the feeling that is supposed to be his secret.*

"If you deem me a liar from the first instance of our conversation, then anything I say will be useless. We might as well end the discussion now."

"All elves lie. It is in your nature."

"And orcs do not?"

"Orcs lie, too."

"So what's your point?"

"I trust none but my blade."

He taps the hilt of what appears to be a red dai-katana.

"Good for you."

"Elf must think he is very funny."

"Elf thinks this is a waste of time." I move to stand up, and the orc chuckles.

"Elf will try his hand at acquiring freedom?"

I must admit—that caught me off guard. To be mocked is one thing, but this old orc finding my refusal to obey amusing? That's another. There is a slight nuance in the way I get offended, and offended I am.

I assume my tektra stance: ready to divert his attacks. I look to see if anything nearby can be used as a weapon, but unless I'm taking a fish as a sword, I'm out of luck.

"Elf will suffer severe injuries. Are you sure?"

"Orc will die by my hand, one way or another."

"Ohhhh, tsk tsk. You must earn the right to fight me. You fight my grandson, DeakGu."

Another grey-haired red orc comes through the back door beside the tank of rainbow fish. He's holding a massive spiked hammer. His body is pure muscle and three times my size. A few moments pass until another red orc enters, this time with black hair. He wields a large battle axe and has a red flag attached to his back. He is twice my size.

DeakGu the axe wielder enters the middle of the arena where I'm standing. He looks me up and down.

"Puny elf should be in the pits," he says in orc.

"Giant orc should be in the dirt," I respond.

"Ohhh, elf really can speak glorious orc tongue. I shall pull it out of your very mouth."

The red orc leader presses a button on the side of a fish tank that turns the entire wall around. An arrangement of various weapons is now on display, most of which are unknown to me. They vary from primitive orc weapons to advanced dwarven-made. It would seem that there are dwarves backing the orcs.

*Not good for elven kind.*

A deep, soothing voice calls out to me. *Come to me when it is time, for I am change, opportunity, and redemption.* My mind flashes to a place I've never been before: a golden pyramid with white gold at the point. Sand flows down the pyramid like water.

While shaking off the voice and the vision, I am interrupted by VerThag, the warlord.

"You may pick two weapons from the board of truth."

Naturally, I choose my two wind scimitars. But for range there aren't any SMGs or plasma rifles—at least none that I can use. What piques my interest is something called a shock rifle. It looks sleek and advanced.

Definitely dwarven made.

My only hope is that it will work well with my elven hands.

After I return to my spot in the arena, DeakGu gives me an awkward bow.

I bow back.

"Duel will be until crippled," says DeakGu.

"Fine by me."

He swings his axe at blistering speeds, connecting with my two scimitars. I'm sent flying into a fish tank, which remarkably doesn't break. But I hear a crunch as I shift positions.

*How is he that fast?*

I shake myself to my senses and watch as he poses with his axe at his back.

*Cocky son of an orc.*

I pull out the shock rifle and aim at his chest. There seems to be three modes on the rifle.

I shoot the rifle at his chest, and three balls of electricity almost connect with my target—but something blocks them. It looks like a giant, glimmering red hand. I see a lightning bolt mark appear above DeakGu's head.

I unleash another barrage of lightning balls upon my opponent, but they are blocked by the giant red hand once again.

DeakGu just stands there posing with his battle axe. Wearing that arrogant grin.

I drop the shock rifle and meteor dash with my scimitars aimed at DeakGu's throat while activating my shield ring. He blasts fire from his mouth, covering me in fire and taking out all three shields simultaneously.

My scimitars are within inches of his thick neck when he grabs them by the blades and snaps them in two.

"That the best elf can do?"

I retreat backwards and assume my battle stance once again. I'm forced to pick up the useless piece of junk shock rifle again.

At this point, I notice the two lightning bolts remain floating above his head. Could they be some kind of timed weaponry? Or a stacking ability? I aim the rifle at his chest one more time and unleash another three-bolt burst. The giant translucent hand absorbs the blast burst once again—but this time a third lightning bolt appears.

"Getting boring," says DeakGu.

I shoot another burst, this time at his big mouth.

A fourth lightning bolt appears around his head. This time, the three bolts connect and a massive beam of blue energy shines down from the ceiling. The shock bypasses the hand shield, and DeakGu takes the bulk of the damage.

He stands there in a daze as the lightning bolts circle his head. I use this opportunity to close the distance and land a combo of punches and kicks on him, but his body is so hard and muscular that my hand breaks in the process. As soon as he wakes from his daze, he grabs my legs and throws me into the wall stocked with weapons.

He sneers as he approaches. I grip the first thing my hand touches and point it at the beast.

He pauses. "Oh, you know the ancient dance of chain blades?"

I look at my hands to see that I'm wielding two sickles attached to a long, reinforced chain. The sickles are exceptionally sharp and have the faint green glow of ethereal magic. It's a rare type of magic. Supposedly, ethereal magic allows one to ignore armor at the cost of one's own life force. They are so light that it feels as though I'm holding nothing at all.

I casually swing one of the sickles in the air, only to strike myself in the nose with the other.

The room erupts into a fit of laughter.

"Put down sacred chain blades before elf kills himself."

I'm about to do just that when a tiny voice in my head says, *You're not the boss of me.*

A juvenile defense if there ever was one. In any case, I twirl both sickles forward this time. As they pick up steam, I approach DeakGu, who backs up slowly. For the first time in my life, I'm seeing fear in an orc's eyes. There is something special about these weapons.

I fling the two sickles at my opponent, catching one on his axe. The blade actually sinks halfway through the hilt of the axe; the other lands on his opposite arm and also sinks in. I yank both. The left easily disarms his axe, while the right slides through him, leaving a large gash on his arm.

Red orc blood leaks onto the floor. His eyes turn a pure red rage. The air in the area heats up, and I feel myself sweating. He charges at me, and the floor rumbles. I wait until he's in range then unleash my two grappling spears. They bounce off his tough body harmlessly. With the hilt of the sickles in my hands, I meteor dash a short distance and duck at the last second, managing to cleave his side with both blades. They move easily through his tough skin like parchment. He slams his fist in my direction, but I meteor dash to his other side.

I swing one sickle out, both cleaving him and getting stuck inside his stomach. I yank it to pull myself in closer. While ducking another blow, I wrap the other sickle around his ankle. I tug the chains, dropping him to the floor. I remove the blades and pounce on him, aiming both sickles at his throat.

He smiles, revealing his ugly yellow teeth and stinky breath.

He grips me closer and reels back to spew fire from his mouth. My helmet takes the brunt of the damage, but the intense heat makes it difficult to breathe. He dashes me across the room into another fish tank, damaging my back. He emits another blast of flames, but I manage to put up the tektra wind shield, reflecting back some of the damage and absorbing the rest.

Exhausted, I use the sickles to pull the shock rifle into arm's reach. I switch the rifle to blast mode and shoot a massive beam of blue energy that bypasses his hand shield and pierces a head-sized hole in his stomach. He stumbles towards me with a sneer. Then he collapses to the ground with a loud thud.

The old man leader starts clapping wildly.

"Elf may prove useful after all. It's time to meditate and ponder today's occurrence."

He glances at his grandson.

"DeakGu you will go one week without food or drink for this disgraceful loss. Come elf who can talk. We have much to discuss."

# CHAPTER 26
## CLASSIFICATION: POLITICIAN

My hands' blue tint is more evident now, but now an odd pattern has appeared. Some kind of advanced code that cannot be duplicated or deciphered by normal elven minds. Even the dwarves are having issues with it.

One thing I do know is that my powers have increased drastically. I can telekinetically lift large objects twice my size with ease and throw them larger distances each day. But I still walk with a limp due to the grievous wounds caused by Leaky Faucet's plasma cannon, and thus I am still in pain.

My cyber elf comrades tell me that there is nothing that they can do. At least not until I am a fully-fledged cyber elf. How much longer I must wait depends on how long it takes to detain the remaining RRA members.

It has become clear that this vagabond of a striker has assistance from a technician. Her knowledge of the hidden areas in the base is well beyond her means. So, like any good Grand Inquisitor I focus my energy, on finding the technician instead of chasing down a striker able to move through walls as though through water.

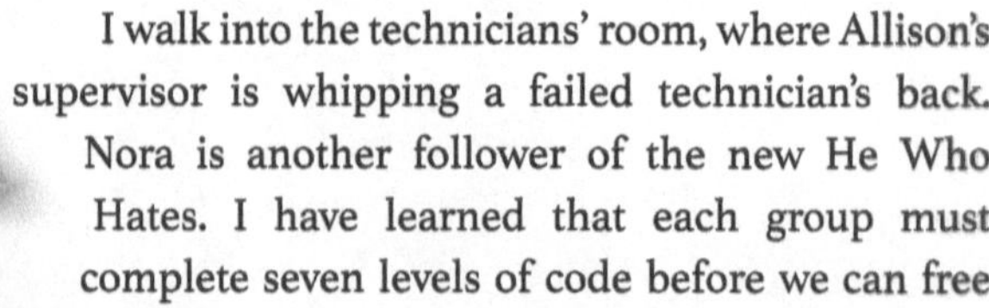

I walk into the technicians' room, where Allison's supervisor is whipping a failed technician's back. Nora is another follower of the new He Who Hates. I have learned that each group must complete seven levels of code before we can free

our god Kuleta Kifo. That is our ultimate task—only then will the cyber realm and our realm fully merge. My suspicions are that the technician helping the RRA will simultaneously be hindering overall operations. Thus, they will be in a group that is behind.

"All hail the entrance of the Grand Inquisitor," says Nora.

"All hail!" says the room.

I turn to Nora. "Give me the status updates on the various groups."

She nods. "He Who Hates is still in the lead at level six. Then there is He Who Sees at level five, She Who Takes at level five, He Who Hears at level four, He Who Knows at level three, and He Who Loves at level three."

"What are the ramifications of these levels? I have noticed some anomalies."

"It's quite simple, really. The cyber realm is about sixty-percent merged with our realm. We are seeing more stats with those who have the vision: health bars, bodies dissolving when killed, item drops including powerful, life-sustaining food, knowledge downloads on others' greatest weakness and strengths, and increases in upgrades to power levels, speed levels, and pain receptors."

"So what you're saying is that the game world has nearly merged with our world. Soon our entire realm will be one giant game universe! Excellent."

"Yes, that is correct."

"What happens to the bodies when they dissolve?"

"We estimate that they feed the economy of the game universe. Essentially any and every death goes to Kuleta Kifo, keeping everything functioning."

"And we, the cyber elves, will sit at the top of the food chain, leading the masses to a new era. No longer will we need to do business with the uppity, drunken dwarves, or put up with the existence of smelly orcs," I say.

"About that..."

"What?"

"The prince's death may have created some complications."

"Complications such as what? Spit it out."

"I have heard that the dwarven empire is up in arms. They blame the IGF for his death and are considering pulling funding for our projects, as well as removing specs from our advanced technology."

"So? Forget those minions. We are so close to our goal. Nothing can stop us."

"Yes, we are close—but not quite there. We still need their equipment. If the equipment breaks or shuts down for whatever reason, we won't be able to fix it. This could just be me being paranoid, but it could part of the RRA's plan."

"You leave the RRA to me, and I will leave the decoding to you and your techs," I say.

Although I don't believe these RRA ruffians to be as intelligent as Nora does, I have come to respect them a little bit more. I would be a fool to ignore their actions up to this point. To be able to infiltrate the Frontier Division and turn several members of HQ to their side isn't a small feat. Because of this, I requested to have six strikers defend the technician room at all times.

*Who knows. Maybe being cautious will pay off.*

I find myself standing in front of the vault that Leaky Faucet managed to blow open. It was supposed to be impervious to most explosives, as well as to any type of phase shifting—including, it would seem, her mysterious abilities.

*Or so we thought.*

"Techno Geek!"

"Y... yes, Grand Inquisitor, sir?"

"What's all this mess? Why is everything wet?"

"It would seem that Leaky Faucet accessed the contents of the vault, sir." I find myself straining to hear her voice, barely above a whisper.

"Speak up when you're spoken to."

"Yes... sir!" She gives me an awkward salute with all four of her mechanical spider arms.

Apparently she is our most intelligent striker. Her scores test in the mid-range for a technician. She is also a decent fighter, but not much to look at. Quite frumpy, in fact, in her dreary grey armor—and downright cumbersome with those long mechanical spiders' arms.

In any case, I'm not here for that. I am here to find this Leaky Faucet.

"What can you tell me about what was taken?" I ask.

"According to the records, nothing."

"Impossible."

"Impossible?"

"I know better than to believe everything that was in this vault was on record."

"Yes, there are rumors..."

"Speak swiftly, or you'll find yourself cleaning toilets."

"Yes, sir! It is rumored that there was a unique dwarven cannon once given as a gift to Legislator Powell. This was a hundred and fifty years ago, when the dwarven-elven pact was first made. There was also a frost-enchanted blade."

"What does the frost enchantment do?"

"They say it slows the movement and attacking speed of anyone struck with it."

"Both sound useful. Why weren't they put into play?"

"Frankly, the gift giver was a loony dwarven tech designer. He didn't give us schematics or instruction manuals with them and died soon after. So, the useless cannon was placed in the vault. The sword was deemed too volatile to be put into action. It's a double-edged enchantment: It can also slow down the user's movement speed."

"All magic has repercussions. That's why we drifted towards technology. But at what cost?"

"What do you mean?"

"Our reliance on technology has made our dependence on the dwarves all the more glaring."

I look around the vault.

Placing my foot on a creaky tile, I lift it up to see an empty slot where a torso-sized cannon and frost blade could have been held.

*What is this rat up to?*

It's been two weeks since we've seen any sign of this Leaky Faucet. It's possible she died of her wounds.

As anticlimactic as that sounds, I am fine with such a resolution. She has been more than a nuisance.

I dress in my best outfit: a green cyber suit with a light blue tie. The legs of the suit glow in a special design. I also clearly display my badge on my chest.

*Grand Inquisitor. As always my title fits me like a glove.*

Today is a conference call with the dwarven empire: the richest planets, controlled by the credit-hoarding, beer-drinking, technological geniuses known as dwarves.

It is my job as Grand Inquisitor to ensure that this secret meeting goes off without any unplanned interruptions. I glance at Sanguine, who gives me a nod. Then I look at Quaint, who shrugs. I take that as her way of letting me know everything is in order.

There are the ten highest-ranked members of HQ in the room, as well as myself. With us are twenty strikers, each trained to kill Leaky Faucet on sight, not including Sanguine and Quaint. If this ragamuffin of a striker shows her face, it will be blown into two.

A hologram pops up in the middle of the room, showing one representative from the five richest planets and one from the next ten. All are dominated by dwarves. But there is no sign of the dwarven royal family.

That's a slight in itself.

*It could mean that this is all a farce, that they have already made their decision.*

"We have gathered you here today to discuss the death of our beloved prince. What say you on this account?" asks the dwarven representative.

The number-one-ranked member of HQ is the first of us to speak. He's a mysterious man who always has his face covered and is represented by a holograph of himself. When he speaks, the heavens part ways in compliance.

"It is obvious what has occurred. This is a plot to create a rift between the noble elves and the glorious dwarves. In this midst of the chaos, the RRA plans on picking up the pieces. We mustn't let them succeed, for to do so would be a disservice to our many-decades-long alliance."

"Well spoken. As expected from…"

The feed freezes and out pops up the face of Sansa, helmetless. She is hazel-colored, with short dreads in a ponytail; her eyebrows, nose, and ears are all pierced. Her earrings are the teeth of some wild animal, and she wears a necklace with shark teeth.

What piques my interest the most are her eyes. These are not the eyes of a seventeen-year-old. These are the eyes of a grown woman trained to kill. Her hazel eyes are as intense as those of any striker in this room—maybe even more so.

"Hi." She beams a smile.

The menace terrorizing the Frontier Division opens with "hi."

The room erupts into murmurs. Grown-ass politicians are at a loss for a response.

"Typically, when someone says hi, you say hi back," she says, furrowing her brows.

"There is nothing typical about this situation. What do you want, Leaky Faucet? Have you come to surrender?" asks the number two politician. Her codename changes with the moon cycle. She is known to be shrewd and highly intelligent—someone I plan on getting up close and personal with.

"I suppose. And no, nothing like that. I just thought I'd list out the crimes of the top ten politicians. Just so the dwarves know who they have been getting in bed with."

Now the room is dead quiet. A single dropped hairpin would thunder like a trumpet blast.

"Do you guys want me to start with number one and work my way down, or start with ten and work my way up?"

There is further silence.

"I suppose it doesn't matter. Okay, I will start with number one," says Sansa.

She clears her throat. "Rank number one is one of the more depraved ones. He is guilty of trafficking children for sex. Additionally, he frequently has sexual encounters with his pets."

"This is preposterous! Lies!" With that, he disconnects his hologram.

"Number two. She has a torture chamber. She lures dwarven men with the promise of sexual encounters and locks them up until they die of starvation. She then feeds these dwarves to her guests."

The number-two politician tries to rise to take her leave, but her striker pushes her back down.

Sanguine approaches me. "This isn't good. We should leave."

Quaint approaches us. "The doors are jammed, and the feed is wide."

"You mean everyone in the Frontier Division is hearing this?"

"No, I mean... wide. Like, every striker, technician, navigator, blacksmith, scavenger, and dwarven delegate in all three divisions near the fifteen wealthiest planets, are all hearing this."

"This cannot be real..."

By the time Sansa has reached number ten, the tension in the room could only be cut with a meat cleaver. A few strikers have thrown up, and everyone's trigger fingers are itchy.

"Finally, I'd like to offer a little bonus! Just because I don't like the jackass. Grand Inquisitor Morange. Guilty of teaming up with Sponge Cake, aka Allison, aka Sugar Cane, to take over the RRA operations of trafficking monsters from the rift for consumption and as pets. Additionally, he has killed several up-and-coming politicians during his rise to Grand Inquisitor. Not to mention the fact that he, like all of you, is a lying piece of shit."

She takes a deep breath and smiles once again. "Well, have a good night, y'all. And remember... the RRA will never die!"

With that, she signs off.

The room is quiet for a few seconds as everyone processes what they have just learned. Many murders were revealed. Politicians' friends, brothers, sisters, and affairs were discussed; adultery, pedophilia, and corruption within the elven HQ all brought to light.

All it takes is one.

Just one striker to raise his gun and aim it at the politician sleeping with the striker's wife—a crime that pales in comparison to most.

The entire room erupts into a blaze of plasma fire, bullets, and explosions.

I use my telekinesis to move a reinforced table for protection. Sanguine is firing at politician number seven, whose child he just learned he's been raising. Quaint is shot in the chest by a missile meant for me. She drops to the floor dead where she stood.

*Should have came with my task carriers.*

I withdraw my shotgun and cradle it in my hands, daring anyone to come any closer to my makeshift defense. Eventually, the explosions and gunfire die down.

I poke my head to see a handful of strikers and politicians still alive.

*The carnage is over, but the damage is done. Fucking Sansa.*

# CLASSIFICATION: ROGUE STRIKER

So, they got me high on some red mushrooms. I'm gone like those ancient flying devices. Kites, I believe they were called. I'm ashamed to admit it, but I tell them everything I know about the IGF and the RRA.

*Everything.*

From my part of the grand plan down to every assassination I committed in the name of revolution. I suppose I'm fortunate that I'm confessing my sins to the orcs and not in a grand inquisition in the IGF. I even give up the names of my cohorts in the RRA.

How they were able to extract the information so easily from my lips, I can only blame on the mushrooms. They ask, and I answer.

The three upper-tier red orcs seem more amused than shocked as I divulge how corrupt and chaotic elven society has become. But twinkles in their eyes tell me that they are prepping for something big.

As far as I know, the only thing keeping the orcs from invading our planets are three things. One: The dwarven and elven alliance is a formidable one. Unless it's broken, the orcs would be wiped out before they stepped foot on one of the IGF-protected planets. Two: They don't have any space-capable ships, and can only access a limited amount of advanced technology. Three:

Although they grow like fungi spores, their population is heavily controlled by the sheer harshness of their planets.

But if even one of these conditions were to change, the tables could turn. The scary part is that I am the hand that may have created such an opportunity.

*The assassination of the prince.*

I find myself being led to the elevators with a collar around my neck. Everything is hazy; I am seeing double, along with various new colors.

The only comfort is that I have my shock rifle and chain blades attached to me. Though I am being walked on all fours like a pet, I feel as though my opportunity for escape will soon be upon me.

We reach a crowded arena filled with orcs of varying colors. All are loud and lively. We take an honored seat up close to the pit.

VerThag, the red orc leader, looks at me with a gleam in his eyes. "I take you to this sacred event because you are my favorite pet. May you rejoice in the battle, and take heed not to disobey me. Keep your eyes fresh, lest anyone try their hand at my life."

I've become a mere guard dog for an orc warlord. My pride has dwindled, but my willpower to escape is as strong as ever.

I glance down in the pit to see Zeal enter the arena with his large spiked club and wolf fur. His movements are sloppy, as if he has also been drugged. From the other side emerges what I presume to be a woman with a very advanced crimson battlesuit.

The two engage each other, and purple and crimson energy clash.

Their movements are swift, making it difficult for me in this state to keep track of them. The woman unleashes a cannon blast that catches Zeal in the stomach. He's about to use his phenome, but one of the orcs tugs on his chain, dropping him to the ground. The female flies up into the air to land a killing blow on Zeal with her war hammer.

That's when my instincts kick in.

I send forth my grappling spears, piercing her armor to draw blood. I reel myself in, swinging my chained blades at her neck. She manages to dodge the left one, but I connect with the right. Blood spurts out of her neck as the blade bypasses her armor and sinks deep into her flesh.

She collapses to the ground.

Just when I'm about to check on Zeal, a faint but familiar voice calls out my name. "Vexation?"

Who could this striker be, calling me in such a delicate manner? I wobble towards her and remove her helmet.

My jaw drops to see Chaos. As I deactivate my visor, feelings rush up to my throat. At a loss for words, I drop to my knees and place my head against hers.

"Don't die on me."

She taps me on the back of my helmet. "Too late for regrets, silly." And with her last ounce of strength, she presses a red button on her suit.

It starts blinking.

I feel myself shedding many tears for my fallen comrade. But who am I kidding? She was more than that to me. She meant so much more.

I look at VerThag, who is making his exit from the arena. I have committed an egregious sin among the orcs.

My fate will be worse than death.

A few minutes pass by as the orcs rain down their food at me, along with their boos. I simply kneel there, dazed.

I barely notice the metal gates opening before Hyper Fairy and another striker called PyroTech emerge.

*Just my luck.*

Hyper Fairy approaches me and presses a red button on her battlesuit. The crazed striker PyroTech uses his flamethrower to create a ring of fire.

I look at Hyper Fairy, my eyes puffy, begging her to say something.

*I must look real pathetic now.*

Finally, she speaks. "Vexation, you're being detained for crimes against elven society." She places two yellow rings around my wrists. Zeal engages PyroTech, but he is too weak and battered to do anything of note. PyroTech grips Zeal in a chokehold, and Hyper Fairy cuffs him as well.

I look up at the sky to see a large carrier ship de-stealth. It places a suction beam on the five of us and pulls us up to the ship. Projectiles fly at us from every direction, but the shields hold up.

"Hyper…"

She punches me in the nose.

"Don't talk to me."

The PyroTech guy chuckles.

I'm alert again. Little good that will do me. Would have been better to stay high.

"So, Vexation, you've finally joined us at last," says Leonidas over the comm.

"I suppose."

Hyper Fairy punches me in the nose again, breaking it. "That was rhetorical."

*I suppose it's as they say. Hell has no fury like a woman scorned.*

We land on an off-grid space station. My best guess is that it's somewhere near Plutos, a wealthy planet in the far reaches of nowhere. How they maintain such wealth has always been a mystery to me—at least until now.

I vaguely remember an RRA briefing where they suspected Plutos was paid richly to house the top deviants of the dwarven empire and IGF. It seems they were right. I immediately abandon any hope of rescue upon being shown to my section. The inhabitants are crazed and despondent at the same time.

*Quite the feat.*

Hyper Fairy gives me a final kick to the groin as a goodbye. It's followed by another chuckle from PyroTech. I'm sure they will be well rewarded for capturing public enemy number one.

Leonidas looks me in the eyes.

"You've been through a lot, Vexation. It's unfortunate for you that things turned out this way. I wouldn't wish this facility on my worst enemy."

He turns to leave when he stops. "Oh, I nearly forgot. Here." He hands me my chained blades and shock rifle. "You'll be needing these." Then he rips the RRA distortion chip from my badge.

This isn't what I expected. I expected to be tortured for information. But all Leonidas did was take a pint of my blood once I entered the transport ship.

*None of this makes sense.*

"Here I thought you guys wanted information from me."

"Things would have been better for you if that were the case. But frankly, you're old news. Your little friend Leaky Faucet is public enemy number one." And with that, he gets on his carrier and leaves.

A light elf with short black hair and a menacing scowl approaches me. He has a raven on his shoulder. His clothing is top of the line, black with an emerald green design across the chest.

"Welcome to my zoo. I'm the zookeeper. You may call me Stifle." He smirks at his own joke.

He continues. "In any case, if I were you, I'd abandon any hope of escape or rescue. The time for such fantasies is over. It doesn't matter who you were before you came here. What matters is who you will become."

He motions for me to walk with him.

The only thing preventing me from shooting him where he stands is the pint of blood Leonidas took from me. My energy levels are nearly depleted.

"There is an old saying, Vexation. New level, new devil. That means as new doors open for you, doors will also close; thus there will be new challenges you must hope to overcome. The sooner you accept your fate, the better. You have enemies, Vexation. Plenty of them. There are many who want you to suffer as much as possible all the way until you die of old age. My job is to make sure that happens."

"How's the food here?"

He erupts into a fit of laughter. "I heard you had a sharp mouth and a lively soul. It will die soon enough."

He points at a small cell where a crazed dark elf is wiping the walls with his feces.

"I'm not going in there."

The raven caws. "Cell."

The most pain I have ever felt surges through my body. It feels as though my skin is being peeled off my flesh, limb by limb. I find myself walking into the feces-filled cell.

"Just so you know, Leonidas paid me extra to make sure I put you in here with Checkmate. He drove his last twenty cellmates to the mad house. Consider going to our madhouse the cruelest of fates."

"I'll be sure to thank him in person."

Stifle erupts into a fit of laughter again. He walks off.

On the bright side, I still have my battlesuit and weapons. But it seems like everyone keeps those. Checkmate is dressed in a blue cloak with gold trimmings and gold bangles. He has two oddly shaped daggers attached to his side. He has sharp golden eyes, but his mind is clearly gone.

"Do you sleep on the top or the bottom bunk?"

He pays me no heed, so I'm moving towards the top bed when he throws a handful of feces at my back.

"Mine."

I struggle to contain my ire, knowing that at these energy levels I will be beaten.

Thus, I go to the bottom bed—when he throws another handful of feces at my back.

"Mine."

I take a deep breath and wash the feces off my back at the nearby sink.

*Watch me and him.*

I hitch up in the corner and withdraw my chained blades. I'm ready to strike, lest he kill me in my sleep.

# CHAPTER 28
## CLASSIFICATION: PUBLIC ENEMY 1

Hi, recently unfrozen judge. I suppose you have been following Vex's story for a while, so you aren't that new. In any case, if you hadn't already guessed, my name is Sansa. I'm also known as Leaky Faucet. Now, I'd like to go on the record and say that I'm not a big fan of that nickname. I mean, it's not my fault my phenome leaves water all over the place. Or maybe it is? Him being my shadow self and all.

Anyways, it's my turn to tell our side of the story, and it's about damn time, if you ask me.

In this universe, they say that it's all one big rich pie. I suppose I just happen to come from the worst slice. My mother died at childbirth, and my father started seeing me as the sole reason for this. Often left to starve and eat pig scraps I was also beaten on a regular basis, hence the mechanically assisted arm. What made matters worse was that my brother, fifteen years older than me, saw that it was happening and didn't do anything about it. As soon as he could, he married rich and hightailed it out of there.

Now, I'm not justifying killing both my father and my brother. But I am not sorry, either. In this world, one must do what they got to do. Otherwise, they'll be taken advantage of for the rest of their lives. It's sink or swim—you're either a lion or a sheep. And I knew from an early age that I wasn't no damn sheep.

Why am I telling you all this? Because it's important that you realize that we all have skeletons. I bet if I were to dig up your past, I'd find a few things you aren't proud of.

Maybe I will.

In any case, who the hell are you to judge anyone? Much less Vex. If he is guilty then so am I.

Speaking of Vex, it's about time I back him up.

"Leaky Faucet to Tech101."

*Tech101 connected.*

 "What's the status on Vex?"

"He has been captured and relocated to an unknown facility somewhere in the Eagle Quadrant."

"I'm going after him."

"That's a negative, Leaky Faucet. We must carry out the next phase of the plan, or it will all be for naught."

"Fine. But afterwards, I'm going after him."

"I will assist in any way I can."

"Make sure you narrow down the location."

"It will be difficult, but I'll figure something out."

"Copy that. Leaky Faucet out."

I check my wounds, which have finally healed. I'm fortunate that I have a regeneration ability unlocked.

My body is telling me to push forward, but my mind is exhausted. I managed to upgrade my phenome to level six, but it still terrorizes me, giving me nightmares. I suppose that's to be expected when you have a past as dark as my own. I find myself nervous this evening, so I summon a forearm-sized green version of my phenome. The green shark eats away all my fear.

It turns me into a fierce killing machine.

I feel my hazel eyes intensify, and my canines sharpen. I look up to the ceiling of the storage room and make a quick prayer to the deity of change, opportunity, and redemption.

*Chenji, you keep me firm and strong.*

I puddle through the ceiling with my new shark cannon. That's something I made, along with my new frost sword, using the dwarven cannon specs. I call it the shark cannon because it looks like a shark and shoots out shark-shaped plasma projectiles. A nice touch, if I do say so myself.

Armed to the teeth, I set out towards the technicians' room: the brainchild of the entire Frontier Division. The report tells me that there are six strikers on duty, along with the supervisor Nora, who neither sleeps nor eats.

I'll have to divide and conquer—or fall, as my comrades have before me. The fact that the RRA has dwindled down to one active striker, one technician, one doctor, and a handful of politicians isn't good. But we are managing.

I aim my shark cannon at the door of the technicians' room. I take a deep breath and *pow pow*, the plasma cannon sends a plasma beam with the face of a great white shark. The door dissolves just as I puddle through the ceiling and emerge from behind two strikers. Two of my three sharks rush out and consume two strikers, turning the sharks red. The third shark remains close to me in its natural blue color. They have minds of their own now, and the leash breaks. The two red sharks are now on the hunt for any potential foe.

One shark bites the neck of another striker who tried to shoot it. The bullets enlarge the shark until it explodes, taking the striker's throat with it.

*Boom goes sharkie.*

The remaining three strikers aim their weapons at me. About to eat kelp, I simply puddle back into the ceiling. The second red shark explodes on another striker. The shark attached to me continues to swim around me, revealing my presence. It matters not: I'm immune to most methods of attack while in this form.

The remaining two strikers unleash their weapons on my position in vain. It's rather amusing. They still haven't figured out how my abilities work.

I wait until their energy runs low then catapult myself at blazing speeds towards the closest striker. My frost blade jams into his neck.

He drops to the floor while feebly attempting to cover the wound.

The last striker is in front of me, Nora behind. Nora flings her flail, connecting on my last shark and turning him red. He charges after her, but she manages to dodge the attack just before he explodes. I use this moment to throw my frost sword at the striker in front of me.

The blade pierces his stomach. I run up and jump kick the blade deeper into his stomach, killing him instantly. I turn around to see a grey rhino charging at me. It connects with my stomach, opening an old wound, and flings me in the air. Nora strikes me in the chest with her flail, sending me flying against a wall.

All eyes are on me: about ten technicians, plus Nora. I manage to dodge roll another charging attack from the rhino and pull out my ray gun.

I aim it at the closest technician.

"Back up slowly."

"Please don't hurt me."

"Shut up and do as I say."

She backs up slowly while I have the ray gun pointed at her head. Now, as I'm holding her between me and Nora, you're probably thinking, "Vex would never take a hostage." And that's true. But lucky for me, I'm not Vex.

"Give it up, Leaky Faucet. I see that your energy levels are low. You can't do your little trick anymore. The patrol team will be here any moment."

"That may be true. Except for one thing..."

Now, as a note: I still don't like the nickname. But it does fit rather well. Every time one of my sharks move, they drop water beneath them. Every time I puddle out of a substance, I leave a pool of water.

*Not without its uses.*

I snap my fingers, and all the water in the room flies to Nora's head, creating a water bubble. She clasps her head, but it's too late. Everyone in the room watches as she drowns.

*A gruesome fate.*

I grab my frost sword again, as well as the floating bananas and various jewelry. Just as I'm about to let off several plasma blasts onto the technicians' control station, I am flung back against a wall and pinned there telekinetically.

Morange walks up to me, withdraws his shotgun. and pulls the trigger. Bullets spray into my stomach. I wince as they singe my insides. He is about to shoot another barrage, this time at my head, when I speak.

"Wait, wait. Don't you want to know how to fix your gimp leg?"

"I don't need you to fix it. It will be fixed when I'm a fully-fledged cyber elf."

He is about to pull the trigger when I see just a sliver of doubt in his eyes.

"Are you sure about that? I mean, if their nanobots can't fix it. What else can?"

"What are you getting at?"

"I'm just saying. Don't you think I've proven myself formidable enough that I might have a solution?"

He squints sizing me up.

"Tell me how to fix the leg, and I will apprehend you like I'm supposed to."

Good to know self-preservation will always trump one's better judgement. My energy has just about regenerated for one last puddle.

"It's very simple..."

"Spit it out."

"All you have to do is..."

"Is what?!"

"Go fuck yourself right around the corner." And with that, I puddle through the wall into someone's sleeping quarters.

I consume a code banana.

It's easily the best-tasting banana I've ever had. Every bite is like a party in my mouth. My energy levels go into overdrive, prepping me for any battles to come. I hear footsteps coming towards the door.

One thing Vex taught me is that avoid is better than engage when outnumbered. Thus, I puddle my way back to the storage unit I have been calling home.

It's unfortunate that I failed to destroy the facility. That would have set them back at least six months, giving us time to regroup and build up our personnel. It's also unfortunate that there is no contingency plan.

# CHAPTER 29
## CLASSIFICATION: ROGUE STRIKER

'm still here. Surprisingly. The mad man known as Checkmate has yet to kill me in my sleep, and I've managed to get a few winks. He simply stays up rocking back and forth repeating chess moves.

I've managed to suss out the place in my time here. The communal area is one large fenced cage with over fifty guards at various vantage points.

While walking around in the "play pen," I noticed that there are four factions here. The largest faction is all women. Each has a green skull tattoo on her shoulder for their leader, Acid Reflex. A former striker Z turned psychopath. As beautiful as she is dangerous, She supposedly holds the record for most prisoners killed. Also has a habit of melting men's peckers off.

Then there are the other two elven factions, split between light elf and dark elf. It seems even in this world there is no escaping one's nature. Such a shame. The light elves manage the drug operation in here, somehow smuggling things in and out. Then there are the dark elves. They appear a bit unpredictable. One day they are fighting amongst each other, the next picking fights with the light elves and losing. They're constantly switching leaders after each leader dies. Pathetic if you ask me.

Next, we have the dwarves. There isn't much to say about the dwarves. They are quiet. Not in that they don't speak to the other factions—that's a given. They are quiet in that they don't speak at all. Apparently the dwarven royalty wants some schematics from their leader, but no one knows who their leader is, so they can't even be tortured. They move as a single unit.

Then you have the vagabonds. They're not a faction in themselves, just what I call the people who are factionless. From what I've noticed, we're the kind that get picked off the easiest. Mysterious deaths, defilement, and whatnot. There have been ten newbs this week, including me and Zeal. Two of us have already been pillaged and murdered. Especially now that people's deaths result in a clean disappearance and an item or two. I know I must join a faction—and soon.

Upon entering the play pen, Zeal immediately joined the light elves. He was initiated by taking on three of their members and winning. He has only said three words to me since we entered the prison: "Escape is possible."

But there has been nothing else since he joined the light elves.

I walk around the play pen with my hands on my chain blades. The fact that everyone keeps their weapons and gear in here is a testament to how unruly this prison really is.

We're each given a job to do. So far, my job has been mining ore for the warden in his private mines. One of the more messed up positions, considering that you only eat if you find the rare rudamentium ore. I haven't eaten since my first day here.

It's time I test out a theory: that this facility, like the rest of the IGF sectors, is more corrupt than it seems. I also have a hunch: that, just like any facility, its weakness is the people running it.

I size up one of the guards. Dressed all in black, he wields a high-powered rifle set on stun. He looks at me looking at him.

"Better watch those eyes, convict."

"Just thought I'd make you a proposition."

"What might that be?"

"I bet you that I can become the leader of the dark elves today."

"Ha, that's not saying much. It's staying the leader for more than a week that's the challenge." He points at the group of dark elves. "I've been watching your people fight amongst themselves for over seven years now, and not one leader has lasted more than a week."

"Fine. I bet you that I can make leader and last more than a week."

"I had heard they shacked the infamous Vexation with Checkmate. I guess you already went mad, huh? You're on. What's the wager?"

"If you win, you get my rifle; if I win, you switch me over to lighter duties. Somewhere I can actually get a meal."

"What if you up and croak during the battle? How am I to collect my winnings?"

"Okay. I'll leave my rifle right here on the ground in good faith. If I lose, I'm sure you can manage to get it from behind the fence."

"Deal."

Now, I know what you're probably thinking. How can I even trust this guard, and won't I need my rifle if I'm going up against the unknown?

This is truly a test of the god Chenji. If he exists, I believe he will provide me the opportunity to change my circumstances. And yes, it would be nice to have my rifle, but it could be worse.

I've been watching the dark elves intently since I arrived. Their current leader is a brute who wields a javelin and stone shield. He won't be easy to takedown, but nothing worthwhile comes easy. Or so they say.

As I walk to the dark elves, I notice everyone in the play pen perks up. The moment they have been waiting for—or so they think. The moment when the infamous Vexation begs to join the dark elf faction.

The dark elves stop working out and gambling to block my way to their leader.

"What do you want, vagrant?"

"I want a word with your leader."

"You don't get to speak to the leader. You get to speak to me."

Up stands a tall, muscular dark elf with an eye patch and a mechanical arm. In his hand he holds an advanced machine gun. He's dressed like those old-time sheriffs—even has a star badge for effect. Maybe he was once a supervisor of something.

I cross my arms. "Listen here, old timer."

"Machinemaster, and if you're looking to join the Shadow Elves, you gotta lick my boot."

"Well, Machinemaster, fortunately for me, I'm not looking to join the Shadow Elves. I'm here lead you."

They all erupt into laughter.

"Doesn't work that way. You have to have someone second your proposal. Then, and only then, can you challenge the Shadow King."

"Good. You're going to second my proposal."

This is when his facial expression turns dark. His eyebrows furrow, and his eye blinks.

"Now, why would I do such a thing? It's my job to maintain order."

"How about I make you a wager."

"A wager, you say?"

Just like any elf, he has a hard time passing up a good wager—especially one this juicy.

"You see these?" I hold up my chain blades.

"Yeah, pretty sweet. Where'd you get 'em?"

"These are orc-made. Can't get anything like this in IGF-sanctioned planets. If I lose to your leader, you get to keep them. If I win, you continue your job keeping order, and you give me the rundown on everything that goes on in this facility."

"You got yourself a deal. I'll be sure to put those to good use."

The dark elves surround me in a circle. Inside, I am met face-to-face with the javelin user.

"No hard feelings, but I'll need your spot. Might be better if you step down."

He doesn't respond, simply opens up his helmet to spit on the ground.

"Very well. If you want to play it that way."

He summons his phenome: a grey mare. He mounts her and charges towards me, pointing his javelin down at my head. The mare flashes forward, and he nearly impales my heart when I phase travel forward. I turn around and unleash Tirade.

*Been a while, old friend.*

She copy-cats me and taunts the javelin user. The mare and the rider freeze in a daze. launching my chain blades at the rider, the blades pierce his shoulder as if his armor was nothing but tissue. I pull him off the mare, making it disappear, and

I meteor dash towards my opponent. He blocks my fist with his shield and flings me into the crowd.

They throw me back into the arena just as he has finished removing the chained blades from his shoulder. I start spinning them in a defensive formation, causing him to circle warily. Eventually he grows impatient and charges forward, javelin aimed for my throat. I meteor dash backwards and cleave with my left sickle, catching his ankle. Then I spin around and cleave with my right sickle, catching him on the neck.

He drops to his knees, blood spurting in every direction. I roll forward, now place both sickles to his throat.

"Surrender and I spare your life."

Machinemaster walks out from the crowd and drills the javelin user with holes, killing him.

The body disappears in a burst of purple code, leaving behind a large floating chain with a shiny rock at one end. I pick it up, and it immediately wraps itself around my neck.

*Interesting.*

All the dark elves take the knee, including Machinemaster. My eyes catch Zeal's in the distance; he nods.

*It's only a matter of time.*

I approach the guard to see that my rifle is still there. True to the bet, he waited.

"Not bad. But this is only day one. You still have six days to go. I actually find myself rooting for you." He lifts up his helmet to reveal that he's also a dark elf, although a bit aged.

I nod, pick up my rifle, then head back to my legion.

The next night, I wake up to the sound of Checkmate whimpering in the corner. He points at the wall, where there is the shadow of a fist-sized spider, but no spider. I peer closer. My heartbeat increases and sweat drips down my head just as the tip of a black dagger rushes out of the shadow, stabbing me in the chest, stomach, and neck.

A voice echoes from my console. *System Warning: You have received severe shadow damage.*

I try blocking with my chained blades, but to no avail: The dagger goes right through, piercing my stomach and shoulder. I activate my ring, producing the three shields.

*System Warning: You have received severe shadow damage. Seek medical attention or Hit Point item.*

"Guard!" I yell out.

As I stumble to the bars, I'm stabbed in the back three times, bypassing the shields and dropping me to the floor. The sting of the blade burns as it twists and turns inside of me. While bleeding out, I'm stabbed several times more.

*System Warning: Hit Points at critical levels.*

The last thing I hear before passing out in a pool of my own blood is: "Check."

# CHAPTER 30

## CLASSIFICATION: TECHNICIAN

I find myself ostracized for my role in the underground operations. However, because I am the lead-ranked technician under He Who Loves, the remaining IGF bigwigs voted favorably for me. Essentially, I am blackballed. I won't be able to move up from where I am now, but I won't be dropped any lower. I am in limbo. My fellow technicians look at me with disgust.

"How could you? Those poor animals." The accursed bleeding hearts of techies find my existence repulsive. Yet I hold them in contempt for not understanding what it's like to come from high status, only to fall from grace. They don't know me. They don't know my story.

If I could, I'd bomb the whole tech room myself. Show them who's boss. I have come to realize that they can make me give up being Sugar Cane, but they can't take the Sugar Cane out of me.

In any case my credit balance is big. Big enough to buy my way out of this blackball. I have decided that I will become a politician and change the way things are done around here. That will show these uppity techies. I don't care who I need to suck up to, fuck, or pay off to get there.

Now that I am hot stuff who could resist my natural charm?

Speaking of which, the all-mighty Grand Inquisitor Morange has wasted enough of my time. I have made the decision to drop him and

find someone better. I say this as I look in the mirror at my low maximum health and low energy bar. If I were to get into a fight with a Frontier Division striker, they'd mop the floor with me. I guess I wasn't designated a tech head for no reason.

*How does one increase their maximum HP?*

So far, I've figured out that the yellow bar is for energy, universal for both friend and foe. There is also a separate blue bar for magical weapons, a green HP bar for allies and yourself, and a red hp bar for enemies.

I walk to the common cafeteria and get into the line for mashed potatoes and stew chicken, along with carrots and corn. My meals are a lot healthier these days. I see a few technicians deliberately leave the line because they are too close to me.

*Damn, these people really take this ostracization thing seriously.*

After getting my food, I see a rare politician eating in the cafeteria. He has two of his striker goons standing behind him, attentive as always. As I recall, he was once the eleventh-ranked politician but has since jumped to number six.

*Not a bad rank.*

He is a light elf, a bit stocky with receding grey hair. He wears a grey fox scarf around his neck, with five rings on each hand and a golden cane. His black suit has all kinds of weird designs on it, and his hat is way too small for his head.

*The perfect mark for my new sensual nature. I can have him wrapped around my little finger in no time.*

I approach the round table, and one of the strikers points her gun at my head. Unfazed, I roll my eyes.

"Back off, Sponge Cake, our Grand Legislator is eating," she says.

"I'm flattered that you know who I am. I am but a humble technician."

He almost chokes on his food. "Hahaha, technicians are anything but humble. Especially ones of your..." he looks me up and down. "Caliber."

I take a seat in front of him and lean in close.

"You know so much about me, and I so little about you. Such a shame. Tell me about yourself."

"Not much to know. I love my food cooked well and my wine chilled."

"How do you like your women?"

His eyes nearly bulge out of his head as I take a fry from his place and pop it in my mouth.

"I love me a woman…"

"Go on. I won't be offended."

"Who likes it rough."

His eyes light up as I maintain my smile, revealing my pearly white teeth.

*Time to do the bait and switch.*

"I'm not sure I can handle all of that… I mean, I've never had the opportunity."

He perks up even more. I'm confident blood is rushing to all kinds of places.

"I can teach you, if you'd be willing to learn."

I nod my head slowly; the woman striker sneers.

"She's poison running through my veins, Mr. Nepo, sir. Don't get involved," says the striker.

"I didn't ask you," he replies.

I smirk, knowing that kind of reaction all too well. Unrequited love. It reminds me of me and Vex, once upon a time. But oh, how the tables have turned. If only he could see me now.

*Belle of the ball.*

"So, Mr. Nepo."

"You may call me Nepo. Only the help must address me as Mister."

"So, Nepo. How did you become a politician—especially one of such high rank?"

He looks up to the blue ceiling of the cafeteria as if reminiscing about the good old days.

"I would say it all started when my parents divorced. I was an eighteen-year-old striker in the planetary division when they split. My father wanted me to be a striker, but my mother wanted me safe, a politician like herself. When they split, she pressured my superiors to release me from duty due to an illness she made up. One day I'm a striker, the next I'm a pupil under a politician."

"You must have been angry."

"On the contrary, I was relieved. Being a striker is a dangerous game. You should know this better than most. All that military stuff gets to the brain and can drive one mad."

"That's true."

"True is that! Now, if you'll excuse me. I must leave the story of how I ranked so high in the Frontier Division for another time," he says.

And with that, he opens his wrist console and transfers his personal number to mine.

*Hooked, line, and sinker.*

I've had a lot of moments that for one reason or another didn't last forever. Fleeting moments in time where the heart fluttered, and the mind went foggy. But those moments were few and far between. Sometimes, I picture myself spiraling down a never-ending tube of despair. It's not like I'm depressed or anything.

Just lonely.

I'd be lying if I said I didn't miss the attentions of Beaver Mouth and He Who Loves. The cold touch of Morange isn't sufficient anymore. Not for one of my caliber. I've upgraded, and it's time that I upgrade my partner.

Although not officially broken up, we haven't spoken since the night Sansa revealed everyone's secrets. It was a quick conversation, but he did call to tell me that everything would be okay.

Nonetheless I find myself scrolling through my console contacts to finally settle on Nepo.

*Allison connecting to Nepo.*

"Hello there, bright eyes."

He sounds rather surprised to hear from me. I suppose I now have that effect on men.

"Hello. Have you been thinking about me?"

"Of course. Every chance that I get. Probably a little more than I'd like to admit."

"How'd you like to come and see me?"

"It's rather late, but I'd love to. I just need to..."

"To what?" I find myself getting a little heated. I take a few breaths.

"To figure out something to tell my wife."

Just my luck, he's married. The good marks are never just available like that. I suppose it doesn't matter. How can a man resist my kind of temptation?

"You're the clever politician. I'm sure you'll figure it out."

"Okay, okay. I'll make something happen tonight. Do you like Silver De Quo wine?"

"Never heard of it."

"It's absolutely exquisite. I'll bring a bottle."

"I'll be waiting."

*Allison disconnects from Nepo.*

*Morange connecting to Allison.*

*Look who it is. Mr. Too Little, Too Late.*

"Hey there, sweetheart," says Morange.

"Ain't nothing sweet but the name."

"Funny," he says sarcastically.

"What's up? I Haven't heard from you in a while."

"I know. I've been busy," he says.

"With all this Sansa stuff, huh?"

"Yeah, this Leaky Faucet has posed more trouble than I could have imagined. You don't have any info that might assist, do you?"

I sigh.

"For the fifth time, no. Is that all?"

"Why are you rushing me off the phone?"

"I'm not rushing you. I'm just wondering why you always talk about business. Less and less about pleasure."

"Haven't we always talked about business?"

"That was when I had a business to speak of."

"So, it's like that?"

"Yeah, it is."

"Very well. Have it your way."

He disconnects.

I get up and look in the mirror, admiring myself.

*Who needs him?*

# CHAPTER 31
## CLASSIFICATION: ROGUE STRIKER

his passing out and waking up shit is starting to get annoying. It's almost as if I can't be left to rest in peace. No matter how close I come to the brink of death, the gods deem me unworthy for the afterlife. Then again, I wonder. *Is the afterlife better than where I have found myself?* The age-old question that is summoned by everyone who has contemplated suicide. The room is dark and smells like rubbing alcohol.

"Anyone there?"

"Check, check, check."

I look to my side to see Checkmate sitting on the bed adjacent to me. He has no wounds on him, but he still seems rather out of sorts.

*I suppose that's normal.*

A doctor approaches me with his hands in his pockets. He eyes me up and down.

"You're rather fortunate to be alive, Vexation."

"Vex."

"Well, Vex. You're rather fortunate to be alive. You were stabbed thirteen times. A shadow blade like that would have killed most people by the third piercing."

"I see. I suppose I am hardier than I look."

"Maybe. Then again, your friend over there saved your life."

"How so? And he isn't my friend."

"Well, whatever you call each other. He sent the blade to another dimension, breaking the connection between the wielder and the dagger."

"I see."

"Very peculiar."

"Why is that?"

"Checkmate has only used his abilities once since coming to this facility. Not even the times when he was attacked by the Shadow Elves. Any idea who wants you dead?"

"Nope. I suppose any number of people could have paid someone to off me."

"Are you sure? Perhaps this has something with you being the current leader of the Shadow Elves. You know those don't last long."

"So I've heard. Fortunately for me, I have no idea what you're talking about. I'm just some guy."

"Oh, the infamous Vex could never just be some guy. In any case, you're being discharged back to general pop. Good luck. You'll need it."

"Sure. What about him?"

"Checkmate? He insisted on coming with you. I figured he wanted to watch over you. Never seen him take a liking to anyone. He's warped all the minds of his previous bunkmates. Maybe you're special."

"Sure. Can I go now?"

"Yes, you may. Just sign here that you're being discharged, and gather your belongings. I'll have a couple of the guards escort you two."

"Hey, doc?"

"Yes, Vex?"

"What's to stop me from taking my weapons and, say, killing a guard or something?"

"I'd love to see you try. Been a while since anyone tried such a thing. You see, the Warden takes care of our safety."

"How vague."

"Vague, just like any chances of escape." He says with a wink.

I'm escorted back to my cell. My battlesuit has all these holes in it, making it less-then-suitable for wear, but my chained blades and shock rifle are still in good shape. I'll have to be more careful. The fact that someone can reach me in my cell is not a good sign.

I'll have to take them out before they take me out.

I'm rehabbing in the Shadow Elf area, Checkmate by my side. He hasn't left my side since the attack. Fortunately for me, he is a dark elf; otherwise, he wouldn't have been welcomed. I'm secretly eying the members of my group. At this point, none have directly challenged me. But it's only been six days.

One more day, and I'll be off mining duty. Maybe I'll actually get a meal.

Machinemaster approaches me. "So, you're alive huh?"

"So it would seem. Any idea who came after me?"

"Maybe, maybe not."

"I thought you were supposed to instill order. Not doing a great job if the leader dies every couple days."

He winces. I clearly struck a nerve.

"Let's just say I'm not sure. We've had slew of newbs come in the last month or so, most of whom have kept their abilities hidden. Then again, you're so infamous that maybe someone from another faction was hired to off you. Ever think of that?"

"Yeah, I have, but it's less likely. In any case, I have a feeling the assassin will show himself one more time before the day ends."

"Whatever you say, boss."

I approach the guard on the other side of the fence with a gleam in my eye. "So, your little friend failed, huh?"

"Perhaps. Doesn't mean he won't try again."

"You're not gonna deny it?"

"Of course not. What you gonna do? Go to the warden? Heheheh."

"Here I thought you were rooting for me."

"I want that rifle more."

"How about we up the stakes?"

"I'm listening."

"You have that friend of yours challenge me in open battle. If I lose, you get my chained blades and my ring of protection. If I win, you get Checkmate and me both into new work positions."

"That's doable... may be challenging, but doable. You're on. That ring of yours is worth at least a year's salary."

The next day, an elf in black light armor with a black katana is in the Shadow Elf section. Shadows fade from behind him. His eyes are glowing blue.

"So, you're the one who came after me?"

He nods.

"Do you have any idea what you've gotten yourself into?"

He nods again. "The name's Shadow Dancer."

"Very well. Let's get this over with."

I immediately send out Tirade, who uses taunt, but it's ineffective.

Shadow Dancer shadow phases behind me to slit my throat, but I phase travel through his katana. I turn around and swing my sickle into his neck, but it goes right through him.

*Not good.*

He throws several throwing stars at me, which I manage to block with my chain defense. Tirade unleashes a wind barrage, swooping Shadow Dancer in the air and shredding his armor to pieces. I follow this attack by imbuing my sickles with my energy. I launch the blades forward, and they pierce his shoulder to slam him into the ground.

He squirms on the ground as I meteor dash to him. He disappears into the gravel, reappearing above me. His katana slices through my right shoulder, nearly cutting my arm off.

Blood spurts out as I jam my left sickle into his neck and tear away flesh.

He bellows out in pain; as blood fills his throat, he begins to gargle.

As I drop the carcass on the gravel, a sniveling scum excuse for an elf runs into the middle of the circle and charges an attack.

"I challenge you for the supremacy of the Shadow Elves."

Too exhausted to protest, I simply look at him with furrowed brows.

Machinemaster steps in front of me and riddles the elf with bullets, downing him instantly.

*Those bullets were fast.*

He turns to me and says, "That's how I keep order."

After my wound heals, Checkmate and I are relocated to the kitchen. It's a fast-paced position that requires you to be on your toes, lest you mess up the meals. But it's a much better position than the mines. Every now and then, I sneak a couple pastries to the leader of the Green Skulls faction, Acid Reflex. I figure if there is anyone that I want to be on the good side of, it's the largest and most influential faction in the facility.

You see, I have come to learn that the women in the prison essentially run things. They control the prostitution ring and the assassination game. And in a prison filled with high-testosterone elves, dwarves, and guards, such things are very powerful. Even more so than on the outside.

Makes sense, if you ask me. It's easier for a woman to lure away a guard while the other sneaks into a cell to eliminate a target. Basically, if you want someone dead, you go to Acid Reflex. Now, my case is a bit different. I don't want to bed any of these criminals, nor do I want anyone dead. What I do want is to stay alive long enough to escape. Thus, I need to make an introduction securing my position as leader.

The problem is that it's extremely taboo for the Shadow Elves to mix with any of the other factions. The Green Skulls provide women, the Shining Ones provide drugs and alcohol, the Dwarven Legion provide information, and the Shadow Elves at the moment provide nothing but large numbers and occasional entertainment.

*That will have to change.*

Now that I'm in the kitchen, it's time for me to secure it. Then, and only then, can I implement operation Cookie Monster. That's where my superior numbers come in. With a bit of order and direction, I can move on the light elves with their shitty food.

Consider it a tactical takeover—that I am sure will one day lead to violence.

"Checkmate do you hear me?"

"Check, check, check." He has a pawn piece in his hand that he keeps moving around on an imaginary board. Must have summoned it from this alternative dimension of his. To think that this man was once the most feared elf in the galaxy.

"Watch my back ok? If anyone comes distract them ok?"

"Check, check, check!"

"Sheesh, say something else already."

I head over to the food replicator and get the baking ingredients that I need. Chocolate chips, flour, baking powder, sugar, butter, et cetera. I then pull out the toxic mushroom from the orc planet. I tuck away the spores for later, mixing in just enough to get you high, but not enough to make you sick. I make four strong batches.

One for each faction and one for the guards.

*Fortunately for me, I picked up a few things from my mom, who was an expert chef.*

I hear the kitchen supervisor, a fat slob of a light elf, approaching. Then I hear the words.

"Pawn takes rook."

And after a flashing beam of light, I turn to see the chef has been turned into a chess piece. A rook, to be exact.

*Now, that's a terrifying power.*

I don't know what's happening with the bodies disappearing after death, but the leftovers seem to be interesting trinkets. So far, I have the amulet from the javelin user and a ring from the shadow user. What use they have, I have no clue, but they look cool. Also, it makes eliminating people much easier. Harder for them to pinpoint who's doing the killing.

The next day during lunch, I slip each member of the Shining Ones a special homemade cookie. One each for the ten top-ranked members of the Green Skulls, and one to every dwarf from the Dwarven Legion. I have spies keeping watch to see who eats the full cookie.

If they don't eat it all, the effects might not take.

I deliver the batch for the guards personally to my contact, who seems to be sulking in the corner.

"Greetings."

"What do you want? Another stacked wager to make?"

"That wager wasn't stacked. I nearly lost my life." I show him the number thirteen tattoo on my shoulder where the scar is.

*Thirteen: for each time I was stabbed and lived.*

"Hmm, perhaps. What's in the box?"

"A peace offering, for you and your fellow guards. I suggest you don't eat too many though. They have a special kick."

He squints from behind his clear visor.

"What's in 'em?"

"Mom's special recipe. I guarantee you it's nothing like you've ever experienced. Trust me."

"That will be the day—the moment I trust a convict in this hellhole."

"I suppose you're right." I turn to leave.

"But hand them over anyways. There are a few people I don't like in here. Maybe I'll give a few to them. Let them test it out."

"Cool."

"By the way, we're having a Letting tomorrow."

"A Letting?"

"Yeah, a Blood Letting. And your name is on the list. It's easily the most painful experience you've ever been through. But it doesn't last long."

"Are these common?"

"Yeah, we have them every month at random intervals. You may think this facility is all cake and lollipops, but that's because you haven't gone through a Blood Letting. Or crossed the Warden. I sure hope the disappearance of the kitchen supervisor wasn't on you."

"No, sir, not at all."

"Good, because he is investigating that one personally. He was fond of the supervisor's cheesecakes."

"Good looking out."

I head back to the relative safety of my faction and watch as the faction leaders consume their cookies. The leader of the Shining Ones takes a look before gobbling it down like the oaf he is. The Dwarven Legion all eat their cookies at once.

*Creepy.*

I watch as Zeal takes his cookie and gives it to his leader, who eats it fast. As we make brief eye contact, Zeal has a sly smirk.

To my apprehension, Acid Reflex crumbles the cookie and sends a quick scowl my way. She must know I've been placed in the kitchen.

*Not good.*

But interestingly enough, she doesn't stop her faction from eating the cookies.

*I'll have to keep an eye on her.*

# CHAPTER 32
## CLASSIFICATION: POLITICIAN

These days, the Frontier Division is running low on both strikers to protect and HQ members to be protected. Frankly, we're in a chaotic state. The cyber elves are growing impatient as some of the technicians are a bit in shock after losing their supervisor.

I myself haven't been left untouched. I feel the noose tightening around my neck.

Once again, I find myself looking for signs of Leaky Faucet, I carry around a new shotgun. It's state-of-the-art and highly destructive. Next time I shoot someone in the stomach, they are dead.

I stalk the halls alert as a falcon, double-checking every nook and cranny in the entire space station. Sanguine is attached to my hip, along with my two V-13 bots.

"This is growing tiresome," says Sanguine.

"If you can't handle the job, then you can stay your ass in your quarters."

"I can handle the job. Just would rather she revealed herself."

"It's not going to be that easy. We have to track her down."

"If I were her, I'd be holed up in as small a space as possible. Like the little rodent that she is."

"Like where?"

"It was just a joke."

"I asked you a question."

"Well, when you think about it. She's small. We've been acting as if she was a fully grown striker male. Maybe she's hiding in a small area that we wouldn't normally search. Like our storage units, perhaps. We have several where we keep explosives. Can't stack too many together, you know? Precautions and such."

"Interesting. Show me."

We make our way to the bottom levels of the space station, and then to one of the storage units. As I limp my way to the door, I sense that I'm being watched. I look up to see a makeshift camera poking its head out in the ceiling.

I use my telekinesis to crush the camera. Pointing my shotgun forward, I walk carefully.

"We're on to something," I whisper.

As we creep deeper into the bowls of the level, I see a blinking device on the floor. It's a pretty obvious position in which to place a proximity mine.

*Maybe she isn't as smart as we think.*

I look at Sanguine, who steps forward and begins to deactivate the proximity mine. He cuts himself, turning his blood into tentacle hands able to pull off the most intricate maneuvers.

A few minutes pass in silence until he nods.

"It's done."

"Well?" I say.

"Well, what?" he responds.

"Go on ahead."

He gingerly steps over the mine. Nothing happens. I send my first V-13 bots next, then I go, followed by my second V-13 bot. As we progress through to the next section, we finally meet a door with an upgraded lock. I used my passcode, but it's denied. My passcode should open damn near any door in this facility, especially a mere storage unit.

*It's been tampered with.*

I look at my V-13 bot.

"Command: Unlock door."

We stand back as the V-13 switches to hacking mode and begins to deactivate the lock. After a few minutes, my V-13 bot overloads and collapses.

*Stupid bot.*

I look at Sanguine, who shakes his head.

"I'm not opening that door. Use your bot."

"That bot is worth more than you are."

"So what? I'm sure you have some elite insurance."

"As a matter of fact, I do."

I look at my second V-13 bot. "Command: Open door."

It moves the other V-13 bot out of the way and opens the door.

Inside the storage unit, we see a letter written on primitive parchment. It reads: *If you're reading this, you're going boom!*

I turn to run, only to be blocked by stupid Sanguine, who didn't get the message. I push him out of the way when the lights in the level shut off.

I telekinetically peel the corundum sheets off the walls and shield myself just as a massive explosion goes off on both sides.

I wake up in the healing quarters, surrounded by several doctors writing things on their console charts.

"Why the crowd?"

"We're studying your nanobots. It's only been two hours since the explosion, and you're fully functional. Quite impressive."

"How close was I to dying?"

"It's hard to tell. The explosion was mitigated by the layer of corundum, but your grievous wound was further aggravated. You'll need a cane to walk."

"What about my V-13 bot?"

"It's toast."

"And Sanguine?"

"He's in critical condition. He will be out for at least a month."

"Get me a fucking cane and move out of my way," I grumble.

*I now have clarity.*

Now with a severe limp and a black falcon-headed cane, I head straight towards the technicians' room.

*I have been going about this all wrong.*

I open the door with my badge and enter the room. The new supervisor is about to speak when I throw her against the wall with my telekinesis, knocking her out.

"All you techies listen up. Get against the wall."

One of the techies, currently, hooked up to the cyber net, is a little too slow for my liking. So I telekinetically summon her to me, then blow her apart with my shotgun, sending her flying back. The rounds pierce her body and explode, leaving bits and pieces of her all of the place. Soon after, the body fades away in a splash of code, and I'm left with a higher-level console chip.

I pick up the chip and place it in my pocket.

Now turning to the eighteen technicians, on duty, including Allison I speak.

"One of you is working with the RRA. You have three seconds to step forward before things get gruesome."

"One."

"Grand Inquisior Morange, you must be mistaken; we have already been cleared to work," says one.

"Two."

"Sir, this is preposterous. Leave our training facility. We are eighty-five percent of the way to summoning the great Kuleta Kifo and fully merging the worlds," says another.

"Three."

I raise into the air the two who had the gall to speak to me and crush their hearts with my powers. Their bodies drop to the floor with a loud thud.

Screams fill the room as the technicians begin freaking out.

"Quiet!" I command. I shake the room to its very core, threatening to destroy all the technology.

Allison steps forward and begins to speak, but I toss her against a wall. I hear a crunch as she lands a bit harder than I anticipated.

*As if I didn't know that she slept with that disgusting cigar-smoking Nepo. He bragged about stealing my partner the morning after.*

*It matters not. Who needs love? Women are like the sunrise. Another one will be there the next morning.*

I patrol the wall, looking each technician in the eyes. An assortment of men and women. All with weak fortitude. Some are shivering, some have defiled themselves. But not one of them has stepped forward. So I move on to the next phase of my plan.

I start with the first one against the wall and squeeze her brain with my powers—an excruciating amount of pain, having your brain squeezed from all sides. The woman covers her head and starts pulling out her hair.

"I'm not an RRA spy, please."

"Maybe or maybe not, but at this rate, every single one of you will die in a pool of your urine."

"Stop!"

I turn to a technician who, if I recall correctly, serves He Who Sees.

My half-brother's assignment.

With tears streaming down her face, she speaks once again. "It's me." She drops to her knees. "I'm the RRA spy."

"Good. That's good," I say, nodding my head.

"What now?" she asks.

I turn to one of the other technicians. "Call in the cleaners to take care of this mess and see to the injured. Everyone else get back to work."

I grab the woman by the arm and tug her out into the main hall.

"You're going to tell me everything you know about the RRA and its remaining members." I grip her tighter and look her in the eyes. "And you're going to do it now."

# CHAPTER 33
## CLASSIFICATION: ROGUE STRIKER

I make my move. I manage to get a few light elves transferred from the kitchen to another duty. The remaining ones see what's going on and reported to their faction leader, Dragoon. It turns out the kitchen is how the Shining Ones bring in the drugs. The logistics make sense; I suppose I should have seen this coming. In any case now I find myself involved in a faction war. There have been murders on both sides, and it doesn't seem like the bloodshed will end soon. Unless I put an end to it.

*This shit is getting out of hand. Bad for business.*

"You're on the wrong side of the play pen, Vexation," says a female with facial tattoos.

"It's Vex."

"Whatever. Get going before I slit your throat."

"I'm here to speak to Acid Reflex."

"I don't recall her summoning you."

"She'll want to hear what I have to say."

There is some whispering among their large group. All are giving me dirty looks.

Acid Reflex steps down from the bench and takes a good look at me.

"You got a lot of balls crossing the play pen to speak to me—especially alone. Last time a darkling did that, he came with ten of his men. He still got dropped."

"What can I say? Maybe I'm special."

"Every man thinks he's special, until he ends up with his balls sawed off. Speak swiftly, while you have a tongue."

"I hear my name is now on a piece of green paper. Courtesy of Dragoon."

"So, what if it is?"

"What do I have to do to get you off my back?" I cross my arms. "I don't need you breathing down my neck while I'm taking care of the Shining Ones."

"You really think you can win this faction war, do you?"

"Dragoon thinks I can. He wouldn't have come to you if he wasn't concerned."

"Perhaps. What's your point?"

"I just need you to hang back, let that note hang on the wayside, and let me do my thing."

"Now, why would I do that? We have a good thing going with the Shining Ones. They provide us with the drugs; we provide them with an occasional kitty."

"Because good can turn to better."

"How so?"

"I currently have a strong grip on the kitchen, and as such, the drugs have slowed down. People are converting to my product. The cookies I have are better than anything the Shining Ones could bring in. All you have to do is two things."

"I don't have to do shit. I run things in this facility."

"True. But think of it like this: a better and more convenient high. You don't have to rely on an outside source. All I ask is you take my name off your list, and get me and Dragoon in the same room."

"Oh, now you want me to play the united fucking galactic force or some shit huh?"

"As it stands, Dragoon is surrounded by way too many light elves. I can't get to him with my numbers. But get us in a smaller space, and I can take care of it. That will even the odds."

"That's assuming you can defeat him in a one-on-one fight. Dragoon isn't leader of those skunks for no reason." She glances over to Dragoon, then sizes me up again.

"What do you say?"

"My thoughts will run on it."

"Fair enough."

I wake up in the middle of the night straddled by Acid Reflex, her hand blaster pointed at my head. She pulls out a jagged dagger and caresses my balls with it.

"What's this about?"

"Shhh, don't want to wake your bunkmate."

*The one time he falls asleep, she enters? She must have drugged him somehow.*

"You've made your decision, huh?" I ask.

"Yup."

'Well, get it over with."

She smiles the most mischievous of smiles.

"I rather like to take my time."

"And I'd rather not have mine wasted. If I'm to die in this rat-infested hellhole, then so be it."

"Oh, we have ourselves a tough guy huh? I've been thinking about that, Vexation."

"It's Vex."

"I'll call you Don Dough if I want."

"Very well. What have you been thinking?"

"How could the most infamous RRA member and rogue striker be satisfied with life trapped in, as you call it, a hellhole? Judging by your profile, you'd rather die than live life a slave to the warden. Then my mind started bubbling on something. And you know what I came up with?"

"No. Please enlighten me."

She presses the flat side of the blade against my balls. "You're planning an escape. The cookies slow you down. Slow you way down. I noticed the guards swallowing them down like water."

"Perhaps. What if I was? What's it to you? It's apparently a suicide mission breaking out."

"Worse than that, the last person to try had the misfortune of becoming one of the warden's ravens. Not the most pleasant of experiences, as you could imagine."

"I'll take my chances. Now, as I said, what's it to you?"

"I want in."

"You want in?"

"What are you, a parrot? I want in on the escape."

"Why should I let you in on my plan when you got a knife to my balls?"

"Precisely because I got a knife to your balls is why you should let me in on your plan."

"That's not good enough. There are worse things than death, and that's being trapped in here. I don't want any liabilities."

"Hmm, do you know exactly what the warden is capable of?"

"No, maybe you can tell me."

"If you let me in on your plan, I'll tell you everything about the warden—and which guards we would need to avoid. The guards here are specifically picked for abilities that prevent escape. We're meant to suffer in this facility until we die of old age."

"Fine."

"Excellent." She removes the dagger from my person and lays beside me, caressing my helmet. "Now tell me. Who else is in on this?"

"So far just you and Zeal."

"The wild elf huh? You're full of surprises."

"Check, check, check." says Checkmate as he stares at Acid Reflex and me.

"And Checkmate."

"I don't like the idea of working with that lunatic," she says.

"Something tells me the sentiment is returned. In any case, his abilities will be useful if I can just get him to focus."

"You don't know what the Warden did to Checkmate do you?"

"What?"

"Checkmate was inches away from escaping when the warden challenged him to a chess match. As you might imagine, that's your boy's favorite game. In any case, near the end of the match, the warden used his raven to trap Checkmate in a loop-the-loop. Essentially, Checkmate is trapped in his own dimension playing the one person that he can never defeat: himself."

"So ever since then he's been half-and-half?"

"Yup. Half here and half there."

"How intelligent was Checkmate?"

"His intelligent and wisdom stats made your high cunning stats look like child's play. But he was arrogant, and that was his downfall. I wonder what yours will be?"

"You can wonder until you're green in the face. As long as I'm breathing, I have a puncher's chance at victory."

"Heh, I like you, Don Dough. It's why I'm letting you make your little schemes and plots. But if you don't get me out of here, I'll show you why I was placed here to begin with." She lets out a little giggle.

And with that, she dissolves in a bubbling green liquid into the bed.

Another crazy chick. It would seem that I attract the crazy ones. My thoughts drift to Chaos. I feel a tear rise up, but I do my best to suppress it. Her death will forever haunt me. Then my thoughts drift to Hyper Fairy. The disappointment she must have felt will forever scar me.

Trapped in this small cell, you have a lot of time to think. You can think until your mind burns out, but it doesn't matter if you aren't put in a position to make amends. It especially doesn't matter when you know you made the right decision with the information you had.

*No regrets.*

One of the guards approaches the metal gate.

"Time for another Letting Vex."

Shivers run down my spine as I think about the first time I went to the Letting.

The guard leads me and nineteen other prisoners to the blood-letting rooms. I'm strapped to a small chair in a tight squeeze. They hook one palm-sized butterfly needles into each of my limbs. As my blood pours into the butterfly needles, a guard take some green fluid and injects it into my neck. The liquid pours into my veins, and I feel an excruciating amount of pain. It feels as though fire ants are biting every inch of my body simultaneously. The green liquid mixes in with my blood, making me sick.

My body is now weak, and the warden manifests in a flock of ravens.

"How are you liking your stay, Vexation?"

"Sucks. Don't you have any entertainment?" I say through blurred vision.

"Oh, still cracking jokes, huh?" Stifle snaps his fingers, and the raven on his shoulder speaks.

"Caw, fifty push-ups." My eyes widen and my blood burns as I do my best to resist, but I drop to the floor and start doing fifty pushups.

It's like the raven has me under some kind of spell.

"You see Vexation, Perky and I control this entire zoo. A simple command, and I can have you put a few bullets in your head. There is nothing you can do about it. But on another note: I know what you've been up to."

"What might that be?"

"Becoming leader of the Shadow Elves, trying to disrupt the order of the factions. It seems like you've become addicted to power. But here is how it's going to go down: If another light elf in my facility disappears, I'm blaming you. I don't care if they trip on their own shoelaces and their gun goes off. It will be your fault."

"Let's just say that were to happen, then what?"

"Then I'm coming for that ass. And it will be sore when I'm done with you."

I'm not quite sure what he means, but I choose not to probe further. When a man can command you to kill yourself at the snap of his fingers, it's best not to antagonize him. Two things I do know. One: my plans will have to be altered, and two: that raven has to go.

I'm find myself sitting across the brutish oaf Dragoon. He kind of reminds me of a bigger and stronger Tyrant. He's wearing heavy dragon-scaled armor, with a dragon cannon on his left arm and a sword made from dragon scales in his right. His helmet is that of a dragon head, and his eyes are a piercing dark blue. Essentially, he is dressed in the scales of a high-level frost dragon.

I have twenty dark elves at my back, while he has thirty-five light elves at his. If it comes to it, there will be a brawl. But I'm hoping I can talk my way out of this. Acid Reflex said she could buy us about ten minutes without eyes on us. It will have to be enough.

"So, you're the infamous Vexation? I expected someone bigger."

"And you're the no-name Dragoon. I expected someone just as ugly."

"I may be no-name to you, but it's me who runs this facility."

"I've been hearing that a lot lately."

"But when I say it, it rings true."

"Enough foreplay. How about we get down to why I called this meeting."

"Yeah, let's. I'd rather not stand in the stench of your people longer than I must."

I grind my teeth. "This isn't about complexion."

"One thing you'll learn soon is that in here, everything is about complexion."

I lean in close and whisper. "What if I told you that you could be out of here in a month?"

"Then I'd think you were as crazy as your buddy."

"If we pool our resources, we can take down the warden and escape."

He tilts his head back and spits. I watch as it lands right beside me. "I don't do business with darkling scum."

"Well, I'll tell you what. You can hear me out or walk away from the deal. But just know that there are people in your camp that would slit your throat for a cookie or two."

He looks behind him, then turns back to me. I see the paranoia in his eyes.

One thing about a place like this is that you're always wondering who wants to clip you and who wants to rape you—especially when you're top dog.

A smirk crosses my face. "I know you've experienced it. The anxiety and the jitters. It's been a while since you guys had your share of cookies. Your guys are slower to the take. My guys are fresh. If we were to brawl now, you'd lose. Numbers and all. If I wait a bit longer and approach the right light elf, they'll do the job for me."

"What's your point, boy."

"My point is this: Work with me, or I'll find someone that will."

"What's your ask?"

"You have connections on the outside. I need you to acquire a fast ship—fast enough to outfly the jets they got here. Something with some firepower."

"Even if I were to get a ship in orbit, there is no one I can trust to pilot it. Ain't no one dumb enough to get involved with a break-out."

"I know someone skilled enough and willing. I just need to get a message to her."

"I'm limited in what information I can get out. I can get you a ship, but if you need a message to your contacts in the Frontier Division, that's dwarven territory."

"Fine. I'll get them on board."

"Hahahah, if it was that easy to get the dwarves on board, I would have escaped already. They have the entire layout to this place. But what you gonna do? Fit you, me, Checkmate, Acid Reflex, and forty dwarves on one ship fast enough to outfly their jets?"

*Good to know he doesn't know about Zeal yet.*

"We just need the dwarf to get the message out and in. After that, we don't need the dwarf. Worst case scenario, we just take the leader."

"Those guys only say two words to outsiders, and those are 'Legion forever.'"

"Leave that to me. Just get the ship ready for this date and time. Now punch me in the face so it doesn't look like we came to an agreement. Time is up."

"Gladly."

He hauls back and punches me in the jaw. I'm launched back into Machinemaster, who catches me.

"Our paths will cross again, ugly darkling!"

"Cut it out, Dragoon. Everyone back to your cells or we'll have a mass Blood Letting," says one of the guards.

I have never seen a group of hardened criminals move so quickly before. This Letting thing truly strikes fear into the hearts and minds of the zoo animals.

I sent another two batches of cookies to the dwarves. This time they analyze them together, then gobble them up together. I watch as the euphoria kicks in, activate my stealth, and then make my approach.

Taking a seat beside a random dwarf, I speak. "So, if I wanted to get a message to the outside world. I hear you guys are the ones to come to."

"Legion forever!" they say, circling me with weapons drawn.

"I'm here to speak to your leader."

"You killed the prince!" they yell out.

"That was then, and this is now. Allow me the opportunity to make amends. What if I told you I could get a one-way ticket out of here for the smart dwarf who sends a message out for me and gets me the reply?"

"Warden!" they all scream simultaneously, attracting the attention of the guards.

"Sure, you could go to the warden. But then you'd have a mark placed on every single one of you by the Shadow Elves. Not to mention no more cookies. I can see how much you guys love them—yet you don't experience any of the negative effects of withdrawal. Must be nice. What if I were to give the remaining dwarves the recipe? You can whip up as many cookies as you want, and you can get your leader out of here. If you really cared about your little group, you'd want to see your leader prosper."

The dwarven collective starts muttering amongst themselves in an obscure dwarven tongue. My helmet is unable to translate.

"Five."

"Five what?"

"Five dwarves will be set free."

"Fine. Five dwarves will be freed."

Now for the final phase of my plan. I need to get the guard in on it.

I approach my lone guard contact with another box of cookies.

"Hey Vex! That another batch for me?"

"Yeah."

"Aren't you the wiz in the kitchen. I hear they call you Don Dough."

"I see nothing here stays secret for long."

"Nothing at all. Now, hand those cookies over. They were a hit with my superiors. I simply left the box on one of their desks, and they pounced on them like wild hyenas."

"Sure thing, boss."

I hand him the box of cookies and begin to turn around to leave before turning back.

"By the way..."

"Yeah?"

"I hear there's an escape plan going on. Supposed to happen at this date and time." I hand him a piece of paper.

"Why are you telling me this? I thought you'd be front and center for an escape. Rushing to a painful end and whatnot."

"I am. Kind of have no choice since I'm the leader of the Shadow Elves. I have to show face. And whatnot."

"Well, give me the names of everyone involved, and there will be a mass Blood Letting. I'll look like a hero in preventing an escape."

"Of course. I got you. Just make sure my name is on that list. I don't want to look like no snitch."

"Volunteering for a Blood Letting, huh? You got some balls on you."

"So I've heard."

On the evening in question, I find myself, Acid Reflex, her lover Sparrow, Checkmate, Dragoon, Zeal, and five dwarves lined up for the Letting. But it seems like we're waiting for one more. Out marches Machinemaster with a broken jaw and a limp. He gives me a wink or a blink—can never tell with those wearing eye patches.

He whispers, "I see all, Vex."

Apparently he decided to beat up a guard at the same time we're about to be taken in for the Letting.

Because there are so many of us, we're escorted by twenty guards, plus the warden.

"Look what we have here. An all-star team of renegades. Too bad your little plan has run amuck. I am going to find out who's the mastermind behind this, and they will get a triple dose of nanobites," says Stifle.

"I think you mean nanobots," says Acid Reflex. The warden slaps her across the face.

"I said what I meant. Nanobites: bots that bite you from the inside and allow us to track your every move. Even if you escaped, we'd find you."

*Good to know. Never underestimate the arrogance of those who are at an advantage.*

"Now, march," says the raven.

We all start marching towards the Blood Letting room. Just as we're about to pass by the main gate, there is a massive explosion, followed by a siren. The guards point their weapons at the gate where the explosion went off.

There are two things I won't tell you. I won't tell you how Acid Reflex got the keys to the handcuffs, and I won't tell you how I got Checkmate out of the loop-the-loop. But what I will tell you is that it wasn't easy, and I will forever be changed because of it.

Acid Reflex reveals the key to her handcuffs on her tongue and unlocks her handcuffs. She then activates her acid abilities and melts all our cuffs. By the time one of the guards notices, it's too late. Checkmate releases all of our weapons from his hidden dimension, and all hell breaks loose: a massive brawl between the elite prisoners and the guards.

The raven is about to speak when Machinemaster riddles it with bullets, causing Warden Stifle to shriek in shock.

Within moments, all the guards are either dead or unconscious—including my guard contact. May he rise in peace.

I turn to the warden. "Open the gate, and you might live to see your children."

"You can kill me; my life is worth nothing."

"Oh, I know that. But why don't you phone home?"

"What?"

"You heard me. Call your home."

He taps his wrist console and up pops the vision of his wife tied to a chair.

"Dragoon, you there? Where you at, Dragoon?" says a voice in the background.

"I'm here." Dragoon steps forward and looks into the console.

"You fucking animals! What did you do to my wife?! She will be avenged. Mark my words," says Stifle.

Dragoon points his hand cannon at Stifle's head. "Nothing so far. But that can change if you don't open that gate."

"Okay, okay." He inputs the code, and the doors swing open to the landing deck. "Just no more, okay? Leave my wife and children alone."

"That all depends on what Dragoon says," says the Shining member.

"Roll out and head to the rendezvous point. I'll see you soon, brother," says Dragoon.

"That wasn't part of the plan," I say, as I grip his arm.

Dragoon shrugs me off. "Plans change." And with that, he punches Stifle to the ground and blasts him in the face with the cannon.

A sudden wave of anxiety washes over me as I realize what I'm doing. I'm letting the worse scum of the galaxy loose into the wild. Murderers, rapists, drug traffickers, prostitution madams.

*Is it worth it? And am I any better?*

Zeal places a hand on my shoulder as if he knows what's going through my head. I nod and push forward.

We make our way towards the ship, where Sansa has already taken out the five guards. How she managed that is a feat in itself.

I rush over and embrace her.

"Been a while, Vex. I knew I'd see you again."

"Of course."

She whispers, "So many?"

"Yeah, think it will work?"

"Maybe, maybe not. Those are state-of-the-art jets under secure force shields. It will take too long if we try to destroy them."

We hop into the carrier craft that Dragoon procured. It's spacious, but it looks like a clunk of junk. How we're supposed to outfly or outgun those fighter jets, I don't know.

'This the best you could do?" says Acid Reflex.

"As if you could do better," he rebuts.

"Let's get the hell out of here," I say.

Sansa launches us out the landing deck, and we're off to the last place they will think to look for us.

My home away from home, Kukosa.

Now at this point, you're probably wondering what I plan on doing about the orcs.

I'll have to make them an offer that cannot be refused.

We blitz across space, the fighter jets on our tail. Sansa maneuvers out of range from their homing missiles, but we're clearly too slow to outfly them, and there is no way we can outgun them.

"We're too heavy!" says Sansa.

"Just my sentiments, exactly. I'll lighten the load." Dragoon steps forward and blasts one of the dwarves in the chest, instantly killing him.

I punch Dragoon in the jaw, sending him flying against the wall. But it's Machinemaster who unleashes fire, drilling holes into the remaining four dwarves.

Their last words? "Legion Forever."

There is a pile of glowing code orbs left from their deaths. I touch one, and I'm filled with that dwarf's entire lifespan in the time it takes to make a single breath. It just so happens that this dwarf was their leader.

Zeal swings his club at Machinemaster, catching him in the stomach. Then he touches two of the orbs. Acid Reflex puddles in and touches the remaining two.

Dragoon is back up and places his cannon firmly against my skull—but Acid Reflex has her acid blaster pointed at his chest.

"Try him, and you try me. I think we've lightened the load enough, don't you think?" she says with a wink to me.

Sansa is in the pilot's seat with Checkmate beside her, me and Zeal on one side, Machinemaster and Dragoon on the other side, and Acid Reflex and Sparrow in the middle. Who would have thought? Complexion barriers break down the instant there is mutual hatred.

*How bittersweet.*

# CHAPTER 34

## CLASSIFICATION: TECHNICIAN

 cracked spinal cord and a booming headache: That's what I'm left with when Morange has finished his little temper tantrum—or, as he likes to call it, his inquisition.

*That asshole. I can't believe he did his mind thing on me. Threw me against the bloody wall.*

I mean, I can believe he did that to the other technicians, but to me? How can you do that to someone you once cared about? Once spent many a night holding and caressing? Once said you'd always be there for?

Maybe his words were just that.

*Empty words.*

The swishing of the doors attracts my attention. The plump Nepo rushes in.

"Oh my, oh my," he says as he grabs my hands.

"You look nearly as bad as I do," I say.

Which is true. He looks a mess. His clothes are all wrinkled, and his hair is out of sorts.

"I've been disoriented after hearing the news!"

"I'll be fine."

*At least someone cares about me. Morange didn't even come to visit me after sending me here. Prick.*

"Of course you will be." He puts his hand on the doctor's one mechanical shoulder. "This right here is an excellent doctor. He knows the technology better than anyone. He's even part machine—how amazing is that?"

"Yeah, he's been quite the delight. Waiting on me, hand and foot."

"My pleasure," says the doctor with a wide-brimmed smile.

"Mind if I walk you to your room?" asks Nepo.

"I would love that."

"You also want some ice cream? I think this calls for ice cream."

"I'm not a child. But some ice cream couldn't hurt."

I didn't notice it before, but there is a cake symbol beside Nepo's health bar. I wonder what that means.

"Why are you looking at me like that?"

"Like what?"

"As if you're analyzing one of your screens."

"Oh, sorry. It's just that there is a symbol beside your health bar."

"Ahhh, I see. It would seem the next level of He Who Loves has been unlocked—as well as that of He Who Sees, for I can also see your health bar, too. But I see what I would receive if I were to kill you where you stand."

"What would you get?"

"A Tɪɪ advance microchip that contains all your skills and abilities. If you were a striker, it would be quite tempting. An instant powerup!"

I lower my head. "Is that all I'm worth?"

"That, and some question-marked item. That's interesting. It is rare for a life to be worth more than one item. I actually saw Morange the other day, and boy, is he worth something valuable."

"What do you mean?"

"Ever since his rampage, his value went up. The cyber elves were pleased."

"You mean to tell me that monster has benefited from all of this?"

"Of course. His demonstration of power and influence impressed the cyber elves. He is now only a few ranks below myself in political rank."

"How far he has climbed?"

"Enough about your ex. Time to talk about your next."

*As corny as that sounds, I rather like his train of thought.*

We bypass the line and head straight to the ice cream machine, which is down for cleaning.

*How upsetting.*

I see Morange walk in with two floozies on his arms. Smiling his patented politicians' smile. Strutting into the cafeteria like he owns the place.

*Who does he think he is?*

I watch as he walks by me without saying a word.

*No hi, no apology, nothing.*

"Hey!"

He turns around with this confused expression. I stand up and point at him.

"So, you're just going to walk right by me like nothing happened?"

"Pretty much."

"You son of..."

The floor shakes beneath us; food flies off the cafeteria counter. I feel my heart rate increase.

"You will speak to me with respect."

"You will get respect when you show some."

"What do you want?"

"I want an apology."

"For what?"

"For what you did in the technicians' room. You didn't have to come in there rampaging like a damn lunatic!"

"Lower your voice when speaking to me."

"You don't scare me."

He walks closer to me, each step aided by his cane. He looks me up and down, then scoffs.

"You think just because you lost some weight and put on some makeup you're something to be idolized? You're nothing but filth from the bottom of the swamp that has bubbled to the top." He spits on the floor. "But you're still filth."

"I can't believe you." I feel tears welling up, but I refuse to let him see me cry. I refuse to let this poor excuse for a man break me down.

"Believe it, Sponge Cake or whatever, you're called these days. At the end of the day, I made you who you are. You'd still be a greasy little piglet if not for me. You'll be wise to remember that the next time you wish for me to grace you with my presence."

"That's enough!" says Nepo.

"Stay out of this, Nepo, or you'll find yourself in a dusty grave soon enough."

Morange is finally showing his true colors. His sly demeanor usually masks his devious, ruthless tongue. I never thought it would come to this, though. Never thought I'd receive the tongue lashing.

He walks off with his two floozies, who seem even more enthralled with him.

*So much for women sticking together.*

This is the day my heart truly turns black. I may be pretty as a peach on the outside, but on the inside, I recognize this as the moment I've become rotten to the core.

"So... how about a slice of cheesecake?" says Nepo.

I find myself deep in the cyber net, surrounded by these weird-looking cyber creatures. They have pitch black eyes and long fingers the length of my hand. Their feet are like smoky tentacles, and on one arm each carries a shield made of void energy.

"What are you?" I ask.

"He Who Loves will meet with you now."

"Very well."

My avatar is transported in a tornado of code to a dark room with green hearts plastered all over the place. I feel overwhelmed with pleasant feelings—like my heart is being filled with love, pleasure, and joy.

I find myself shedding tears of happiness, picturing every good thing that has ever happened to me.

"You see, my dear Allison. Life is all about perspective."

"What do you mean?" I say, my head bowed low.

"When one shifts their perspective to the positive things in life, they can achieve great things. I have brought you here because I sense a deep change in you, Allison. Your deepest, darkest desire has shifted from wanting love to wanting respect."

"I didn't know there was much of a difference."

"Love is all-encompassing and all-accepting. It can be selfish, yet liberating at the same time. But respect must be earned. It comes from taking what is yours and giving what one deserves. If what you truly desire is respect, I can transfer you to another."

"Such as?"

"She Who Takes or He Who Hates."

From what I know, He Who Hates is who Morange serves—although his half-brother is He Who Sees. I suppose that's off the board.

"Tell me more about She Who Takes."

"If you choose to align yourself with She Who Takes, you will achieve great things in this life. You will reach heights unknown. But you will never know true love, never know what it's like to hold your own child. And you will never know who to trust. You will lose your sight even as you gain vision."

*Who needs love anyways?*

"Sign me up."

"As you wish. May it be everything you desire it to be and more."

# CHAPTER 35
## CLASSIFICATION: ROGUE STRIKER

ansa manages to land the ship where the remaining IGF ships lay. Fortunately for us, we lose the fighter jets in an asteroid belt; unfortunately for us, the ships on the planet were all scavenged. Their most vital parts are plucked apart, leaving us with one ship between the eight of us.

Sansa turns to me. "What's the plan, Vex?"

"He doesn't have a plan. We're here on a toxic planet. What kind of messed up atmospheric levels are these?" says Dragoon.

"Of course, he does. Right Vex?" asks Sansa.

"But I do. I take my ship and head back to my home planet, where my crew is waiting for me," says Dragoon.

"That's a stupid idea. That's the first place they will look for you. Besides, can you even fly that piece of junk?" says Acid Reflex.

"That piece of junk got us here in one piece didn't it? Also, I'm taking your pilot."

"Over your dead body," replies Sansa.

*If only these people knew how wicked and cruel I have become in my time in that facility. The gruesome things I would do to them if they laid a finger on Sansa.*

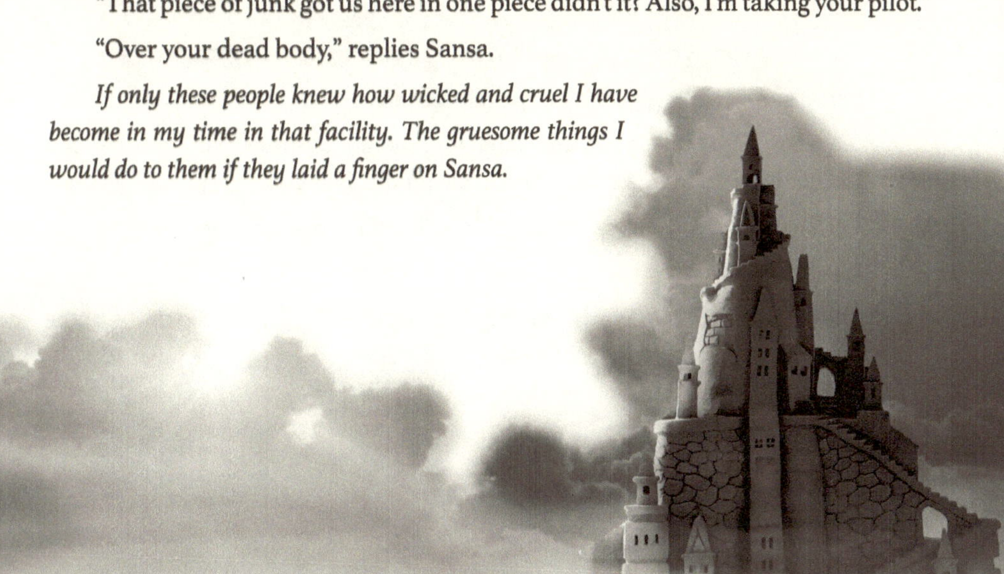

I point to the large black tower approaching us. "That's where we're going. Zeal, Sansa, Checkmate. The rest of you can rot here if you want. The planet will kill you in due time."

"Not if I kill you first." Dragoon points his cannon at my head, but I ignore it and start walking towards the orcs' tower, followed by my group of renegades.

By the time we reach the area directly surrounding the tower, the scent is unbearable. The toxins that the orcs give off have increased in potency, and there is a distinct green fog enveloping them.

"I sure hope you know what you're doing. Orcs are bad business," whispers Acid Reflex.

"They have more honor than your average elf."

"If you say so."

"I know so." And with that, I increase my pace, slightly distancing myself from the group—just to be alone in my own thoughts.

*If this doesn't work, we're all screwed. It must.*

By the time we get close enough to see the slave elves, the new group members are appalled.

"What is the meaning of this? Light elves in shackles?!" Dragoon's voice thunders like a storm.

"Yeah. Ignore it for now."

"What do mean, ignore it for now? What are you up to, Don Dough?"

That's a show of disrespect if there ever was one.

"Keep running your mouth, and you'll join them. I didn't ask you to come. But since you're here: Fall in line if you want to get off this planet in one piece."

"You have one try to get me off this planet. Then I'm doing it my way."

"Sure."

A blaster goes off, but I dodge it. Dragoon wasn't so fortunate. He drops to the floor, seizing up, then goes unconscious.

The war cry of several orcs echoes, causing a large portion of my group to soil themselves. We're surrounded by blue orcs—including their leader, Zalthu, the giant blue orc with a massive war hammer.

"Elf has returned. Pet of VerThag."

"I'm nobody's pet. Take me to WarBlade."

"Dead or alive?"

"Alive."

"Elf makes a funny."

"Orc is the funny."

He lifts his giant war hammer into the air and summons a massive amount of energy from the sky. The clouds crack open, revealing dark blue.

"Elves will perish here and now, make good soup."

"What if I told you that we can make you ships and more advanced technology. More armor, weapons, and fighter jets than you can handle. You won't have to rely on the scarce amount you've gained from dwarves—you'll have them made in house for you."

He squints, looking at me and then at my group. "Fine. Come."

We make our way to the top floor of their tower.

"How can the orcs have such advanced technology? I thought they were primitive beasts," whispers Sansa.

"No more primitive than you backwater elves. Orcs once great army with great technology. But our best and brightest wiped out by IGF betrayal." says Zalthu

"We're here to change that," I say.

"We will see."

When we arrive in WarBlade's throne room, it is filled with green, blue, and red orcs. VerThag and BugGug are already in their seats.

Upon seeing me, VerThag closes his eyes and lowers his head.

"The shame you have brought upon me. Yet you return?"

"Pretty much."

Just as he's about to strike me down, WarBlade enters the room to orc trumpets.

"So many smelly elves. A gift from Zalthu?" she asks.

Zalthu takes his seat below WarBlade and leans his war hammer against the throne.

"We have come here to make a deal," I say.

"Elves want deal with orcs? Last time elves betrayed orcs, set us back thousands of years."

"So we have heard. We can fix that." I look WarBlade directly in the eyes. "We have dwarven knowledge and elven knowledge. We can create armor, weapons, and ships for you to fight the IGF with."

"You are elves. Why would you betray your kind?"

"Not all elves are alike. The IGF is a tyrannical organization. We wish to see it thrown to the ground beneath our heels."

She squints. "And you wish to use orcs to do it."

"We wish to align ourselves with orcs, for the greater good."

"If this can be done, first elves must prove their abilities by defeating two-thirds of my warlords."

"Very well."

I step forward, along with Dragoon and Acid Reflex. It seems old habits die hard—not a coincidence that it's the faction leaders who are up to the challenge.

BugGug, the green orc, stands and looks Acid Reflex from top to bottom. He licks his lips.

"When I am finished with her, she will be unrecognizable."

"Begin!"

Acid Reflex bubbles into the ground, leaving behind a pool of acid, and pops up behind BugGug to pierce her jagged dagger into his lower back. He chuckles and grabs the blade, melting it with his own acid. The stench is horrendous.

Quicker than one would expect, he backhands Acid Reflex, sending her flying into his throne. She swiftly gets up and sends several blasts of acid at his head. They're blocked by what I can now recognize as a floating green version of his ancestor.

*The dwarven knowledge is proving to be useful.*

The ancestor throws five dice at Acid Reflex; she acrobatically catches them, imbues them with her own acid, and throws them back at him. She dissolves her body into another pool of acid to appear above the orc with her cannon resting on his head. She fires a massive blast of acidic energy that washes over him like oil over water.

BugGug chuckles again. "That's all? Weak elf."

Acid Reflex sweep kicks BugGug to the ground, then releases a large green viper that pierces the orc's neck. He writhes around on the floor, clutching his neck as the venom moves through his body.

"Interesting." WarBlade looks at Zalthu. "I trust you will not disappoint me," she says to her lover.

Zalthu gets up and makes his way towards the middle of the room. Dragoon steps forward.

"This will be quick."

I grip his arm. "Don't underestimate him. The green orcs are gamblers, trackers, and slave drivers. Not fighters. It's the blue and red that we must concern ourselves with."

Zalthu raises his war hammer to the sky, and the grey ceiling breaks apart to cover him in a ray of sunlight.

He twirls his war hammer, then slams it against the floor.

Dragoon catapults himself forward with his dragon thrusters and unleashes a massive cannon blast from his dragon arm. Zalthu swings his war hammer against the blast, sending it right back. Dragoon eats the blast, charging his body more.

But once they're within striking distance, Zalthu's ancestor grips Dragoon with two hands, lifts him in the air, and bends him.

We hear a loud crack as Dragoon's sturdy armor is broken. It's followed by Zalthu pummeling Dragoon in the stomach with his war hammer.

*These ancestors seem to be quite the nuisance.*

VerThag steps to the middle of the arena in a blazing fire.

Sweat streams down my face in bullets. My armor is still in tatters, and I know VerThag is not someone I can defeat in a straight-up battle. That's when my dwarven memory kicks in.

"VerThag, do you recall the ancient ritual of the duelist stance?"

"Of course. From once upon a time when elves, dwarves, and orcs were at peace."

"May we initiate it now? In the name of honor."

"What does Vexation know of honor? He run away like a coward. Leave VerThag to punishment."

"I'm nobody's pet. But I understand where you're coming from. You treated me well and taught me many things."

"That I did. What is Elf's point?"

"My point is that you should allow me to return the favor. There is much technology to be gained, should you choose."

"Enough talk. Fight now!" commands WarBlade.

"Very well. Duelist stance it is."

I combine my chained blades into a large two-handed crescent blade. For this to work, I have to down VerThag in one explosive move.

He stands there with his dai katana sheathed, charging as much fire energy as he wills, while I stand with my crescent blade behind my head, gathering as much wind and ethereal energy as I can.

He's about to make the first move when I meteor dash towards him, ready to use the special cutting technique Speedster from the Planetary Division taught me a while back.

I flash forward in wind armor while VerThag flashes forward in fire armor.

My blade bypasses his blade and cleaves him right through ancestor and fire armor both, while his blade pierces me through my stomach. I walk a few steps then drop to my knees, leaking blood. He walks a few steps, then drops to the floor.

*Thank Chenji for the opportunity.*

Sansa approaches me with her brows furrowed and her thumbs twiddling.

"Are you sure about this, Vex?"

"Why? What's wrong?"

"I mean. If we give these orcs this technology, they will be on equal if not greater footing to the strikers. What if, after they wipe out the IGF, they don't stop there? What if they turn on us?"

"Then we deal with it. Don't tell me you're having second thoughts now. It was your idea to begin with."

"What are you talking about? I never said anything about arming the orcs."

"Yes, but you thought about it."

"How do you know?"

I lean in closer. "The dwarves... they communicate via a mind link. After I absorbed that lead dwarf's orb, I can hear things."

"Eek! You're a thought rapist!"

"What? No."

"What else have you reaped from my mind?"

"Just that. It comes and goes; I can't really control it."

"Well, stay out of my thoughts, pervert!"

She marches to the front of the room and begins the unveiling of the first set of orc armor. Made by elven minds with dwarven schematics: state-of-the-art S+ grade armor and weapons.

"Hi, green orcs, blue orcs, and red orcs. Greetings, orc warlords and orc leader," decrees Sansa.

"Get on with it. We don't have all night," says BugGug

"Don't rush me. This is a very special moment for me," she rebuts. "Anyways, we are gathered here today to unveil the armor of the three orc warlords. Special S+ grade armor that will deflect the majority of projectiles. The armor is supercharged by sunlight—so there is no need to use one's energy to fuel it, like with elven armor."

"Interesting. What are those things on the shoulders?" asks BugGug.

"I'm getting to that." She pouts, putting both her hands on her hips. "Each armor is tailor-made to its warlord leader, enhancing their battle acumen and ancestral connection fivefold."

She places her palm in the air. "You heard that right! Fivefold."

BugGug gets up and analyzes his Ooze Mecha Suit, as it's called. He enters from the front compartment and hops into the suit, which is four times his size. The mecha suit has one cannon arm that shoots out a sticky projectile or an acidic projectile. Elf-sized tubes on each shoulder are filled with the acidic and sticky substances. The other hand is capable of incredible crushing power. His mecha suit has ridiculous range and guided accuracy.

I feel the tower shake; the reinforced glass window shatters. Another explosion goes off, and the tower begins its descent towards the ground. As it tilts over, the orcs grab their weapons and rush to the elevator, but it's been deactivated.

*One way or another, we're going down with the ship.*

I activate my shield ring and brace for impact.

The tower rumbles and shudders as it tumbles. I'm thrown in the air momentarily, then with a loud bang I hit the floor.

By the time I regain my senses, I hear jet fire and homing missiles. I stagger outside into the bright light to feel a spotlight on me. The fighter jet revs up its gatling gun and is about to riddle me with bullets when Zeal launches himself like a wild animal into the air and lands on the jet. I watch as he slams his club into the reinforced glass, breaking it easily. The jet tumbles to the ground after he disposes of the pilot.

I look into the distance to see something I never expected to see. Something that sends shivers down my spine. Who would have thought I could still feel fear after all that I have been through?

*One thing I do know is that they won't take me back alive.*

The Frontier Division and the Eclectic Division have both formed one army. Together they are a wave of death, prepared to eliminate anything in their way.

My hands quiver as I take a deep breath. I had hoped we would have time to remove the tracking bots inside of us. But it seems I was wrong. Perhaps I should have made that my number one priority—not prepping the orcs for battle.

It's a critical mistake that may have cost everyone their lives.

*No time for regrets, and no tears left to cry.*

The orc army is on the defensive; we are severely outranged and out-teched.

Meanwhile, the elven army has massive artillery cannons. They're wiping out a dozen orcs at a time.

I turn to Sansa. "We need to get rid of those artillery cannons or we're dust."

She nods her head. "Easier said than done. Any ideas?"

I look around, and I'm hit with a flashback to my day in the meditation room when I fought with DeakGu. When I had the vision of Chenji. He said to come to him when it was time.

*Why am I thinking about this now?*

I find myself pushing past the many orcs, all charging to their deaths, back into the tower. I hear Sansa calling out to me, but I ignore her. What I'm doing is more urgent. I just feel it.

When I reach the ruined meditation floor, I see that all the weapons have been ransacked.

*Why am I here?*

I feel tingles all over my body. I sit down in the rubble and meditate just as VerThag taught me. It's supposed to connect one with something called their highest self: the aspect of themselves that is closest to their governing deity.

*Whatever mumbo jumbo that is. I was never good at clearing my mind, so I choose to opt for the other way to meditate. I focus my mind on a single thought related to the present. But what?*

*Think, think, think.* My mind eventually settles on the thought of opportunity. I mean, this deity is supposed to be the god of opportunity, change, and redemption. So give me an opportunity. I'll take it.

I'm showered in a beam of sunlight. I try to move my body, but it's frozen within a moment of time.

"You may not be ready for that kind of opportunity. Perhaps your destiny is to fail. What makes you worthy enough to receive my blessing?" says a deep soothing voice.

"Listen here. I may not be a noble person, but I do what I believe is right. And right now, I believe the IGF needs to be stopped."

"Do you know what it would mean, were I to bestow upon you change, opportunity and a chance of redemption?"

"How am I supposed to know that? What I do know is that I have people I need to protect. Zeal, Sansa, and Checkmate. I don't want to lose anyone else. I have people I must protect by any means necessary. I want a future that isn't filled with blood, death, and treachery."

"Well said, Vincent. Just as the sun rises, so shall you—or die trying. Your shadow runs deep. Let us see what happens when the doors that have been blocked are shattered."

I feel a sudden urge to withdraw my sickles and slit my throat. But I resist. As I collapse to the floor, I look around and I see these weird-looking beetles crawling towards me.

*Disgusting things.*

The room is now filled with odd beetles of varying colors: gold, purple, blue, red. They swarm me as I thrash around. Their touch is hot like the sun at its peak. My skin burns and begins to peel off. I watch as my arms dissolve into flakes of light, followed by my legs, then my chest.

"What is happening to me?"

"You're dying, Vincent. You're letting your true shadow consume you. Such a pity. I had high hopes for you."

"I refuse to die like this."

"Show me."

I focus my mind on opportunity, change and even redemption. Opportunity to protect my comrades, opportunity to become something greater than I am, opportunity to achieve great things. Change in my circumstances, change in the world around me, and change in myself. Redemption for every life I've taken, every drop of blood I've shed, and for all the pain I have caused those around me.

"I need more time. I am not done with this life yet!"

A feminine voice speaks back to me.

"Resurrection!"

My body floats in the beaming sunlight. What was once burning now tingles, all over my body. It feels amazing—as if my DNA is being rearranged. My heartbeat intensifies, and my shattered battlesuit washes off my body in flakes of light.

Grains of sand rise up from the ground to cover my naked body.

She continues. "Just like your father, you will control the flow of the sands. But will you be consumed by them as he was?"

"I am nothing like my father."

"Poor little Vincent. You grow to be more and more like him every day. But are you worthy of me? He was not, and perished at your hands, for that was his destiny. You are now forever stained with his blood. His very essence stands behind you, and his powers now flow through you. What shall you do? Will you break your generational curse?"

"I will do what is necessary. Now show yourself. For you must be my true phenome."

*Tirade will always have a special place in my heart, but it is now time I meet my true shadow. The deepest and darkest manifestation of my mind. The thing that will make my heart rumble in fear.*

The beetles turn into sand and cling together to form a giant armored scarab beetle with sharp claws, a protruding horn, sharp teeth, and purple glowing eyes. Smaller scarab beetles drop from underneath the armor and turn back to sand on touching the floor.

Whereas Tirade was cute and fluffy, this thing is hideous, monstrous.

I look down at my body to see that I am covered in gold armor, with purple bandages at key points for good measure. The armor is light and flexible, but made of a material I have never seen before. At my back is a golden spear with purple gems attached.

*My true weapon.*

I am filled with a new knowledge of what I must do and who I must become to achieve my goals.

"You know nothing, Vincent," says my new phenome, a darkness passed down from generation to generation. Perhaps she is the source of my mutation.

"You will obey me," I command.

"For a time, yes. Until you show your weakness. Then I will devour you like I did your father. Those who bathe in the shadows are destined to drown in them."

"We will see about that."

Returning to the battlefield, I am met with plenty of item drops where orcs once lay. The orcs are still on the defensive, getting picked off in groups by the artillery fire.

I hop atop my phenome Resurrect, and she launches herself into the air to fly at blitzing speeds. She dodges the wave of artillery, lasers, and blasters that come my way. Once in range of the first artillery cannon, she releases burning sand that covers it. The cannon tries to fire, and the explosion is trapped within the sand.

I jump off my phenome to land on top of a striker, impaling him with my spear.

It feels like home, wielding this weapon—as if every weapon I have held before it was being used by the wrong hands. Surrounded by five elves. I spin my spear to release burning sand in every direction. A sandstorm manifests where I'm standing, protecting me from their projectiles. I rush forward like the monstrosity that I am and pierce the heart of another striker.

I turn to see Hyper Fairy, who emits a blast of cannon fire into my tornado, only to have it reflected back at her.

"Lay down your weapons, Hyper Fairy."

"Vex, is that you?"

"Yes, it is."

"It seems not even the depths of hell can hold the infamous Vexation. I will do what I should have done the moment I met you."

*It's as they say. A lover crossed is an enemy for life.*

Hyper Fairy activates her wings and takes to the air, where she starts unleashing hyper charged blasts of energy at me. They bypass my sandstorm, forcing me to dodge the projectiles. I'm struck in the back of the head, but it has no effect on me. I turn to see a striker from the Eclectic Division.

*No match for my newfound power.*

I uppercut him in the jaw and he flies through the air. As he lands, I summon sand spikes. I have seen my father wield these powers enough to know how they work.

*It is one with me, and I am one with it.*

Just as I'm about to turn my attention back to Hyper Fairy, I'm pinned against a broken artillery cannon.

I look for the culprit. Finally, my eyes find Morange, who is now blue. He pulls out his high-powered shotgun and blasts me in the chest. It slightly dents my armor, but other that I'm left unaffected.

"So you've beefed up a bit," says Morange.

"I suppose so."

"No matter. Tonight, you dine with your ancestors."

Resurrect, who has systematically eliminated every artillery canon, comes barreling into Morange and leaves him bloody. She disappears, but not before bathing me in a shower of golden light.

A thin golden layer of energy surrounds my entire being. It's some sort of special shield. Hyper Fairy unleashes a barrage at me, but the special shield absorbs it. As I charge towards her, I'm struck in the back with such great force that I'm brought to my knees. My armor is dented, but I received little physical damage.

I turn to see Leonidas rounding up for another blow when Sansa pierces him in the lower back with her sword. He turns and grabs her by the neck, squeezing, threatening to end her right there and then.

I cover her in a burning sand shield, preventing Leonidas from harming her further. He drops her and sneers just as he is struck with several stun blasts from an orc rifle. He is completely unfazed. A swarm of orcs rush towards our location.

The frontline of elves has been breeched, and their cannons are down.

Leonidas summons his lioness, who roars, stunning us momentarily.

"Retreat back to base camp!" He turns to me with his eyes burning. "Until we meet again, Vex. You may have grown more powerful, but Kuleta Kifo will be upon you soon enough. And then we will see who wins this little game called life."

# CHAPTER 36
## CLASSIFICATION: POLITICIAN

I look at Leonidas, who doesn't even have a scratch on him. Then I look at myself. My physical wounds are still a problem but my mental wounds are what concern me the most. All the power I've gained, and I am still weaker than Vex—still weaker than Leonidas.

As I look at my hands, I am disgusted by what has transpired.

Leonidas approaches me with his hammer at his back. "We will have reinforcements soon enough. That was just the first phase. This entire planet will be wiped off the map when I am done with it."

"Who perished and made you leader of this war?"

He chuckles. "You may be a bigwig up there. But down here, this is my army. Get used to it."

He turns and walks off without bothering to hear my rebuttal. My hands shudder as I squeeze them, attempting to close off his breathing.

He turns back to me and chuckles again. "Your little telekinesis trick will not work against me."

"Who do you serve?"

"I serve Kuleta Kifo directly." He takes his hand and waves it against his face; his skin turns a distinct purple.

"It cannot be!"

"Yes, it can. I have achieved the hidden level eight in the cyber net and thus have bypassed the mere cyber elf council. You will see what I am capable of soon enough. A storm is brewing, and if you are not careful, you will get swept up."

With that, the level eight cyber striker walks off, leaving me with my metaphorical hat in hand like a beggar.

*More power. I need more power.*

A cargo carrier ship lands in our base camp, and I turn to see Convert stepping first off the ship. The dark elf wife of Leonidas, and as gorgeous as they come. Then out steps a striker I never thought I'd see in action, a striker rumored to have been in slumber for many decades. If they unfroze him, then things really are changing.

I bring up my wrist console.

*Codename: Salvation. One of the legacy strikers, capable of eliminating a hundred opponents at a time while protecting a hundred allies. The sweetest thing to walk the planets. Decked out in white-and-brown heavy armor, armed with a holy mace and a massive impenetrable shield, he is the most holy of all strikers. Last known activation: the last time Checkmate was on a rampage.*

They must really fear this Checkmate. But why?

I pull up the file on this Checkmate guy.

*Codename: Checkmate. Genius level intelligence—levels that surpass anything known to elven, dwarven, or orcish kind. Often speaks in chess moves. Plots things out ten moves ahead. A former legacy Striker. Went rogue for unknown reasons.*

Another heavy hitter steps off the jet: a striker that I don't recognize. I use the laser camera of my console to slyly scan her devil's badge.

*Codename: Punk Rock. Legacy Striker. Lightning user and mechanical user. DO NOT ENGAGE.*

She has short red hair, red eyes, and blue lipstick. She has a mechanical forearm and a mechanical leg from the knee down. Blue code circles her left side, and occasionally static manifests around her body making it appear as though she is only partially there.

*What do you mean, do not engage? This thing doesn't know who I am. I'm the bloody Grand Inquisitor. I must know everyone in my army.*

I walk past Salvation, making a beeline towards this so-called Punk Rock.

"Greetings. I'm Grand Inquisitor Morange."

She looks at me with the same expression she departed the carrier with.

I repeat, "I said, greetings. I'm Grand Inquisitor Morange."

"She heard you."

I turn to see who spoke.

"She doesn't speak to lesser beings," says Salvation.

"Who are you calling a lesser being?"

"You."

"You'll put some respect on my name."

"My heavens. With a title like Grand Inquisitor you must have a tiny pecker. Overcompensation and such. In any case, if it makes you feel any better, I can barely get a peep out of her most times."

"Not really." I ignore the pecker joke and turn my attention to Punk Rock. "Do you understand the words that are coming out of my mouth?"

She nods.

I smile. "Good. You see, with people like this you just have to be—"

With one smooth motion, she pulls out her lightning katana and slices my right hand clean off. My jaw drops while I bellow out in agony.

"My hand!"

I see a slight smirk cross her face as she walks by me without a word. Salvation turns and leaves as well.

After the debacle on orc planet twenty-one. I was sent back to the Frontier Division for medical attention—a blatant excuse to get me out of the way. It would seem that both Salvation and Punk Rock deemed my presence a nuisance. One complaint to the remaining bigwigs, and I was gone. Just like that. I guess it goes to show who has the most say.

*When it comes to the beast or the handler, the beast wins every time.*

Now using a mechanical hand, and still walking with a permanent limp, I find myself hovering more days than not. Using my energy in such a trivial way is something I once thought I was past.

Floating through the halls one day I am met with Allison, who is looking absolutely delicious. But my pride will get the best of me this evening, and I will simply float on by. Truth be told, I miss her. I miss her ambition and her wits. But above all, my demons played well with hers. It's our angels that couldn't get along.

Just as I'm about to pass her by, she grips me by the hand and pulls me in closer.

"When I heard what happened, I was so worried."

"It's not as bad as it sounds. Mechanical limbs and such are the way of the future."

*Look at me, trying to play it off. When in actuality, I'm fuming. It's a sad day when you learn that the power you gained is not enough—that you've essentially reached your limit, and everyone around you passes you by.*

"I missed you." I hold her tight. She lifts her head up and peers into my eyes. She gives me a wide-brimmed smile.

"You know what I miss?"

"What?"

"This."

The blood rushes towards my johnson as she grabs it. She leads me to her room, which I happily enter. A rendezvous is exactly what I need to clear my mind. I will find a way to achieve more power—and soon. I will make sure I rise higher in the ranks and eliminate all who stand in my way.

She pulls down my pants and looks up at me once more, smiling with those gorgeous green eyes of hers.

*I thought they were yellow.*

"Your eyes—they changed color again."

"Yeah, they're different. You know what else changed?"

"What?"

"Me."

A green dagger manifests smoothly in her hand, and she slices off my johnson. I live just long enough to see it fall to the ground as she rises and jams the dagger in my neck.

My blood spurts out, turning into code, as I feel my body flake away.

*What a bitch way to die.*

# CHAPTER 37
## CLASSIFICATION: ROGUE STRIKER

I walk up to Sansa, who is working on creating a ship suitable for space flight. This kid is always working on something. Though I suppose she isn't a kid anymore. She's accomplished a lot these past few years. The leaves flow in the wind; the mushrooms glow ever-so-slightly under the moon's glimmer.

"Hey."

"Hey." She stops what she's doing and gives me her undivided attention.

"How is the progress going?"

"It's going well. I'll have about four cargo ships and two fighter jets up and running in no time."

"Look at you, always thinking ahead."

"Well, what can I say. I don't like the idea of being stranded on this planet."

"It's not so bad."

"Easy for you to say. You've been in worse places."

I cringe, thinking about the Blood Letting, the cramped spaces, the mines, the never-ending routine, and the moments I was on the brink of death—never knowing what was around the corner. Not being able to find the right words to reply, I stay silent.

"I'm sorry. That was in poor taste," she says.

"It's okay."

She looks at me and starts twiddling her thumbs.

"Something on your mind?" I ask.

"Well, what was it like?"

"Let's put it this way. You have a lot of time to think about how your destiny brought you into a box. You have time to think about the ones who deserted you, the ones who didn't deserve you, and even the ones you did dirty."

"And yet, here you stand. Shining brighter than ever."

"Yup, here I stand."

"How did you do it?"

"It all starts with faith. Faith in yourself—that you can overcome any obstacle that life throws at you. That's followed by the knowledge that your happiness is created from within. You learn to appreciate every breath, every waking moment, and every opportunity."

"What about Chenji?"

"Chenji played a role as well. Just understanding the concepts of change, opportunity, and redemption is enough to keep one poised to succeed."

"I like that. You've certainly grown, Vex."

"What about you?"

"What was it like being public enemy number one?"

She blushes slightly. "Oh, you heard about that?"

"Yeah, even in the depths of an uncharted prison, word gets around."

"It was scary at times, exhilarating at others—but mostly depressing." She grabs my hand. "Vex, I couldn't stop them from cracking the code. It's only a matter a time until..."

"It's fine. How bad can this Kuleta Kifo be? Besides. They have their deity, and we have ours. We will persevere."

"Oh? Since when did you become a believer?"

"Since I was freed from that prison and gained newfound powers."

"I must say, the gold does look good on you."

"It feels right. Especially the sand—I used to watch my father when I was a child and marvel at all the things he could do."

"Vex?"

"Yeah?"

"Don't leave me like that again."

"I won't."

"Do you promise?" she asks, her eyes calm.

"I promise."

With my head held high, making sure to maintain eye contact, I walk up to WarBlade. The leader of the orcs places her hands on my shoulders and kisses me on both cheeks.

WarBlade makes an announcement. "With your assistance, we have dealt a massive blow to the IGF. Now we will strike at their hearts, and drive them off our planet. We will forever show them that we will not be bullied any longer!"

The orcs roar in unison, and the earth beneath our feet trembles.

"They may have the numbers, but with this new technology, we have evened the odds."

I look at the fifty new state-of-the-art battlesuits Sansa made for the elite orcs out of a special material they have been hoarding for a day like this: the day the knowledge of how to create orc technology returns to them.

*Who would have thought the dwarven schematics had orc elements to them?*

Orc battlesuits are either large mecha suits with heavy artillery or bulky battlesuits. They also prefer lasers over plasma energy.

In any case, I have a nagging feeling that this still isn't enough. It will take a miracle to fully eradicate the elves off this planet. It hurts me to say, but the IGF is a pestilence that spreads across a planet, devouring everything in its wake.

"Perhaps we should do a reconnaissance mission first?"

"You mean, spy?"

"Yes, spy."

WarBlade sneers. "Orcs don't spy. We track, hunt, and trap. But we do not spy. Sneaky elves spy. Hide in the shadows like rats."

"That may be so, but did it ever occur to you that gaining information before rushing in is smart tactics?"

She squints. "Elf calling orcs stupid?"

"No."

Acid Reflex steps up and speaks. "What he is saying is that you should allow us sneaky elves to sneak in their camp and get information before you go in and eliminate them. It's been several weeks. Without knowledge of the right mushrooms, they should be feeling the effects of the atmosphere."

"True. Elf in green makes sense."

She squints at me again. "Go. Move swift as wind, and strike if necessary."

With that, me and my vagabond strikers make our way to the outskirts of the planet. With few food provisions, we're not much better off than the rest of the IGF. The good thing is that we have an expert tracker in Zeal, who knows the terrain very well.

After two days of tracking the IGF footprints, we run out of rations after Dragoon feels the need to devour everything left.

*I suppose his motto is feast today, famine tomorrow.*

I'm not completely unaware of my situation, though. I saw him eying those cargo carriers like a hawk. He is only playing along until he can get off this planet. It's like he said: This isn't his war. He owes allegiance to no one.

"Now you have me trotting through the jungle, starving, eating bloody mushrooms," says Dragoon.

"You're not really starving if you have mushrooms to eat."

"See, I've been thinking. What do you think our heads are worth?"

"What do you mean?"

"I mean, how bad do you think they want us dead? You three, they must really want bad." he says, pointing at Sansa, Checkmate, and myself.

"But the rest of us. What we've done isn't so reprehensible, now is it?"

"So, what's your point?"

"What if we take this spy thing to another level?"

"I'm listening."

"Say we surrender ourselves to the IGF and pretend to sell you guys out. Leak them a little information here and there, then set them up for a trap. How does that sound?"

"Could work."

*Maybe elves really are naturally sneaky rats.*

Dragoon looks at Machinemaster, who nods his head.

*Clearly the two of them have been talking.*

Eventually, we make our way to the IGF base camp, where we see a massive army almost twice the size of the orcs'. It's worse than we thought. They have heavy-hitting mech suits, more of those artillery cannons, and there is an eerie electric static pulsating throughout the camp.

Dragoon looks at Machinemaster again, and the two of them bust out running with their hands in the air.

We watch as they are met by a slender red-headed striker with a devil badge. Dragoon speaks, while Machinemaster stands there nodding his head.

Acid Reflex grips her lover Sparrow. "This isn't good."

"What do you mean?"

"That's Stifle's sister."

"Shit."

I summon a sandstorm on their location as I dash forward, but I'm too late. She draws out her katana at lightning speed and decapitates both of them with one strike. I watch as their bodies dissolve into flakes of code, leaving a gold-and-blue machinegun and a golden assault rifle. Resurrect barrels through the sandstorm and into the katana wielder, pushing her away from the golden assault rifle. I touch it, adding the weapon in my arsenal.

*This new item drop thing is pretty cool.*

My console pops up without my command and reads out loud:

*Item Acquired: Legendary Golden AK13. Projectiles adapt to the element of wielder. High-powered, high-recoil weapon, capable of piercing even the toughest of armor. Sand Magic, Primary Effect: Each bullet has ten percent chance of turning opponent into ally sand walker. Duration sixty seconds. Secondary Effect: Five percent chance of creating Sand Turret. Permanent until destroyed. Tertiary Effect: Unknown. Three modes. Burst, automatic, sunbeam.*

By the time the console is finished dictating to me, the katana user has defeated my phenome. She tilts her head back, and lightning flashes behind me. I send up a near-impenetrable sand shield, which her sword slashes halfway through before being stopped.

The fact that she managed such a thing means the strike that would have sliced right through me, golden armor and all. Sansa lets loose her new legendary machine gun, which spews out a string of water bullets that nearly pierce myself and the katana wielder both. I send up another sand shield, which blocks the barrage with a loud thud. Meanwhile the katana user lightning flashes towards Sansa with her sword held high. Sansa pools into a puddle of water just in the nick of time.

At this point, the alarm has been sounded, and a group of elves is making their way towards us.

"Retreat!" I say.

The katana user lightning flashes in front of us, blocking our way. But Zeal appears to save the day. He leaps out of the bushes and swings his club, knocking her into the air several hundred meters. I watch as her body twirls and tumbles to the ground.

We make our way into the bushes, back towards base camp. Although we gained a limited amount of information, we did manage to gain two very valuable weapons. This item drop on death is scary. Your best friend could betray you for a chance at something good.

*I'll have to sleep with both eyes open now.*

As we run through the bushes, Checkmate makes sure to leave many traps in our wake, ensuring that we won't be followed—at least, not for long.

By the time we have reached the outskirts of our base, we're exhausted.

I find myself looking at Checkmate as he eats his mushroom soup. I haven't heard him say a word since the prison. It's as if he's forgotten how to speak. The odd thing is that I sense a storm brewing within him. As if his mind is still fighting a battle I know nothing about.

I catch Acid Reflux eyeing Sansa's new weapon with envy, breaking my attention.

"You know, there will plenty more weapons to drop. Imagine if we were to take down that lightning katana user," I say.

"Pfft. Take down Punk Rock? Do you know what you're getting yourself into?"

"I suppose you'll tell me," I say, rolling my eyes behind my helmet.

"Punk Rock is one of the legacy strikers. A striker who has defied the normal aging process. One whose stats aren't recorded because they would skew the records. In any case... it's about time Sparrow and I take our leave."

"What do you mean take your leave?"

"Exactly what it sounds like. You can play hero and try to free the galaxy from the grasp of the IGF. I will not waste my newfound freedom on such shenanigans. I have a business to look after."

"Where will you go?"

"It's best that you don't know."

"Very well. I won't stop you. But you do know the IGF will be monitoring any spacecraft. Chances are they have the planet surrounded."

"You let me worry about that. Goodbye, Vex."

"Alright."

Acid Reflex hops on one of the cargo ships alongside Sparrow, who gives me a nod. Sparrow heads into the cockpit, and within a few minutes they are off to some planet unknown.

I can't help but feel a little a twinge of sadness. She was an integral part of my escape. Even Dragoon and Machinemaster played their roles to perfection.

Shaking off any residual feelings for my past, I focus on the task at hand.

We make our way to WarBlade, waiting for us on her broken throne. The orc, now wearing a distinct scar on her face, watches me intently as we approach.

"Elf will make report now."

"Yes."

"Elf has shiny new weapon."

"I suppose."

"I want shiny new weapon. Give me."

"I'd rather not."

"I said, give me now!"

Every orc in the vicinity turns their attention to us, brandishing the weapons we made for them. Wearing the armor that we put together for them. And above all, holding us in contempt for a legendary grade AK13 and a legendary grade machinegun.

"Elf will give weapons over, or orc will take," says WarBlade.

# CHAPTER 38
## CLASSIFICATION: TECHNICIAN

After killing Morange, I feel better than ever. His telekinesis powers transfer to me, and I also gain access to a phenome. I will have to keep that secret for now. A technician with a phenome is a dangerous thing. We're supposed to be the passive tech heads, not the frontline.

This particular phenome suits me very well—though I suppose that can be said for all phenomes, them being your shadow self, and all. One thing I do know is that from now on I will take what I want, when I want.

"Sponge Cake, care for some more cheesecake?" asks Nepo from across the cafeteria table.

"No, thank you."

"What are you thinking about? Wondering about who made Morange disappear?"

"No, he's old news."

*No need to wonder.*

"Well I am. It's not every day a Grand Inquisitor disappears."

"What's so special about his position?"

"The Grand Inquisitor position is one of the few positions that can serve as both frontline personnel and pencil pusher like myself. Also, you're able to launch an investigation into almost any member of the IGF, including most of the bigwigs. Then there is the access to the funds."

"What funds?"

"Well, the Grand Inquisitor position pays very well. It's their attempt to keep that person as honest as possible. A politician that polices other politicians—that kind of power that can go to someone's head. Say what you will about Morange, but he did his job to the best of his abilities. He will be missed."

"Sounds like the position has now become available."

"That is true. I'm sure they will fill it soon enough."

"Perhaps they will fill it with my own two shoes?"

He coughs up a storm, nearly choking on his cheesecake.

"I beg your pardon?"

"You heard me. Get me that position."

"It's a highly coveted position, and they wouldn't dream of giving it to the likes of you."

"The likes of me? What's that supposed to mean?"

"You know. A technician. You're meant to surf the net and what not. It's best if you stick to pushing your buttons and playing your games. It's critical that we summon Kuleta Kifo soon. There are rumblings that the Arunkai are making their move."

I feel my hand trembling as I decide what to do with this pompous politician. Do I dare risk killing another high-ranking member of the IGF? It is then that I remember something Morange once told me. In politics, there are often multiple ways to get the same result.

"How is your wife doing?"

"Hmm, what a peculiar question. She is fine. Feeling a bit neglected lately, but none the wiser. She thinks it's because we're still shorthanded."

"I see. It would be a shame if she found out what we're up to."

"What are you saying?" He raises his head and clenches his jaw.

"I'm just saying it would be a shame. That's all."

"Well, you'd be wise to keep such comments to yourself."

"And you'd be wise to tread lightly. The ice you're on may not be able to handle your weight."

I stand up to leave, taking my piece of cheesecake with me. I see him eying me with an expression aflame. But what is he really going to do? Besides comply, and get me on the council.

A deep raspy voice whispers in my ear, waking me up out of my deep slumber. "Someone is at the door."

I jolt up out of bed, my MP5 pointed at the door. The security code has been bypassed, and the intruders rush in.

My MP5 sizzles as I fire it in full-automatic. I hit the first intruder in the neck and chest. They send back plasma fire as I roll off the bed. I fling the bed towards the two intruders with my new telekinesis abilities, then release my phenome.

A warty green frog with a purple tongue hops out from its realm and lashes its tongue, swallowing the bed instantly. He gets even bigger and puts up a green reflective shield that sends back the projectiles.

He opens his mouth, this time spitting out puke-yellow acid. It connects with the striker I already shot, who dissolves into flakes of code. My phenome lashes his tongue to devour the second, fleeing intruder, but she sends out her phenome, slowing down the tongue lash drastically. It gives her enough time to get away.

*Some kind of sloth.*

I get a good look at it because it waves at me before disappearing back to the shadows.

My phenome turns to me, dripping saliva onto the nice tiles. "You better get your act together. I don't want to have to save your ass every time someone so much as sneezes your way." He disappears.

A little rattled now, I hear the footsteps of two security officers come rushing in after hearing the commotion. Now I must explain how a mere technician managed to take on two well-trained strikers, and even kill one of them.

I rush to check the item that dropped and find some kind of green grenade. I stuff it in my pocket just as my console pops up without my summoning it.

*Item Acquired: Short Circuit Grenade. Capable of short-circuiting all advanced weapons in a room, as well as disrupting all mechanical devices, for several minutes.*

The two security officers knock on my door. "We heard plasma fire. Is everything ok in there?"

"It is now," I say as the door slides open.

They enter and analyze the situation. "Who attacked you, and how did you fend them off?"

"I don't know. I sleep with an MP5 PDW. When they broke in, I let loose. I must have scared them off."

"A technician that sleeps with a high-powered SMG?" says one.

"Who can fend off more than one assailant?" says the other.

They look at each other. "How peculiar." says the second one.

"I know how this sounds, but maybe it's technician-on-technician crime. I recently moved under a new cyber elf, and it's a lot more competitive. I've also bumped quite a few people from that section. Most likely they wanted to scare me away, but they got more than they bargained for."

"Hmm, makes sense."

"I suppose it does make sense," says the second one.

"Yeah, so maybe you guys can run along and take care of the investigation? I can't do it all for you, now, can I?" I say with a wink.

"Cute," says one of the officers.

I'm left to clean up while they take their leave.

There is only one person I know with reason to send people to come rough me up. That would be that slick Nepo.

Hmph. He's in for a scare when he finds out that he lost one of his precious guard dogs in the process. Teach him not to mess with good old Sugar Cane—a name I will proudly wear. Forget what the IGF tells me. I'm going as Sugar Cane, and they will let me become a politician. One way or another.

I find myself storming towards Nepo's room. I haven't been there yet. It's over in the nice section of the space station. Decorated with fancy lights, illegal recording devices, artwork all over the walls, and a lot of security.

"Where do you think you're going, ma'am?"

"Ma'am? Do I look like an old lady to you?"

"You look like you're lost."

The guard scans my ID badge. His console speaks:

*Allison Ravenguard, Codename: Sponge Cake. Technician ranked fourth under She Who Takes. Level six clearance.*

"Hmm, impressive for someone formerly in the Eclectic Division to make level six clearance. But I'm afraid you need level seven for this sector of the space station."

I give him my widest smile and speak in the most innocent of tones. "Can't I take a little peek? I'm so close to level seven, and I just want to see what I'm working so hard for."

"I'm afraid it would be my head if I let you in. But I do assure you, the elite sector of the space station is quite amazing. Even safer since that whole Leaky Faucet debacle. We have entire portal and anti-phase technology, as well as recording devices. Safest place in the galaxy."

"Wow. Now I really want to see what's so amazing about it."

"That's a no-go."

"Hmmm. Are you sure there isn't anything I can do to sway that stubborn mind of yours?" I touch his shoulder lightly and caress his arm.

He looks me up and down then licks his lips.

*I mean, how can he resist an exotic level-six light elf. With my green eyes and green skin designs? Even the horns granted by She Who Takes are considered glamorous and attractive.*

He grabs me by the waist and pulls me into his muscular arms. Turning to his comrade, he says, "Hold down the fort. I'll be back."

His comrade nods.

The head of security takes me to one of the vacant rooms and throws me on the bed. I let out a little giggle as he takes off his shirt, revealing his well-structured frame.

*The weakness of most men is their second head. That's something She Who Takes drills in our minds from level one.*

*I will make use of this pawn as I rise to the top. Everything is within my grasp, and I will not let pride be my downfall as it was with Morange. Nor will I let wrath overcome my good senses as it was with Vex. Hell, I won't even permit gluttony to end my reign.*

*Someday, this will be my world.*

# CHAPTER 39
## CLASSIFICATION: ROGUE STRIKER

I look at Sansa, who gives me the most *I told you so* smile I have ever seen. It's so *I told you so* that I can't help but chuckle to myself.

"Elf thinks this is funny?"

"Somewhat, yeah."

"WarBlade no joke," says WarBlade.

"WarBlade the biggest joke."

Zalthu steps forward and pushes me away from WarBlade.

"Hand me the spear, too."

I sigh. "Greedy-ass orcs. No wonder your people have been systematically dismantled. You're like crabs in a barrel."

Zalthu leans back to strike me down when Sansa presses a red button on her console. The top fifty orcs, all decked out in their fancy new armor, drop to the ground unconscious. WarBlade recoils back just as I riddle her with bullets from the AK13 she wanted so bad. The recoil is intense, causing me to miss a lot, but the sand bullets rip through her tough skin like tissue paper.

She slumps down into her broken throne and dissolves into fragments of code. Zeal leaps over my head and does a front flip onto the throne. He picks up the light purple bow and arrow.

His console goes off:

*Legendary Sparkling Bow and Arrow: True Shot: Impossible to miss target in daylight. Chance of striking target is reduced to 70% during night. Spirit Arrow: Bypasses all shields, obstacles, and energy fields 40% of the time. Damage heightened during daytime; projectile speed heightened during night.*

"Mine, mine, mine!" He looks around shiftily as if expecting someone to take away his new toy.

The rest of the orcs are in shock as they watch us walk back to our sector of the camp. None decide to make a move to avenge their orc leader. As is orc custom, there is no pity for the dead and no vengeance for the fallen. Only a progression in objectives.

"Who will be their new leader?" asks Sansa.

"Most likely Zalthu. VerThag despises the spotlight, and BugGug is too cowardly to challenge for leadership."

"He won't be much easier to deal with."

"He isn't as stupid as he looks. He will comply—if only until we push the IGF off their planet. Then he will turn on us."

"Crabs in a barrel, huh?"

"Yeah.

"That's a shame."

"Yup."

The next morning I'm up early due to a night terror. I dreamed that I was enclosed in a tomb of sand, but not one of my own making. But one built by my father. I remember when I was a child, he used to find different ways to punish me when he found me lacking.

The sand tomb, the sand hound, the pyramid of death, and so on. Ironic that I will use what once terrorized me as a child to strike fear into the hearts of my enemies and bring them to their knees. But I have to ask myself one important thing.

If and when I do remove the IGF from power, then what? As far as I know, there are no other high-ranking members of the RRA. Maybe a few sleepers here and there. I know there is the doctor, and at least Alterna. But do I really see myself putting them in charge after Sansa and I have done all the heavy lifting?

*I think not.*

I find myself patrolling the camp, only to find footsteps heading towards enemy base camp.

*We may have a spy in our midst. But who?*

By the time I reach the enemies' camp, the footsteps have disappeared. But now that I'm here, I might as well observe what is going on. I poke my head out the bushes to see they have marked some kind of giant triangle inside a large circle on the ground. It seems to be made out of blood. Additionally they have added a sick camp where they take the sick and starving elves.

*Good. The environment is getting to them.*

I take a bite out of my daily mushroom rations. While munching away, observing the IGF camp I hear it. "Check."

I turn around to see Checkmate holding a bishop piece. He throws it at my head, and my battlesuit and weapons change. I'm now camouflaged as one of the Eclectic strikers. A no-name regular guy. I have his polearm and sniper as well as his belt of grenades. Everything feels and looks authentic.

Checkmate looks at me with a straight face. He then throws a bishop piece in the air, and it lands on his forehead. "Check."

It turns him into another generic striker. Someone that most would not pay any mind. I suppose this is his way of doing reconnaissance. It appears effective if you ask me.

We walk into the IGF base camp as if we belong and blend in with the other eclectic strikers.

Upon closer inspection, the base camp isn't doing too well. There are a lot of sick strikers, and the blacksmiths are having trouble keeping them alive. I see Punk Rock, the lightning-katana wielder. Not wanting to blow my disguise, I keep it moving. We head over to the food tent, hoping to get a good meal and pick up on some stray information.

*Everyone knows the food tent is where all the good gossip occurs.*

We sit down with big bowls of ramen noodles and pork meat. I start digging into the delicacy as if my life depends on it. Meanwhile, Checkmate pulls out a small bat carving and throws it into the air. The carving expands, comes to life, and flies to the top of the tent to hang upside down.

*What an odd way to summon a phenome.*

The bat lets out a low screech that no one seems to be paying attention to. A few seconds later, my mind is flooded with the noise of more than twenty different conversations. I clutch my head; the noise is overwhelming. Eventually, the voices die down to only about three different conversations, mixed with static. It's as if Checkmate is fine-tuning an ancient radio.

Eventually, he narrows it down to one conversation—between Leonidas and a striker by the name of Salvation.

"It's been a long time, Leonidas," says Salvation.

"Yes, you've been in a deep slumber for quite a while. What's it like?"

"It has its pros and cons. You have this vivid dream of a world where there is no war, death, or pain. You think something, and it happens right away. You want to create an ice cream that tastes like chocolate, pizza, and fries all in one, and it happens."

"Sounds like an upgraded version of the cyber net in some ways."

"Yes, being frozen is similar. But the thing is that while the cyber net and realm are real places. The dreams of a frozen entity are just that. Dreams. I'm reminded of it every time they wake me up."

"Perhaps. But what really is the difference between reality and one's imagination?"

"The difference, my good friend, is that imagination is a gateway to passion, and passion eventually becomes reality. When you're frozen, you're constantly reminded that everything is just a figment of your internal world. It has no effect on the outside world. Frankly, there is no challenge. When everything comes in the blink of a thought, there is no fun in achieving it. Life is truly about the progress to one's goals, not in the actual achieving of them."

"Interesting. Very interesting. In any case, reality and imagination will merge once Kuleta Kifo is free," Leonidas says as he looks around.

"In many ways, yes. I mean, I can gain a legendary power upgrade if I kill you where you sit. How is that for a merger?" says Salvation.

"Hehehe. Yes, I had noticed the upgrade in the mirror as well. My wife made a quip about it. Fortunately for me, you're on my side," says Leonidas.

"That is true. This war will be over as soon as the planet devourer arrives. We can't afford to waste good fodder by killing them by our own hand now. When he manifests, his hunger for death will be insatiable. It would be best if we corral the fodder closer together."

"Hmmm, yes, boxing them in would be best. Right now, they are spread out a bit too much. What do you have in mind?"

"I'll take a small portion of our army, perhaps the Eclectic Division, and let the orcs loose on them. That will force the orcs to gather once again. If we do not, Kuleta Kifo may see our weakened soldiers as a prime feast," says Salvation.

"Heh, he may very well see that as the case regardless. You know how unpredictable this god of games, deceit, and trickery is."

"Unpredictable, yet unwavering in his vision."

"This is true. Anyways it's about that time," says Leonidas.

Leonidas stands up and surveys the cafeteria tent. "Everyone get up, it's time for the ritual."

Not wanting to stand out, we get up as well and follow the group for this ritual. Deep in the IGF camp is a giant wooden cube roughly the size of a house. The IGF army surrounds the cube, sitting down with their legs crossed. Everyone has their head bowed and their eyes closed.

I peek to see Leonidas, Salvation, Punk Rock, and Convert standing atop the cube. Leonidas connects his console to every T7-and-above chip. Fortunately for Checkmate and me, we had Sansa deactivate those tracking nanobites. My only concern is that my RRA tag will give us away. Leonidas tore off my distortion chip but the tag is still in my DNA.

When one joins the RRA, they piggyback off the server information on the IGF console, but if someone is smart enough, they can tell the difference. The higher the upgraded chip, the easier it is for detection when a bigwig connects to my chip directly. It's a rare occurrence—but it is happening as we speak.

Before I left the IGF, they implanted a T9 chip. It was one of the more advanced chips available, granting me access to a lot of inside information.

I watch intently as Leonidas looks through his console.

"It seems we have two spies in our midst."

I watch as Punk Rock grips the hilt of her katana.

Checkmate stands and turns in the direction of our camp, where he throws a knight piece on the ground. It turns into a black stallion with orange flames flowing from its hooves. We both jump atop the stallion, and it charges forward quickly, trampling every striker in our way.

By the time we reach base camp, we have ditched every striker who dared to follow us.

I'm not sure what to make of this Checkmate who apparently can wield two phenomes at the same time. It makes me wonder what the other pieces can do—and just how powerful he is. Not to mention his motives and goals.

*But such things will have to wait. I have battle plans to prepare.*

# CHAPTER 40
## CLASSIFICATION: TECHNICIAN

The exclusive section of the space station is quite a marvel. I'm overwhelmed by the various pleasant scents. They have their own cafeteria, a zoo, a pet house for their illegal pets, and even their own casino ward. Why any high-ranking politician would want to leave these quarters except for official business is beyond me. It's by far the safest place in the space station.

I can go on and on, but you get the point.

I look at the directory board on the wall. I scroll down to see where Nepo and his family lay their precious heads at night.

*I'll have to pay them a visit.*

While strutting through the halls, I notice that I'm turning a few heads. I blush slightly. Getting all this attention is nice. It's amazing what a cyber makeover can do.

I arrive at Nepo's quarters and press the buzzer.

When he opens the door to see me, he widens his eyes.

He speaks in a low whisper. "What are you doing here?"

"You mean, what am I doing alive?"

He scrunches his face up. "I don't know what you're talking about." He pokes his head out then looks around in the empty halls. "Come in, my dear, come in."

"Sure thing."

"Would you like me to take your jacket?"

"No, it's fine. I won't be staying long."

"Good. So answer my question: Why are you here?"

"I'm here because I've been doing a lot of thinking."

"About what?"

"About our future."

"Our future? As far as I'm concerned, we don't have one."

"And as far as I'm concerned, we do." I look him dead in the eyes and smile the most innocent smile I can muster.

"Guards!" He yells.

I lift my right hand and backhand him in the mouth. "The guards are preoccupied with their impromptu meeting."

"What did you do to my guards?" Nepo says.

"Nothing a little call from the head of security can't handle. In any case, I'll lay it down like this. You're going to get me on the council, and you're going to do it with a big smile."

"Now why would I do that?" He laughs.

I place two of my fingers on my left temple, causing my eyes to swirl clockwise. As we make eye contact, I see his eyes spin counter-clockwise, indicating that he is open for communication.

"You, Nepo Tingden, will acquire the Grand Inquisitor position for me. By any means necessary." I place my left hand on his shoulder, sealing the pact. "Do you comprehend?"

He nods his head, still in a trance.

The next morning, while in the shower, I get a private call on my wrist console. I tap the button to accept the call.

"Allison speaking."

"This is the council adjudicator calling. You're on the short list for the Grand Inquisitor position. You have five minutes to make it to the council chambers."

"Copy that."

*Call disconnects.*

I dry off, get dressed, then rush over to the council chambers where the bigwigs have their meetings.

By the time I arrive, the vetting process has already begun. I join the short line and wait my turn. I watch as they question the first person on the list, a male with long purple hair and a trench coat. He's sweating buckets under the scrutiny of the questioning.

The adjudicator has a high-powered shotgun aimed at the guy's face.

"What is code violation number twenty-three of the code book?"

The guy clenches his jaw, then looks up to the ceiling.

"Umm, breaking oath without... without."

"Time!" yells the timekeeper.

*Boom* The shotgun goes off, blasting the candidate in the knee. He rolls around on the ground.

"Next question. We don't have all day," says one of the high-ranking politicians.

"When can the Grand Inquisitor initiate an inquisition on a member of HQ?"

"You shot me in the knee, man. How am I supposed to remember that?"

"When can the Grand Inquisitor initiate an inquisition on a member of HQ?" the adjudicator repeats.

"I don't know man. What the hell kind of question is that?"

"Time!"

The adjudicator takes the shotgun and shoot the guy in the chest, dissolving him into a flurry of code.  He picks up what appears to be a blue shock glove.

"Nice. I've been waiting to get my hand on one of these." He looks over to the line and bellows out, "Next!"

A couple people in front of me leave the line and walk to the exit.

*I don't blame them.*

The doors lock, and the adjudicator faces them. "If you want to leave, drop your badges on the counter first. The Grand Inquisitor position isn't for the light-hearted."

"Screw this, and screw the IGF," says one man. He rips off his rank badge and dashes it onto the floor. The others hesitate. The doors unlock, and he makes his way outside. A few seconds later, we hear his screams.

*No one leaves the IGF unaffected. Everyone knows that. It's either death or retirement.*

After a few more failures, one person passes the questionnaire portion of the test. It's my turn next. If I fail, I'll perish—as many have before me. If I succeed, I'll be pitted against a striker in a duel of skill.

"Interesting. A technician applying for the role of Grand Inquisitor. Must have pulled some major strings to gain entrance to the exam. I fully expect an egghead like you to pass the questionnaire part—but the skill challenge is another thing," says the adjudicator.

"Heh. We will see about that." I smile, trying my best to exude as much confidence as possible. In reality, my legs are shaking, and my breath is shallow. I studied every question, and even the hidden questions that Morange had mentioned in passing. But the Striker that passed the question portion is no joke.

"Let us begin."

"Fine by me."

"What is the protocol for investigating a striker with a chip of T9 or above?"

"I must first send my suspicions with at least three valid arguments to an IGF HQ member rank fifteen or higher."

"Good. Who is the current top-ranked legacy striker?"

"That's a good question. One of the hidden questions. That would be the currently inactive Raise the Banner. Also known as The Summoner."

The room erupts into murmurs.

*I'm not supposed to know this person's second name.*

"Interesting. You think you're smart, huh? Must have hacked your way into the Tier 15 records. I supposed it's to be expected from a former criminal."

I look the adjudicator dead in his eyes. "I didn't hear a question in that sentence."

"Hmph. Next question. What happens to those who betray the Grand Inquisitor position?"

"They are either sent to an unknown prison location with regular Blood Lettings, the most painful experience known to elven kind, or they are offered a chance to redeem themselves. It depends on the level of betrayal, and the level of the Grand Inquisitor."

"Why is that second part allowed?"

"Because the Grand Inquisitor position, although often lower than a top-ten political position, is one of the most difficult to maintain."

"Time!" screams the timekeeper.

"Interesting. You did well. We will see how you do against this particular striker in battle."

"I suppose we will." I say, making sure to beam another wide smile at him.

My heart is rumbling. This will be the first time I've fought a striker head on. Not to mention the room is kind of cramped, so I might get caught in melee. The two things I have going for me are the element of surprise and the fact that She Who Takes trained me in the forbidden arts.

Equipped with tome, grenade, poison dagger, and magical staff topped by a purple frog, I step forward to face Sanguine. Morange's former striker protector.

*I wonder how things would have gone down if Sanguine was with him the night he passed on?*

*No matter.*

Sanguine walks into the middle of the circle. "I know what you did to Morange. No one believes me, though. A technician taking out the Grand Inquisitor. I was laughed out of the office."

"What's your point? Don't tell me you're still caught up in that?"

"So you admit it?"

"I admit that you'll meet an early grave on this day."

"We will see about that."

"Begin!" bellows my future adjudicator.

Sanguine makes the first move. He jumps into the air and unleashes an onslaught of blood bullets from his revolvers. The blood lands on my witch's gown, which diminishes the effects of elemental attacks.

Unfortunately for me, blood isn't considered an element.

He snaps his fingers and the blood spots explode, throwing me back. My console goes off, giving me a status update. *Severe damage received: HP at 50%.*

Sanguine sends forth another barrage of blood bullets, but this time I'm ready for him. I raise my staff, putting up an absorption shield. The damage is absorbed by my shield, restoring my health back to full.

*Though that isn't saying much.*

I summon my phenome, Sluggish. He rolls forward and slowly sets up for an attack. Floating above Sluggish with my absorption shield still up, I point my staff at Sanguine and lift him in the air with my telekinesis strangling him. Just as Sanguine is holding his neck for breath. Sluggish lashes out his tongue for a devastating combo attack.

Sanguine manages to summon his black-and-blood-red tiger. The tiger jumps out and cleaves my phenome's tongue in two, dissolving it into a pool of poison liquid. My giant frog burps, unleashing a toxic gas that quickly fills the room, causing several HQ members to cough.

Sanguine, whom the attack was directed at, drops to his knees before turning into a pool of blood. He appears behind my phenome and pincer-attacks my precious with his tiger. My phenome disappears in an explosion of sticky liquid, slowing down Sanguine's movements.

Still levitating high in the air, I rain down a flurry of poison bolts that expand upon impact. They connect on Sanguine's chest and arms. He drops to his knees once again, and this time the poison paralyzes his body.

I drop to the ground, withdraw my poison dagger, and slit his throat. It imbues my dagger with another kill.

"How brutal," the adjudicator whispers.

The rest of the HQ members shower me in their applause.

The adjudicator approaches me.

"How did you manage to unlock a phenome?"

"She Who Takes grants many things—when she favors you."

"Quite the effective liar you are." He looks at the hologram of the number-one HQ member who nods.

"You're conniving, brutal, and above all seductive. You will make an excellent Grand Inquisitor. May none hide a secret from your watchful gaze."

I bow and say my thanks.

Just as I'm about to take my leave, I glance at Nepo, on whom my hypnosis has now waned. It's no matter. His mind will be blank. I have a new target to set my eyes on.

*I shall scheme and plot as I claim that number one spot.*

As I patrol the halls of the space station, I experience various reactions from members of the IGF. I never noticed it when I used to walk with Morange. Some fear me to no end, so they avoid my eye contact. Others are weary and watch my hands as if I'm going to eradicate them on the spot.

Above all, I experience the respect that I damn deserve.

*It truly is better to be feared than loved. Even hated is better.*

I smile to myself as I enter the common cafeteria to see people adding pep to their steps. I scan the room in search of my future security detail. Every politician is required to have one.

Fortunately for me, I already know exactly who I want. I've decided to stack poison damage together making a deadly trio.

The first one I approach is Spite: a fourteen-year-old girl with an augmented scorpion tail and scorpion hands. She has also imbued her body with toxic venom. It was a miracle she survived the procedure. She is currently a striker Y, so I will have to work on getting her to Z status.

"Hello."

"Hi! Miss Grand Inquisitor."

*Quite the cheery scorpion girl.*

"Good, you know who I am."

"Of course. Virtually everyone was watching the duel between you and Sanguine. I was rooting for you myself. I'm all for female empowerment."

"That you are. How about you join me as my security detail?"

"Oh, is that why you've joined me on this occasion? Here I thought it was about the missing people."

"Missing people?"

"Oh, nothing." she says with a sly grin.

"What do you say?"

"It would be my honor. Who do you have in mind as my partner?"

"Serpentine."

"Ew. You know scorpions and snakes don't get along."

"That may be true. But together, we can create a toxin so powerful that it will surpass what the IGF sprays on the orc planets."

"That would be amazing. Will it be painful and make people tremble like babies?"

"Yeah... sure."

"Count me in!"

"Excellent. I'm glad to have you on board."

She follows me to the table where Serpentine is eating alone. She is a fifteen-year-old striker Z known for controlling a myriad of serpents, some of which are said to hide in her long flowing purple hair. She is currently the youngest striker Z in the organization. I take a seat in front of her.

*Another loner. Reminds me of Vex.*

"Hello."

"What do you want old hag?"

"Old hag? Do you know who I am?"

"Yeah, you're the new Grand Inquisitor. What, do you want a cookie or something?" She lifts up a purple cookie towards my face.

"No, it smells like it's been tainted with snake venom."

"What you call tainted, I call a good meal. My answer is, go suck on a lollipop."

"You don't even know what I'm going to ask you yet."

"If you think I'm going to join you and... that thing. You're quite mistaken."

"Are you sure about that?"

"Positive."

"What if I told you that you'd be able to hunt down rogue strikers and test out a newly created toxin on them?"

"Hmm, that would be fun. Give me a sample."

"We haven't created it yet. But in due time."

"Nah."

"What do you mean nah?"

"Do I need to spell it out for you? N-A-H."

*How would I get a spoiled version of Vex to join a group?*

"Oh, I get it. Maybe you think your venom is stronger than my own toxins. Maybe you think you're a match for me."

"I know I'm a match for you. I'm not Sanguine."

"Fine. Let's do a swap. Whoever can resist the other's toxin the longest wins. If I win, you swear loyalty and join my security detail. If you win, you can have my staff, dagger, and tome."

"What's in the old scraggly book?"

"Forbidden knowledge."

"Deal."

She hands me a cookie, and I put out my hand.

"What am I supposed to do with this?"

"My toxin is on my skin. Like a frog. Kiss my hand."

She squints. Then she obliges as I gobble down the cookie.

*It's good. Like chocolate raspberry, with a slight aftertaste. If I didn't know any better, I'd say it was a regular cookie.*

Thirty seconds pass until she is convulsing on the floor and I'm on my third cookie.

I watch as she twitches. Then I raise her up with my telekinesis, lick my finger, and tap her forehead to place my saliva on it. Soon the convulsing stops, and she is back to her senses.

"How?" Is the only word she musters.

"Join us, and I will teach you all about the toxic arts. Things that you couldn't imagine."

# CHAPTER 41
## CLASSIFICATION: ROGUE STRIKER

They have tanks, heavy artillery, and the numbers. We have knowledge of the terrain, knowledge of how they operate, technology designed for short fights, and devastating war cries. Thus, we find ourselves launching a surprise attack on the elven camp. Instead of waiting for them to corral us together like the animals they make the orcs out to be, we take the fight to them.

The strategy is simple. We take out their medical ward and cafeteria tent, then leave traps on our way out.

I'm accompanied by Zeal and Checkmate, leading the vanguard with the red and blue orcs, while Sansa heads the trap unit with the green orcs.

I look at the camp to see them taking care of their sick. My main concern is these legacy strikers. We must have really pissed off the bigwigs. For them to unfreeze two legacy strikers at the same time is nearly unheard of. Then again, there is our mysterious comrade called Checkmate.

*Perhaps I will regret the day I find out why they fear him so much?*

I yell out, "Advance!"

The vanguard descends on the elven encampment like a flood of locusts. We set fire to their food tents and medical ward, causing confusion. As the majority of sleeping elves wake up, we strike at their hearts

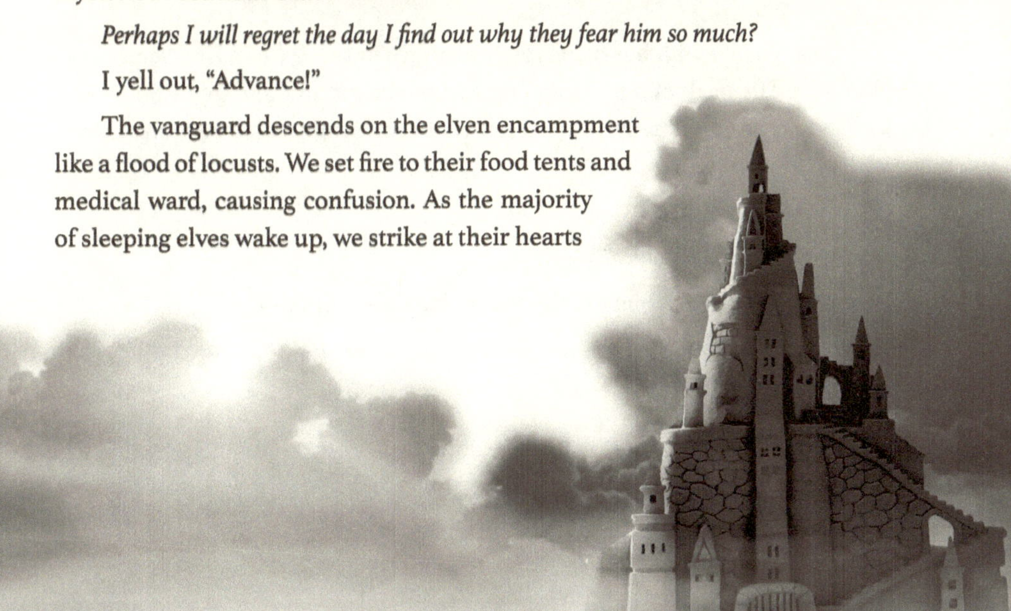

in a flurry of bloodshed. The well-equipped orcs cleave through the elves like butter. Their war cries working to unsettling effect.

In the distance, my eyes lock onto Punk Rock and Salvation entering the battlefield. I tap Zeal on the shoulder, and he follows close behind me. Checkmate has already activated his chess ability and has captured over fifty elves in his game of death. They will most likely perish soon enough.

Zeal and I engage Punk Rock and Salvation. I mean, how deadly can these legacy strikers be?

Punk Rock taps Salvation on the head and points at Checkmate's game. He nods and makes his way there. As I'm about to intervene, Punk Rock lightning steps in front of me and slashes at my neck. I dodge backwards, but am forced to put up a sand shield. Slowing down her attack giving me time to dodge. She is faster than last time.

*Perhaps she was a bit rusty after the unfreezing?*

I watch as she twirls her lightning katana, sending sparks flying everywhere. I summon another sand shield, which absorbs the attack. Zeal dodges by jumping high into the air then crashing downwards with his club, creating a massive crater. Punk Rock sidesteps the attack with ease. I follow up Zeal's attack by erupting sand spikes from the ground, forcing her to leap in the air.

"I got you," I whisper. Closing my hands, I create a sand tomb around her. The suffocating sand tomb tightens around her. I watch as blood leaks out, followed by blue streaks as she slices the tomb into four pieces.

"Impossible..."

She lunges at me with her blade ready to pierce my neck when Zeal sends forth his phenome. His pack of wolves emerges from the ground and grips onto Punk Rock's legs and arms. I aim my AK13 at her chest, unleashing a barrage that riddles her with holes.

She drops to her knees.

Then she cackles maniacally.

"Death, decay, all in a blaze of lightning! For Kuleta Kifo."

Blue energy shines down on her, healing all her wounds and freeing her from Zeal's pack of wolves.

She opens her mouth to release about ten fireflies, all of which land on Zeal. Ten flashes of bright light flicker as he drops to the floor in a crumpled heap of his own blood.

I rush forward with my spear slashing wildly like a madman. She dodges each attack with ease, donning a smirk. As she is about to retaliate, I summon my phenome. The golden scarab beetle spins out at enormous speeds, pushing Punk Rock back into a tree. Then my phenome bounces off to flutter above my head. She shines golden light on both Zeal's and my heads, granting increased regeneration, shield, and speed.

I watch as Zeal slowly gets to his feet.

The crazy Punk Rock cackles again

"Been a while since I've had this much fun." She inhales deeply before lighting stepping in front of me, forcing me to block with my spear. Then she sweeps my feet from underneath me dropping me to the ground. As she is about to slit my throat, Zeal fires a true short arrow that pierces her lower back. She looks down at the arrow, then turns around to catch the next one. The spirit arrow fizzles in her hand.

*So fast...*

Using the time she's distracted, I imbue my fist with sand and punch Punk Rock in the back, sending her flying toward Zeal, who smashes her in the face with his club. A random elf striker rushes towards me, so I turn the ground underneath his feet into quicksand, sucking him in. Then I fire a burst round into his head.

To my amazement, he turns into a sand walker: a large sand man with suffocating attacks and plenty of disables.

The sand walker turns into a sand tornado, sweeping up Punk Rock in the process. I create a giant pyramid of compact sand over the eye of the sand tornado. We watch as it drops on her.

A few minutes pass by as Zeal and I both breathe heavily.

Cracks start to form in the pyramid, and Punk Rock bursts forward, bloody on one side, but untouched on her mechanical side. She grips me by the throat and jams her mechanical hand into my stomach, twisting my organs. Zeal tries to help, but she pulls out an electric revolver and shoots him in the chest. It instantly causes him to fall, twitching, to the ground.

I'm starting to lose consciousness when my phenome spits out a burst of twenty scarabs to surround Punk Rock, clawing and scratching at her. By the time she releases me, I'm staggering backwards, blood leaking all over the place. I seal the wound with heated sand.

At a slower pace than normal, I lunge forward to pierce her thigh with my spear. I activate my spear's hidden power to turn her leg into sand. Her elven leg now drops to the ground in a pool of sand, leaving her with one mechanical one.

She clenches her jaw. Other than that, she doesn't say a peep. Losing a leg that way is supposed to be very painful—yet she stays silent.

Beads of sweat fill my helmet and undershirt.

For a few moments she just glares at me as I try my best to regain my energy with my advanced regeneration.

She dashes back, then lunges forward, gaining even more momentum with her katana. When she reaches within striking distance, she dodges my spear attack and shoots her revolver from her hip, dealing severe electric damage to me as she sends several fireflies at my phenome, taking her out.

And then, just when my sand walker is about to deal a devastating blow, it disappears.

*Time limit is up.*

Punk Rock hovers over me with one leg.

She sneers, pulling back her katana to strike, until Sansa's sharks pour out from the ground, forcing her to dodge.

"Until next time," she whispers, and she makes her retreat.

By the time I take in my surroundings, a large portion of the elven army has been wiped out. It seems the orcs were more effective than I could have imagined. Checkmate is still in his game mode, and Zeal is knocked out like a log.

Sansa rushed towards me, helping me to my feet.

"Do you have enough energy to heal?"

"Not yet. Soon."

"Can you walk?"

"Yeah."

She rushes over to Zeal and picks him up.

How she has enough strength to carry a plasma cannon, a frost sword, and a machinegun plus Zeal is amazing to me.

*Could be that mechanical arm of hers. Might have some other mechanical augments.*

The dark sky gives way to many clouds surrounding a bright ball of light. I have sudden shivers as I'm filled with fear. I'm stumbling back to base camp, but it's farther away than it should be. For some reason, every step I make seems to be in slow motion—as if time has slowed down.

I look up at the sky again to see the clouds circling a giant orb inside of a larger cube.

*This isn't good.*

Sansa turns back; she is also moving too slowly.

We're accompanied by Checkmate, who teleports to us by throwing his pawn across the field, then switching places with it. He seems untouched.

He looks up at the sky, and then for the first time, I see a new expression on his face. Something like fear, mixed with excitement. Kind of like how one would feel in their first time in a plane.

He whispers words that send shudders through my entire being.

"Kuleta Kifo."

I look at the sky once more to see the clouds circling more rapidly.

"Sansa, go on ahead and come back with a space craft. We will only slow you down."

She nods and places Zeal against a tree.

I watch as she summons her three sharks, and they tug her along.

I hear the screams of orcs. Not daring to turn back, I keep stumbling forward.

# The End

*"Power doesn't change you;*
*it brings out the side that you always*
*wanted to show the world." – Negus Lamont*

# REVIEW + OTHER WORK

I hope you enjoyed this novel, and I would love to hear your feedback. Please leave an honest review on Amazon, and Goodreads. Reviews help very much, both with rankings and in making me a better wordsmith. The next novels in this series will be:

Striker Z, released TBD 2021.

Striker Unleashed, released TBD 2021

If you want to keep up to date with releases and other goodies, please join my e-mail list:

*E-mail List Signup*

https://www.neguslamont.com/subscriber-freebies

✉ E-mail: neguslamont@gmail.com

# AMAZING LITRPG/ GAMELIT GROUPS

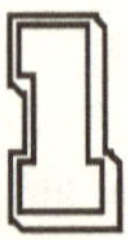

*To learn more about LitRPG, talk to authors including myself, and just have an awesome time, please join the* <u>LitRPG group.</u>

# AMAZING LITRPG/ GAMELIT GROUPS

*Another great group that is friendly and welcoming.* LitRPG Books *is another wonderful place if you are fond of LitRPG/Gamelit.*

# AMAZING LITRPG/ GAMELIT GROUPS

An amazing LitRPG/GameLit group where one can enjoy deep and mesmerizing conversations on the genre. GameLit Society is a wonderful place for readers and authors alike.

www.ingramcontent.com/pod-product-compliance
Lightning Source LLC
Chambersburg PA
CBHW050150120726
47903CB00002B/568